REQUIEM

For The Assassin

Russell Blake

First edition.

Books@RussellBlake.com

ISBN: 978-1503048799

Published by

Reprobatio Limited

Chapter 1

Ensenada, Baja California, Mexico

Cars clogged the Transpeninsular Highway that stretched along the waterfront, running from the border all the way to the southern tip of the thousand-mile-long peninsula. Military vehicles added to the confusion, and troop transports filled with masked soldiers lined the sidewalk adjacent to the naval base as a cadre of marines waved the morning traffic past a temporary roadblock. A procession of limousines wound from the checkpoint to the base gates, where naval personnel directed them to a parking area near the administrative offices.

A cool morning fog had ceded its dominance of the harbor to the ascending sun, its rays glinting off the water like yellow flame, the surface a greenish-blue with hints of petroleum sheen and its depths cloudy with pollution and runoff from the growing metropolis of three hundred thousand. The air smelled of salt and decaying sea life tinged with the noxious odor of exhaust belching from the stacks of nearby cruise ships tethered to massive docks. A concrete pier jutted into the harbor, where several naval ships tugged gently at their dock lines, the destroyer and battleship on the one side drab and gray beside the futuristic vessel on the other, its topsides decorated with colorful banners and streamers straightened in the sea breeze, its new paint gleaming, its lines aggressive and predatory.

A contingent of marines in full dress uniform stood at rigid attention along the jetty road, ignoring the crowd of well-dressed locals making their way to the harbor. An occasional golf cart meandered between strolling families, ferrying dignitaries to the small stage that had been set up by the waterfront, where last minute sound checks of the public address system squealed in the air like wounded birds. Scores of brown sea lions lined the rocks, staring curiously at the ruckus, their slumber interrupted by the unwelcome feedback. A large bull raised its head and called out, his bark competing with the amplified noise, and the surrounding cows gathered closer, the male's primacy reestablished in the din.

At the cordoned gathering point near the stage, a harried officer checked his watch as he surveyed the surge of humanity approaching for the ceremony. The event had made his duty harder during a difficult time, with the city beset by a wave of violence as several cartels battled for dominance over Baja's largest port. Captain Alvarez was overseeing security for the launch and had argued against allowing the general public on the base. But he'd been overruled by his superiors, who had insisted that a moment of pride like the christening of Mexico's newest naval vessel would not be diminished by thugs with popguns.

The spectacle would be attended by busloads of government bureaucrats, as well as any naval officer with enough clout to arrange for a long weekend in the port city. Dozens of private yachts floated nearby, decks lined with revelers for whom the relatively early hour was no deterrent, and the surrounding harbor was clogged with *pangas* – open-decked water taxis and fishing boats equipped with wheezing outboard motors and filled with the curious and the bored.

Under ordinary circumstances Alvarez wouldn't have been particularly concerned about the event, but the prior month's series of grisly beheadings and mass executions had him jumpy, even though the victims had all been cartel-related.

He was on edge because, in spite of his most compelling arguments, his commanding officer had decided not to search the spectators for weapons, reasoning that only a madman would try to start trouble on a naval base surrounded by armed men. Alvarez didn't disagree, but his job was to plan for the unexpected, and right now he had a couple of thousand unknowns headed for the stage, the huge new high-speed warship looming behind it.

Alvarez wiped a trace of sweat from his face as his subordinate Lieutenant Barrera approached, a handheld radio glued to his ear as the younger officer marched toward him.

"The VIPs are arriving. Estimated start time's been moved to ten thirty," Barrera announced.

"Figures. Everyone's half an hour late. Some things are uniquely reliable," Alvarez said.

"So far everything's pretty calm. The only wrinkle was a couple of guys in the parking lot who almost came to blows."

"Let's hope that remains the case," Alvarez muttered, and then his gaze shifted beyond the lieutenant to an advancing older officer, his bearing ramrod straight despite his corpulent physique. Alvarez stiffened and offered a salute, and Barrera mirrored him.

The heavyset officer returned their salute and continued past, trailed by two aides. Alvarez watched the group move to the side of the stage, and squinted at Barrera.

"I guess the admiral didn't get the memo about the show not starting on time."

Barrera nodded. "He looks like he's ready to break the bottle and have done with it."

"Let's hope he doesn't decide to do so prematurely. He's not the only important person who's shown up for this."

Admiral Torreon was one of the top officers in the Mexican Navy, in charge of Pacific operations. His reputation was of a sybarite, but a scrupulously honest one, and he'd earned the respect of his subordinates by being fair in his dealings and orders. He cut an imposing figure in his dress uniform, his gray hair gleaming like gunmetal in the sun, his girth somehow befitting a man who made momentous decisions. He'd come up the ranks the hard way, earning his commission rather than being favored through family connections or nepotism, and had an indomitable reputation that he wore like a medal.

Pelicans wheeled overhead as the admiral engaged in a heated discussion with several other naval bigwigs by the stage, and after a few moments he shook his head and mounted the steps to take his seat in the shade, alongside a dozen other waiting chairs, all empty. One of his aides moved to his side and offered a water bottle, which he waved away, clearly unhappy at the delay, judging by his scowl.

Barrera's eyebrows rose as he studied the crowd, and he leaned toward Alvarez and spoke softly. "Holy mother of God. Would you look who showed up…?"

A woman, accompanied by a cameraman and two grips, sashayed toward the stage. Her white linen pants and red silk blouse molded to her curves. A gust of wind tousled her chestnut hair, and Alvarez realized he hadn't breathed for several beats as she neared.

Carla Vega was one of the most recognizable faces in Mexico, and for good reason: she'd been a star reporter for the nation's top network for a decade and had been linked to a Who's Who of eligible bachelors – film and TV stars, soccer players, industrialists. Now in her mid-thirties, her stature as a celebrity was well established, and she was envied by her peers and desired by every male over the age of ten.

Carla stopped in front of Alvarez and removed her Prada sunglasses. Alvarez swallowed hard. Her hazel eyes seemed to glow from within as she assessed him, and then one corner of her mouth tugged up in a half smile.

"Captain Alvarez?"

"Yes," Alvarez said, noting that she smelled like vanilla and nutmeg.

"Captain, I contacted your people about interviewing the admiral but never received a response other than being directed to you as the one in charge of everything connected to the ceremony. But your office didn't return my calls," she said, her voice musical but with a hint of steel in the tone. A woman accustomed to getting her way, she was clearly unimpressed by a mid-level naval functionary.

"Ah, really? My apologies. I was unaware you'd contacted us," he said, frowning.

She eyed him with barely concealed ennui. "Well, I'm here now, and I'd like five minutes of the admiral's time."

Alvarez and Barrera exchanged a glance. The admiral had been clear in his instructions: he was off-limits to the press.

Alvarez smiled disarmingly. "Miss Vega, may I first say how honored we are to have you at our event?"

"Right. But what about the admiral?"

"Regrettably, he isn't available for any interviews today. I'm terribly sorry. My office should have told you—"

"Yes, well, they didn't respond, and I've traveled halfway across the country to speak with him."

Alvarez shook his head. "Which is most unfortunate, although again, it's humbling that you would think the launching of our newest ship worth your attention."

Carla studied Alvarez's polite expression. He could see her calculating how to sidestep him and go directly to the admiral, and resisted the impulse to speak, to fill the uncomfortable silence with stammered apologies or dissembling. This was the admiral's turf, and if he didn't want to talk to one of the most beautiful women in Mexico, that was his prerogative.

"Could you have a word with his staff and at least ask?" she purred, switching gears as she took in his blank gaze, her voice all honey and promises of paradise.

Barrera caught his eye, and Alvarez nodded. The lieutenant moved out of earshot and murmured into his radio as Carla and Alvarez faced off like gladiators. Alvarez tried another friendly smile, but the expression never reached his eyes.

When Barrera returned, he looked glum. "The admiral extends his apologies, but he doesn't do unscheduled media appearances. He invites you to contact his office during business hours."

"I tried that and got nowhere," Carla said, her tone as stiff as the pole behind her, from which a massive flag billowed in the wind, the golden eagle in the center, a snake in its clutches, rippling like a living thing.

"I'm truly sorry, *Señorita* Vega. I wish there was something I could do, but he is the admiral…" Alvarez said, spreading his hands and offering a helpless shrug. "The good news, such as it is, is that I'd be more than happy to personally escort you to the media area and arrange every courtesy."

"That's very hospitable of you," Carla said, her voice glacial.

Alvarez ignored her demeanor and gestured to an area on the far side of the stage, where several other camera crews were in position. She sighed and followed him to the press section, with its unobstructed view of the stage and the ship beyond. Barrera watched them walk away, she with the hypnotic gait of a prowling cat, and was glad that he wasn't the one who'd had to disappoint Mexico's media queen.

He reluctantly tore his eyes away from Carla Vega crossing the grass and resumed his scrutiny of the gathering crowd. Alvarez had made it clear that he wanted the area locked down, and Barrera had full authority to detain anyone suspicious. As his commanding officer had said, "I'd rather apologize for you being wrong than you not act and have a bloodbath on my hands."

A trio of young men with shaved heads moving along the periphery of the throng caught his attention. They wore baggy jeans and loose jackets – which could have been to fend off the morning chill or to conceal weapons. Barrera whispered into his radio, and moments later four marines materialized and instructed them to step aside for a search.

Barrera watched as his men herded them to an area by the water and went through their belongings. The ensign in charge of the unit radioed back.

Nothing.

Part of Barrera's problem was that cartel thugs often looked like anyone else – construction workers, laborers, merchants, young men out for a little diversion on an otherwise boring day. The christening had been scheduled for a Mexican holiday, so in addition to families and older couples there were plentiful unattached men and women in groups of two or three, any of whom could spell trouble. He could still vividly recall seeing footage from a grenade attack in a crowd several years ago in Morelia, which had killed a hundred innocents with one explosion, and his worst nightmare was a similar tactic used at this gathering.

"Anything?" Alvarez asked from immediately behind him, startling Barrera. He instantly recovered and concealed his surprise.

"No, sir. We're stopping the more suspicious, but you know what it's like in a group this size with no funnel to pass through."

"I do indeed. Let's fall back to the stage and concentrate on security there. If anyone's going to make a play, that's where they'll do it."

They moved toward the PA speakers and took up position near the riser. Five minutes turned into fifteen, and once the area around the stage was packed, a young officer strode to the microphone and announced the beginning of the event.

Alvarez's gaze moved to where Carla was talking earnestly to the camera, giving a blow-by-blow of the event. He wondered what the hell she was doing at a ship launching, and then an ear-splitting wail of feedback screeched from the speakers, shaking him back to the present.

The mayor did his obligatory five-minute speech, followed by a navy minister from Mexico City and then the Baja California Norte governor. Polite smatterings of applause greeted their proclamations, which managed to be entirely self-serving, and then it was the admiral's turn.

Alvarez caught motion out of the corner of his eye to his right and, after a quick glance, shouldered through the assembled mass of humanity to where a man was pushing a wheeled cart near the water. Barrera was right behind him as they converged on him, and his eyes widened when he saw the two navy officers rushing his way, one with his hand on his service pistol. The man tried to turn his cart, but it was too late, and when Alvarez reached him, he was sliding his hand inside the fold of his black windbreaker.

"Stop. Remove your hand from your jacket, slowly. This is your only warning," Barrera said, his weapon drawn, the ugly muzzle of his Beretta 9mm aimed at the man's head.

The blood drained from the man's face as he slowly removed his hand. In it was a laminated blue card on a soiled lanyard – a vendor's license. Alvarez glared at it, then at the cart, which he could now see was a white ice cooler with a hand-painted depiction of a penguin wearing a multicolored beanie and holding a Popsicle aloft. Barrera stepped forward, his weapon steady, and ordered the man to put the license on top of the box and to remove his jacket, but Alvarez had already lost interest and was scanning the surroundings for anything out of the ordinary. An enterprising treat vendor who had talked his way past the perimeter security wasn't the sort of menace he was concerned with, and the lieutenant was more than capable of dealing with the man.

Alvarez made his way back toward the stage, where Carla had managed to push the other media flacks out of her way as her cameraman filmed the last speaker: the admiral, who was rising heavily from his seat, a few notes in his hand.

A loud pop exploded from Alvarez's left and he spun, his heartbeat trip-hammering in his throat, hand on his pistol. A toddler's laughing face met his glower as she reached for another balloon to pop, this one clutched by her tiny brother. Her mother pushed the little girl aside, hoping to avoid a meltdown when her daughter was denied her sibling's treasure to destroy.

Alvarez took a few deep breaths. His discomfiture was unusual, and he made a mental note to avoid a third cup of coffee on the mornings of big events. Barrera rejoined him as the admiral delivered a terse speech commending the shipbuilders for their miraculous achievement, and rattled off a series of specifications that Alvarez knew were far below the ship's actual capabilities.

Another round of applause greeted the end of his statements, and then it was time for the champagne. The admiral waddled at the head of an entourage of dignitaries to where an honor guard stood by the ship's bow. An ensign presented him with a colorfully festooned bottle attached to a ribbon, and after turning to the crowd and making another short statement, the admiral loosed the bottle in a swinging arc.

The glass shattered against the steel hull, and the gathering cheered. The navy band struck up a rousing song, the governor and mayor shook hands with the admiral, and Alvarez relaxed. The dignitaries would be whisked away from the area in the armored SUVs in which they'd arrived, and then that most dangerous moment – where a cartel assassin could make a play for the governor or mayor – would be over, the only remaining concern mundane crowd control.

Alvarez oversaw leading the men back to their vehicles and was standing with the admiral when Carla's voice called out. The admiral leaned into Alvarez without acknowledging her and spoke softly. "I'll be taking a boat out of here. Some of my friends are out on that yacht, and I've been asked to lunch," he said, nodding in the direction of a three-hundred-foot white behemoth near the harbor mouth – the ostentatious and well-known floating plaything of a telecommunications mogul who was one of the wealthiest men in Mexico.

"Very well, sir."

"I arranged for a tender to pick me up. Just keep the jackals off the pier while I make my escape, Captain," the admiral said and then turned and ambled down the length of the jetty to where a Sea Ray 44 express cruiser waited, its exhausts burbling, the crew standing by the cleats in preparation for his arrival.

Alvarez watched him approach the boat, and then his attention was pulled away by the sound of Carla's voice arguing with two of the guards behind him.

"It's imperative that I speak to him, damn it," she repeated, as if by sheer force of will she could stare down the Mexican Navy.

Alvarez had to hand it to her – the combination of her imperious tone, absolute self-assurance, and complete absence of shame might have worked on him only a few short years before, but now she didn't stand a chance.

"Miss Vega, you've been told the admiral isn't available. Let's keep things civil, shall we?" he said as he turned, a placid smile affixed on his face.

She glared daggers through him, but it had no effect, and she knew when she saw the resolute look in his eyes that she was beaten.

The Sea Ray's engines revved, and the boat pulled from the dock, trailing a wake of white froth. Vega's shoulders sagged as she conceded defeat. Alvarez was just about to offer a conciliatory platitude when a look of shock flitted across her face, and she pointed over Alvarez's shoulder to where a helicopter was racing across the sky toward the departing admiral – a gunman leaning out the open door holding a grenade launcher.

CHAPTER 2

"Shit." The gunman in the rear of the helicopter cursed as the first projectile missed the Sea Ray's stern by a few feet. He loaded another grenade into the M320 launcher and tried again, but with the same result – a near miss. "This damned thing is worthless," he said, tossing the launcher aside in disgust and shouldering his assault rifle. His companion in the copilot's seat did the same, and the pilot kept the aircraft behind the boat as they opened fire, strafing the topsides with high-velocity rounds.

The Sea Ray's captain reacted quickly by firewalling the throttles, and the boat launched forward as rounds tore through the fiberglass. The admiral ducked below deck into the illusory safety of the cabin.

The first gunman exhausted his magazine, ejected it, and slapped a new one in place to resume his merciless onslaught. Spent brass shell casings littered the cockpit as the copilot emptied his rifle, and he was reaching for another magazine when the pilot swore.

"Damn. We've got company," he hissed and banked the bird south. The first gunman looked at where the pilot was pointing; to their right, a Mexican Navy Messerschmitt-Bölkow-Blohm Bo 105 helicopter was bearing down on them.

"I thought we were guaranteed no pursuit!" the gunman yelled.

"We were. But that was the police. This is navy."

"Can you outrun him?" the copilot asked in a strained voice.

"That thing has eighty knots top end on us. Best we can hope to do is lose him in the mountains south of the city. Better strap in – it's going to get ugly," the pilot warned and plunged the helicopter into a steep dive at the buildings south of the base.

"What the hell are you doing?" the gunman barked.

"We don't want to get shot down, do we? If we're right above the rooftops in populated areas, they wouldn't dare shoot. Otherwise, we're the piñata and they're the stick."

They dropped eight stories in as many seconds, and the men's stomachs were in their throats by the time they leveled off. The pilot pushed the speed to the limit. The helicopter raced over the roofs of the two- and three-story buildings in a blur, but when the gunman checked behind them, he could see the navy bird gaining on them.

"How long until we're in the hills?" he yelled over the roar of the engine.

"Maybe another minute or two."

"Then what?"

"Then we run up the canyons until we spot a good place to set down, hoping that the navy pilot isn't as crazy a bastard as I am."

The gunman snapped a full magazine in place. "I'm going to give them something to think about."

The pilot shrugged. "Can't hurt. Maybe if they have to fly through lead, it'll make them think twice." He tacked further east as the green of the hills rose before them, the sun crimson over the crests as it burned through a layer of airborne dust and pollution.

The assault rifle jackhammered as the gunman emptied a thirty-round box magazine in two seconds and then loaded a fresh one. The navy helicopter gave no indication of slowing as it continued to gain on them, its malevolent snout locked on their tail rotor like a hunting dog on a game bird, and the pilot jerked the stick and turned the bird south again, keeping it over populated areas in case the urge to return fire was too much for the navy helo.

"I thought we were headed for the hills," the copilot said, eyes bright with borderline panic.

"We need an area with canyons and ravines. That rolling stuff's not going to do it for us."

"Then where?"

"Down by the country club. San Carlos Canyon."

The helicopter began to vibrate as it reached and then exceeded its maximum advisable speed, but the pilot held it steady, roaring only a few yards over the power poles and roof tanks of the neighborhood below. The gunman had exhausted his ammunition and was now sitting with his eyes closed, lips moving in silent prayer through the deafening pounding of the rotors, the paradox of a hired killer begging a benign deity for mercy lost on him.

Glass shattered inward as the windshield collided with a big bird – a turkey buzzard, every bit of eight or nine pounds, the rough equivalent of slamming into a bowling ball at the helicopter's speed. The pilot screamed as the aircraft dipped, but he was able to steady its flight seconds before it crashed into the ground. His sunglasses shielded his eyes, but beads of blood bubbled from his face where small chunks of glass had punctured his skin before being blown into the void by the howling wind.

"Gah…" he exclaimed and glanced next to him, where the copilot's head lolled to the side at an unnatural angle.

"Are you all right?" the gunman screamed at the pilot.

"I…I think so. Look. There's the canyon."

"Damn. We might make it after all."

~ ~ ~

The naval pilot nodded as he received clearance in his headset to fire on the enemy helicopter and gave the copilot a thumbs-up. "You see him hit the buzzard? Stupid prick."

"Time to put him out of his misery." The copilot flipped up the cover on the armament control and zeroed in on the helicopter as it flew over the last of the houses and made for the canyon. The lock indicator blinked and beeped at him, and he released a Hellfire missile with a whoosh.

The damaged helicopter never had a chance. A split second after the missile struck, it exploded in a white-hot supernova, vaporizing the cabin and sending what was left of the craft spinning crazily toward the granite below.

~ ~ ~

A CB-90 fast assault craft pulled alongside the Sea Ray, which was floating in a shambles near the breakwater. The hail of bullets had shattered the decks and riddled the topsides, and two of the crew lay dead in sticky pools of drying blood. The captain clutched his abdomen where a round had caught him. The pungent smell of diesel fuel drifted from the bilge, and the first two seamen who made it aboard from the naval vessel exchange worried looks.

"Shut the engines down," the first one ordered, and the captain nodded but slumped to the deck before he could oblige. The sailor pushed past him and turned the keys.

The rumble of the engines died, leaving only the dim hum of the blower fans.

"Admiral, are you down there?" the second seaman called. "It's safe. The attack's over, sir."

The first sailor peered into the cabin. Beams of sunlight pierced the gloom from dozens of bullet holes in the deck. A rustle followed by a groan emanated from the depths, and then the admiral moved into view, his jacket stained crimson, his color gray. He tried to make it up the few stairs to the deck, but gravity proved too much, and he fell backward, clutching his chest, his eyes rolling into his head as he passed out even before he hit the carpeted floor behind him.

CHAPTER 3

Guadalajara, Mexico

"Imbeciles." The speaker was a thin, dark-haired man in his early fifties with leporine features, whose intelligent mahogany eyes darted restlessly from object to object. "Not only do they manage to blow the whole thing, but they do so in a spectacularly visible manner." He pushed his coffee cup aside in disgust, his color rising as he spoke. A light wind from the mountains blew across the veranda, freshening the air, which was heavy with the smell of grass and horses from the nearby barn and adjacent field.

His companion was his physical opposite: thirties, muscular, fair complexion, hair the color of wet sand, lucid blue eyes that seemed ever at peace as he gazed across the pasture at the corral, where several ranch hands were mending one of the outbuildings. The younger man took a contemplative sip of his coffee and nodded wordlessly, having nothing to add to the discussion.

The dark-haired man's eyes narrowed as he checked the time on his white gold Rolex President. "And now he's forewarned. So what was already a difficult target just got impossible because of these bumbling cretins. Christ. If they weren't dead, I'd kill them myself with my bare hands." He frowned and shook his head. "For all the sloppy histrionics, our problem remains. And we're no closer to a solution than before."

"It's unfortunate, to be sure."

"That's the understatement of the year. How did we wind up with these, these…buffoons? Remind me why we hired them?"

The younger man turned his attention to his host, his expression flat, and fixed him with a neutral gaze. "The cartels are the go-to people for this kind of thing."

"Apparently they're the go-to guys for screwing up. I hope we didn't pay them."

The younger man shook his head. "It wasn't on a best-efforts basis. The agreement was that we'd pay upon successful execution." He smiled at his small pun.

The dark-haired man stood, as if uncomfortable in his own skin, and began to pace, his Gucci loafer heels clicking on the Saltillo tiles. "So now what?"

"It would seem we're out of options."

"That's unacceptable. We can't be. This is too important."

The younger man considered his fingernails, lost in thought, and then acquiesced. "There is one possibility. But it would be more expensive."

"Than failure? So far, failure's been cheap," the dark-haired man spat. "Tell me what you have in mind."

"It would mean calling in favors. And considerable cash, I'd think."

The dark-haired man scowled, his face wrinkling like he'd drunk vinegar. "What are you thinking?"

The younger man exhaled, took a final swig of his coffee, and then leaned back in his chair, a single vertical crease in his brow the only indication he was concerned. He described in a soft voice what he had in mind, his sentences concise and his words crisp, and when he was done, steepled his fingers and waited for a response.

The older man eyed the tall grass at the edge of the tree line, shimmering from the breeze. The mature oaks sighed as the wind blew through their branches. "And you think you can bring this sort of pressure to bear?"

The younger man smiled, his expression almost embarrassed, and allowed his attention to drift back to the vaqueros and their chore. "Oh, I know I can. I've been cultivating this contact for years. I've done favors in the past without asking for any reciprocation, but there's always been the unspoken. Still, as I said, it will be expensive."

"At this point I'm not price sensitive. That went up in a fireball in the Baja hills." The dark-haired man sat back down and grunted. "Fine. Put it in motion. But I want the whole list handled. No more amateur night."

"The cartels are hardly amateur."

"Could have fooled me."

CHAPTER 4

San Isidro Huayapam, Oaxaca, Mexico

The last of the group of four men pulled himself through the narrow passage that ran at a ninety-degree angle and then lowered his torso through the treacherous dogleg section. His arms shook from the exertion of negotiating the last hundred meters of a hitherto unexplored offshoot of the Cueva Rey Condoy cave system. The weight of the line he was dragging, including the thin Teflon-coated telephone cable connected to the base camp at the surface, had grown heavier as he progressed, the friction from the longer pull contributing to the difficulty.

His feet slid out of the shaft, and a pair of strong hands steadied him as he got his footing on the rubble that formed the cave floor, a towering heap caused by the upper reaches of the cave collapsing over time. He unclipped the line from his harness and sat by his fellow cavers, glad that the most precarious passage was now behind him.

"Took you long enough," *El Rey* said from his seated position by one of the walls, his helmet-mounted LED lamp throwing a white glare of light in the newcomer's direction. "We were getting ready to set up camp for the night."

The new arrival, Crisanto Aguilar, a professor of geology at the Colegio Nacional in Mexico City and the oldest of the group, smiled at the good-natured ribbing – part of the camaraderie of cavers, who, while competitive, were mainly testing their own limits when they went underground. Still, it never hurt to have peer pressure to force you on when your stamina was wavering, and Aguilar appreciated the prodding by their most recent team member.

"Ramón, so much impatience. The cave's been here for a long time. What's a few extra minutes so I can appreciate its nuances?" Aguilar chided.

El Rey was using the name Ramón Palermo with the cavers, one of numerous aliases he'd created with an eye toward self-preservation. Although he was out of his former life, ghosts and old enemies could surface at any time. His career as the world's deadliest assassin had made him a marked man with Mexico's most dangerous cartel kingpin, whose ten-million-dollar contract for *El Rey*'s head was still a concern. Even with a presidential pardon and carte blanche from CISEN, the Mexican intelligence agency, which had blackmailed him into reluctant employment, he never let his guard down.

"I forgot you're a sightseer," Alain DuPré, a French expat living in Puebla, said with a grin. He and Aguilar had been in the group the longest, seven years, with the fourth member, Jesus Salgado, having joined three years earlier. "Some of us are Ferraris, built for racing, not for cruising." He winked at *El Rey*, who nodded and took a drink of water from his canteen.

The assassin had grown intrigued with caving while recovering from the concussion he'd sustained during his last CISEN assignment, and once he'd mended, he'd made discreet inquiries with like-minded groups via the internet until he'd met Aguilar in person. This was the second cave system *El Rey* had explored with the group, and while the physical aspect hardly posed a challenge for his hardened, toned physique, the mental demands suited his appetite for challenge and adventure. He'd quickly discovered that he enjoyed being a half-mile below the earth's surface, surviving by his wits and driving himself to impossible feats, far more than he'd ever enjoyed rock or mountain climbing. Something about the complete darkness and occupying spaces that nobody had been in before appealed to him in a way he couldn't have explained, but it was a sentiment he shared with the other three members of his team.

His team. A misnomer, because each member was entirely dependent upon his own strength and stamina, albeit within the context of working together – a prudent concession to very real risks like injury, hypothermia, equipment failure, and flooding. Their lifeline was the support personnel at the base camp, three of Aguilar's students who were hopeful to become part of the subterranean group once they'd put in their time on the surface.

The men settled in for a brief rest before moving deeper into the cave, each lost in his thoughts. A jarring ringing shattered the silence, echoing off the walls in a series of reverberations that seemed to go on forever. Aguilar peered down at the telephone that was one of the many safeguards he insisted upon for his well-equipped excursions and raised it to his ear.

"What is it?" he demanded.

"There are some men here to see Ramón. They say it's important." The voice of the youngest of the base camp workers sounded tinny and distant over the tiny speaker.

Aguilar looked at *El Rey*. "What? Who are they?"

"Government. Is he there?"

"Of course. Where do you think he is?"

"They want to talk to him. Can you put him on?"

Aguilar sighed and handed the handset to *El Rey*. "It's for you."

El Rey reached out, his face a blank, and took the phone.

"Hello?"

"Your uncle has had an accident. You're needed immediately." The voice was flat and mechanical, but the code words had the intended effect.

"An accident?"

"Yes. We were sent to escort you to the hospital."

El Rey checked his watch. "I can be back at the surface in four hours. I trust you can find a way to keep occupied until then?"

"See you when you get here."

El Rey thumbed the phone off and shook his head. "My uncle has been in an accident. His friends say it's bad. I need to get back to the camp immediately."

Aguilar's eyes narrowed. "I'm sorry to hear that." He studied the rest of the group. "Well, gang, looks like that's it for today. By the time we make it back, it's over."

"You don't have to all come with me."

"That's not how this works. The whole point to going in as a group is for safety – not that I don't enjoy your company. But if you were to slip halfway up, you could be dead by the time we returned, and worse, blocking one of the shafts at the narrowest point. Believe me, Ramón, it's purely self-interest in play here."

"I can make it. Really. So far nothing's been that tricky."

"Afraid not, my friend. Those are the rules. And I'm not going to let you destroy my perfect record of no catastrophes." He paused. "Sorry about your uncle. It must be serious to drag you back, not to mention warrant sending someone to fetch you."

"He's got a lot of clout. Let's hope for the best. You know as much as I do at this point."

The sky was darkening when the group emerged from the cave, high streaks of russet and mauve backlit by the sun dropping behind the hills like a dying red ember. Two men waited for *El Rey* beside a black Humvee, and he made short work of packing his few belongings and saying his good-byes before joining them at the big vehicle. The taller of the two shook his hand as the other climbed behind the wheel.

"Nice of you to join us," the man said, his voice soft, aware the others were watching.

"I've had a long day. What can you tell me?"

"Nothing, other than that we've got a plane waiting in Oaxaca. But we've got to get moving, because on these roads it will be the longest eighty kilometers you've ever seen."

The man wordlessly got into the passenger seat, leaving the rear for *El Rey*. The assassin slung his packs onto the floor and slid in, and soon they were bouncing along the dirt track, little more than two ruts in the lush grass that rose from the dirt road at the bottom of the hill. Fog was creeping into the valleys between the mountain peaks, and the sun's dying rays lit the white blanket that stretched below them like a fresh snowfall. Once over the nearby pass, the big vehicle had to slow. Visibility had diminished to twenty feet, and the driver was obviously keenly aware of the steep drop should he misjudge one of the curves in the thick haze.

The men exhaled a collective sigh of relief when they arrived at the Xoxocotlán airport, where a Lear 35 waited by the terminal, ready for takeoff. Five minutes later the jet was climbing on a parabolic trajectory into the night sky, the G-forces pushing *El Rey* back into his seat as the pilots urged the plane to its limits.

CHAPTER 5

Mexico City, Mexico

A delivery van wended its way through traffic on the Calle Miami near the World Trade Center building in Mexico City, ignoring the dissonant symphony of car horns that greeted its aggressive moves. A smattering of pedestrians ambled down the dimly lit sidewalks, most of the illumination coming from retail outlets open late to cater to an evening crowd.

Captain Romero Cruz sat at a curbside table outside a small restaurant, enjoying the pleasant cooling breeze. He took a bite of his *torta* and gazed across the table at his wife, Dinah, who was eating her *tacos al pastor* with considerably greater finesse. He wiped traces of cheese and mayonnaise from his mustache and smiled. "I'm hoping things ease up in the next couple of weeks and we can get away for a few days."

Dinah smiled, and the light on the sidewalk seemed to brighten. "Maybe someplace with a beach."

Cruz nodded with a serious expression. "And cold beer."

"Although tequila's been known to do in a pinch," Dinah agreed.

Cruz raised his bottle of Bohemia beer in silent toast. Dinah matched the gesture with her water, her eyes dancing with playful happiness.

"Seriously, though, we need a vacation," Cruz said. "I've been going nonstop for months. And I know it's been hard on you, with me gone all the time, working."

"The pool boy hasn't been complaining."

"Is that why he's looking so tired?"

She nodded. "I was worried you'd figure out our building doesn't even have a pool."

"Ah. It's the little things. Always the little things." He stifled a yawn. "I'm sorry they were able to drag me back into this sewer. If it had been anyone but the president, I would have said no." Cruz had quit his job after tracking and stopping a German assassin who'd been trying to execute the visiting Chinese premier, but fate had intervened, and the President of Mexico had made a personal appeal to him, imploring him to continue with his duties. Cruz had agreed provided one condition was met, and within forty-eight hours he no longer reported to his nemesis Godoy, a pompous bureaucratic ass he despised.

"The pay raise and getting even with Godoy didn't have anything to do with it?"

Cruz smiled, took another large bite of his sandwich, and sighed contentedly, allowing her question to go unanswered. "It's been eight weeks since we last moved. You know what that means."

"Time to find another pool boy."

"Correct. We'll have a new condo next week."

She finished her taco and sat back. "Do you think we'll ever have a normal life?"

Cruz had been relocating every few months for so long he'd grown inured to being in a new neighborhood, a new building, six to eight times every year. It was all part of the toll he paid as the head of the Federal Police anti-cartel task force, which made him enemy number one to the powerful narco-traffickers – and which was a constant source of stress on his relationship with Dinah, who, while accommodating, had also tired of the impermanence of their living situation.

"You didn't marry a normal man," Cruz said softly, pushing his plate aside and reaching across the table for her hand.

"No, I suppose not. Still, a girl can dream, can't she?"

"Maybe a long weekend on the Mexican Riviera. Someplace quiet, but high-end. Like Tulum. That area has gorgeous beaches."

She nodded. "And beautiful water. Oh, how about Cozumel? Alone on our own tropical island…"

"Well, hardly alone if it's Cozumel, but still, I get your point."

The traffic light blinked red down the block, and the stream of vehicles ground to a stop. Cruz was considering the wisdom of a second beer when he saw two young men running toward a gleaming ebony BMW near the light. He glimpsed a flash of metal in the hand of one of the men, and was already reaching for the shoulder-holstered Glock under his windbreaker as he pushed back his chair.

"Romero—"

"Dinah, stay here," he said, freeing his weapon.

The pair was at the vehicle, and he could clearly see the one by the driver's window wielding a nickel- or chrome-plated revolver, pointing it at the driver and yelling. Carjackings were a common occurrence that plagued Mexico City as the global financial situation continued to erode, a by-product of living in one of the most populated cities in the world, with many millions at or below the poverty line – which in Mexico was a hundred and fifty dollars a month.

Cruz wasn't in uniform – he'd changed into civilian clothes before going for dinner – and for a split second he considered the wisdom of getting involved in a street crime without backup. But by then he was already halfway to the car, his pistol trained on the thug, and was fumbling for his shield wallet as he closed the distance.

Cruz could hear the carjacker screaming at the driver, threatening to shoot him if he didn't get out of the car. The driver was opening the door when Cruz's commanding voice boomed down the street.

"Drop the gun. Federal Police."

The thug's head swung around, searching for the source of the warning. He was younger than Cruz had initially thought, no more than a teenager, and the look of menace on his face transitioned into one of fear as he spotted Cruz bearing down on him, weapon steady in his hand. Time seemed to slow as a series of expressions played across the youth's face, and then he sprinted away, ducking low as he dodged between cars. His companion darted to the far sidewalk and bolted, and as quickly as the street had become a war zone, it returned to normal, crisis averted.

Cruz arrived at the car, where the driver was still sitting with the door open, in shock. Cruz's gaze followed the running gunman as he rounded the corner and disappeared, and then he turned his attention to the driver.

"Are you okay?" he asked.

The driver was nervous, his expression frightened, and when he answered, his voice was shaky. "Yes. Thank goodness."

Cruz glanced at the man in the passenger seat – a clergyman – and shook his head. Nobody was safe anymore, even God's anointed ones. He followed the driver's eyes to his gun and quickly holstered it, aware that a man standing in the middle of the street at night in Mexico City clutching a Glock might not be the most comforting sight, even under the circumstances.

"That was a close one," Cruz commented, shaking his head.

"Unbelievable. We were just minding our own business…"

"I know. I saw the whole thing." Cruz paused. "Do you want to file a police report?"

The driver's eyes widened. "No. It wouldn't do any good, would it? I mean, they didn't steal anything, and they're already long gone."

Cruz sighed. "It's true. Sad, but true." He felt in his pocket and found a business card. "Here. If you change your mind, call me. I can sign it as a witness."

The driver took the card. "No, I don't want any trouble. I'll just chock it up to experience."

"Driving an expensive car at night can be a dangerous proposition these days. It shouldn't be that way, but there it is." Cruz gave a parting look to the passenger. "You're lucky. I hope your night calms down from here."

The driver nodded. "Thank you, officer" – he peered at the card and then corrected himself, his tone respectful – "I mean, *Capitan* Cruz. It was our good fortune you were nearby."

A car several back honked its horn, and then more of the cars joined in, unaware of what the holdup was but annoyed to be stalled, kept from important destinations. Cruz waved at the honkers and turned back to the driver.

"Are you okay to drive?"

"What? Oh. Of course. I'm just a little shaken up. That's all."

"Well, I'd tell you to pull over and relax for a few minutes, but after what happened, I'd suggest you get out of this area of town. Just be careful on the road."

"Yes, *Capitan*. Good thinking. Thank you again."

The driver closed his door, and Cruz stepped back. The BMW surged forward, and Cruz returned to his table, ignoring the black stares of the other motorists as they passed him. When he sat down, Dinah's eyes were wide.

"I suppose that's all in a day's work for you, isn't it? Chasing down gunmen…" she said.

Cruz smiled. "Hardly. The biggest danger I'm in most days is of overeating. Or getting a paper cut. I'm pretty sure it's impossible to get much safer than behind my desk at headquarters."

She eyed him skeptically. "You remind me of that American movie star. What's his name? The one with the big gun? You know, 'Make my day'?"

"Clint Eastwood? Hardly. Although I have been told I resemble him."

Dinah held his gaze and then leaned forward and wiped an errant crumb from his mustache with her napkin. She raised an eyebrow and considered him gravely. "It's uncanny. You could be twins."

They both laughed like schoolchildren, and Cruz ordered another beer. Dinah picked at her final taco as he devoured the remainder of his *torta* and then paid the bill. They walked arm in arm back to where his car and driver were waiting around the corner, and he sighed contentedly. "I'm the luckiest guy in the world, you know that?"

Dinah pulled him closer. "I'm glad you feel that way. Me too."

CHAPTER 6

El Rey was greeted at the air charter terminal at Benito Juárez International Airport by Jorge Tovar, his CISEN handler, a field intelligence analyst who'd been assigned to run him following his earlier mission. The agency had left him alone for the last six months, only interrupting his solitude with his scheduled injection of the antidote for the neurotoxin with which they'd inoculated him in order to guarantee his performance. With any luck he only had one or two more of the semiannual injections to go, and then he'd be free – assuming the CISEN spooks had told him the truth about the agent.

The little man had reminded *El Rey* of a weasel when he'd first met him, and the impression was reinforced in this, their second meeting. Tovar led him to a waiting limousine, its opaque privacy glass raised so whatever was discussed wasn't overheard by the driver. Tovar had a brief discussion with the chauffeur and then got in after *El Rey*, who sat facing him, awaiting whatever bad news Tovar was bearing.

"So. You made it. Water? Something stronger?" Tovar offered, taking in the assassin's muddy, disheveled appearance without comment.

"No, thanks."

"Very well. We have an assignment for you."

"I gathered that. We're still a few weeks off from my next injection."

"It's right up your alley."

El Rey nodded, his expression stony.

28

Tovar opened a slim ostrich-skin briefcase and removed a file. He handed it to *El Rey* and flipped on the interior dome light so he could read.

Inside were three photographs, each with a dossier attached. *El Rey* eyed the images and read each report carefully before closing the folder and handing it back to Tovar. The assassin sat back, thinking, and when he spoke, his voice was soft as velvet.

"Why?"

"I beg your pardon?" Tovar looked honestly surprised at the question.

El Rey repeated it. "Why?"

"What do you care?" Tovar snapped, obviously irritated.

"Didn't Rodriguez explain our arrangement? I think it would be best if I spoke with him."

"I'm your control officer, not Rodriguez. You work for us. You'll do what I say."

El Rey shook his head. "Not exactly. I reserve the right to ask questions, and if you leave anything out or I don't approve of the sanction, I can decline. Perhaps you should make a call and get clear on this, to either Rodriguez or Bernardo." Rodriguez was the assistant director of CISEN, Bernardo the head of section who'd taken over managing the assassin after the last operation. *El Rey*'s eyes darkened as he held Tovar's stare. "And I'd caution you about your tone. You seem to have forgotten who you're talking to. I'd advise you not to. I don't tolerate insolence, no matter what the source."

Tovar swallowed hard and lowered his gaze. The temperature seemed to have dropped twenty degrees while *El Rey* was speaking, and Tovar's arrogant confidence had suddenly abandoned him. He cleared his throat and shifted.

"It wasn't my intention to offend. Here's what I can tell you. These men are part of a drug trafficking and distribution network that needs to be shut down. Obviously, based on the players, it's much different than the typical cartel situation. These are untouchable players because of their prominence. It will require a delicate approach."

"Drugs? That makes no sense. What could these three possibly have to do with drugs?"

"Admiral Torreon oversees the ports. He's in charge of importation into Mexico. The archbishop is getting it across the border. And the American is coordinating the U.S. distribution."

"Why not just take them out using your people? Or here's an idea: build a case and prosecute them."

"Due to their positions, they'd never see the inside of a jail cell. So that leaves us with no alternative. However, there is an important caveat: the sanctions must appear to be accidents or natural causes. And I don't mean the sort of Wall Street 'accidents' we've seen where bankers shoot themselves in the head multiple times or throw themselves through unbreakable windows to commit suicide. There can be no hint of foul play."

"That obviously increases the difficulty level."

"And there's a further element to consider. All three need to occur within a short time frame. If there's latency between the deaths, it will open the door for the others to set up alternative partners, which defeats the purpose."

El Rey studied Tovar's face. "Since when is CISEN in the antidrug business?"

"That's outside of the scope of this assignment. But we're in the do-whatever-the-president-says business, if that's a broad enough hint, and the decision has been made, for whatever reason, that this group has to go."

"Timing?"

"Within the next ten days."

"Impossible. It will require careful planning. Can't be done in that time. Sorry."

"It has to be."

El Rey shook his head, as if admonishing a child. "You're asking the impossible, and I'm not going to rush into anything and get killed because of poor planning by clueless bureaucrats. I want to see

Bernardo. If you don't have the stomach to tell him he's dreaming, I will."

Tovar frowned, and then his tone softened, conceding defeat. "How much time do you think it will take?"

"I need to research the particulars. The admiral's still in the hospital?"

"Yes. He has multiple gunshot wounds."

"I saw something about that on the television. Was that you?"

"No. Apparently he has many enemies. The cartels included."

"It was sloppy enough."

"We agree on that."

El Rey opened the file and stared at the photograph of the admiral for several long moments. "Is there anything else?"

"I need your commitment."

"As I've said, I can't do it on your schedule, and I won't know how long it will take until I'm able to do some research."

Tovar looked unhappy, but nodded. "When can you let me know? Time is of the essence."

"I'll need a few days. And some logistical support."

"Such as?"

"Access to your database. This will require as much information as I can get my hands on."

Tovar considered the demand. "I can arrange for you to have remote access, but they don't want you anywhere near headquarters. You don't exist, and we don't want to do anything to change that."

"Yes, I can appreciate that if something went wrong and it were to become known I was connected with you…well, it wouldn't play well." He glanced out the window. "Drop me off two blocks up, on the right. There's a Greek restaurant there. I'm hungry and tired. I'll find my own way home."

"Contact me tomorrow morning, and I'll get you into the system."

"I'll call you in three hours. No point in delaying."

Tovar depressed a button, activated the intercom, and instructed the driver to pull over at the restaurant. *El Rey* sat forward as the big car moved over two lanes.

"What's the budget?"

"There's no set figure," Tovar said, his eyes darting to the side.

"Any time the sanction is international, it introduces expenses that are orders of magnitude greater than a domestic action, especially on a high-profile target."

"We are not without experience in these matters," Tovar snapped.

"Good. Then you won't be surprised when I have costs calculated. There will be no negotiation. Whatever I think will be necessary will have to be provided without question. Is that a problem?"

"No. Within reason."

El Rey's voice was almost inaudible as the car slowed.

"You want me to take out one of Mexico's top naval officers, the archbishop of Tijuana, and a celebrity American film star, and do it without anyone suspecting anything. There's nothing reasonable about that."

"As I said, we understand what we're dealing with. You'll have whatever support is necessary."

Tovar watched *El Rey* collect his bags and melt into the procession of pedestrians on the busy sidewalk near the restaurant. He waited until the car was moving again, slipped a cell phone from his pocket, and made a call, his voice a murmur as the limousine continued along the wide boulevard. The vague sense of unease the assassin's presence inevitably caused lingered like the taint of ptomaine, and his eyes roved over the liquor bottles in the side compartment as he considered flushing the sour taste of fear away with a few swallows of liquid courage.

CHAPTER 7

Carla Vega strode across the busy floor of the network, nodding to several colleagues as she went, everyone in their usual mad scramble and too busy to slow down. She approached the corner office where a black-haired woman in a tailored cream-colored blouse and designer slacks sat behind an imposing desk in a glass-enclosed lobby.

"Good morning, darling. You look fabulous today. You have to tell me where you got that outfit," Carla gushed as she greeted her friend Lupe, the receptionist for the network boss who ran the news division. They kissed each other's cheeks, and Carla whispered to Lupe, "What's this all about?"

"I don't know. He just said he needed to see you first thing. Beats me. You know how he is."

"Nothing more? Sounds ominous."

"I wouldn't be too worried. He worships the ground you walk on. You're a ratings diva, as if you weren't aware."

"Well, we'll see what the Gorgon wants."

Carla took a seat on the contemporary leather slab sofa in the antechamber, prepared to wait the obligatory five minutes required for her superior to establish whose time was the most valuable, and was surprised when Lupe's line buzzed and she looked up.

"He says to go right in."

Carla glued her famous smile in place and breezed into Silvino Galindo's office, trailing a cloud of expensive perfume. Galindo rose as she entered and motioned to his conference table.

"Carla, as always, a pleasure. Please have a seat. I've ordered coffee."

"Thank you, Sil. You know the way to a woman's heart."

"Hardly. If I did, you'd think I'd have mounted a better offensive in any of my three marriages."

"Their loss. And what's that saying? Number four's a charm. How is Adriana, anyway?" Carla traveled in the same social circle as her boss, and liked the newest *Señora* Galindo, who was three years younger than Carla and thirty fewer than her husband.

"Oh, full of energy and ambition. Just what the doctor ordered," Galindo said, and they both pretended that the office gossip wasn't filled with rumors that the enigmatic Galindo would soon have an opportunity to explain to the hungry tabloids why his latest romantic entanglement had crashed and burned. Adriana was an actress of marginal abilities but renowned libido, whose magnetic performance in the telenovela *Corazón Valiente* had attracted the powerful division head's eye. Love had found a way to bridge the age difference, Galindo's considerable family fortune and the exposure he could bring to an enterprising thespian's career in no way responsible for how quickly and deeply Adriana had been swept off her feet.

"Be sure to give her my regards."

They made small talk until Lupe entered with the coffee service and deposited it on the table, and then Galindo got down to business with none of his customary circumlocution.

"I couldn't help but notice you all over the news yesterday. That was spectacular footage of the attack on the admiral."

"Yes, it was rather, wasn't it? But it was more Blasio's doing than mine. I just stood there and looked pretty while he caught the shot," she said, crediting her cameraman.

"You certainly have a talent for being in the right place at the right time, though, don't you? But I don't recall green-lighting a trip to Ensenada," Galindo said, his casual tone always a warning to those who knew him well.

"Well, I don't bore you with all my whims, Sil. I'm fully aware that you have more important fish to fry than my every human-interest story."

Galindo poured her a cup of coffee, the fine china cups gleaming in the fluorescent office light, and they sat quietly as they attended to their drinks like chess players before an important move.

"Still, I do like to know what my star reporter's up to. A boat christening is hardly the stuff someone with your stature should be wasting her time with," Galindo said with a fake smile, the reprimand clear in spite of the flattering words.

"What's that American saying? All's well that ends well. Our footage was by far the best of the attack on the boat. We'll get a lot of mileage out of it. Providence blessed us, which is all I can ask."

"It was brilliant, no question. But I do have a concern. You can't help but be aware that we're grooming you to be the next anchor for the evening news, ahead of several of your colleagues who have considerably more experience. I think you're perfect for the job, but it's not an easy sell to the stodgy old farts I have to convince, and it doesn't help when I'm blindsided by your having disappeared to Baja, regardless of how well it turned out. To be a real contender for the job, you can't be involved in controversy. I thought we'd discussed that."

Carla nodded, seeming to agree even though her pulse was thundering in her ears. So this meeting was all about control. She hadn't told him because he would have sent someone more junior, and she had ulterior motives in trying to get to the admiral. But this wasn't a battle she needed to fight – she had other, more pressing objectives.

"A very valid point, and believe me, controversy was the furthest thing from my mind when I went to a boat christening. Obviously I had no way of knowing it would turn into a battle zone." She fixed him with doe eyes and beamed a megawatt smile. "Perhaps we should discuss some of my upcoming projects, to make sure I stay out of trouble?"

"I'd like that. What does your month look like?"

She took him through three stories she wanted to pursue, knowing he would shoot two of them down – as with their neighbor to the north, the media in Mexico was largely a public-relations machine for the pecuniary interests that ran the country, and each network was owned or funded by one of the political parties whose coverage of their political adversaries was always so lurid and exaggerated that nobody believed anything they reported. Carla's network was fortunate enough to be the apparatus for the sitting president's party, but in spite of the position of relative power from which it operated, she still had to tread lightly on certain topics, which were usually the ones that interested her the most.

After he had predictably declined the decoy stories, she arrived at one of the ones she really needed approval for: covering an awards ceremony in Hollywood in six days, which was the type of vapid fluff she despised but Galindo ate up. He was a career man who viewed his role as one of providing entertainment, which conflicted with her belief that the job of a news reporter was to investigate real issues – topics that were sensitive, even dangerous. They'd butted heads over it, but had arrived at an uneasy truce where she sought approval for anything of consequence, even if she often misrepresented her reasons for wanting to cover a story.

Both were comfortable with the game of cat and mouse that ensued, Galindo's role to try to figure out the level of discomfort one of Carla's tangents might produce with his masters and quash the more inflammatory before she could pursue them, and Carla's to offer only the most innocuous of reasons for wanting to dig into anything. The relationship seemed to work, even if occasionally her famous temper got the better of her in volcanic flare-ups that were the delight of the gossip columnists that covered the trade.

"The People's Choice Awards? What's the local angle?" he pressed, probing for anything that might reveal her true motives.

"Several of our stars have important crossover roles and have been nominated for honors. It's an important stepping-stone to the Oscar coverage, which I'll also be doing."

"How long do you foresee being in Los Angeles?"

"No more than two days. The usual red-carpet thing, some interviews, party coverage. I'd really rather you send someone else, but I know how you like to stick me in evening gowns," she teased.

"That's better than you wanting to tackle one of the *narcotraficantes* or take on state-level corruption," he said, referring to her last two bombshell research projects, the latter of which had resulted in enough public outcry to bring about the arrest of a state governor for corruption – unfortunately, one of the president's party's brighter lights. Galindo had let it be known that his ass had endured a roasting, although she thought he was secretly pleased that his star reporter had proved her mettle.

"This will be commentary on whose shirts the celebs are wearing and how short the starlets' dresses are."

"You had me at short dresses. Consider that on the schedule. What else do you have?"

She floated two more ideas, the second of which tied into her trip to the U.S. He approved both, and they spent a comfortable fifteen minutes bantering about who was rumored to be sleeping with whom and at which soirees they could expect to run into each other. Carla actually liked Galindo, their differences notwithstanding, and because of their status in the Mexico City entertainment hierarchy, they saw more of each other at events than they did at work, which was fine with her. She'd lulled him into lowering his skepticism over her story choices, and had gotten approval for both of the jobs she secretly wanted to cover, without tipping her hand. Carla had no doubt that he would have blown a gasket had he suspected the truth, so what he didn't know was actually best for them both.

"Well, as always, a pleasure, Carla. Do keep me in the loop if you decide to take any more unscheduled trips," Galindo said as they parted.

"Absolutely, Sil. I mean, what are the odds that another helicopter will be shot out of the sky on my watch?" she said with a wink and a toss of her hair, leaving him off-balance, as always, wondering what he'd missed in their discussion. "See you tomorrow night at the museum opening."

"Oh, is it Tuesday already? Yes, will do. See you then."

He watched as she strode out of his office, her butter-soft chocolate leather pants doing justice to her every graceful move, and shook his head. She was a thoroughbred, but like all stars, could be a handful. His thoughts turned to his wife and her latest demands, and the banal discussion with Carla receded into the soup of office mundanities swirling around in his head.

Carla stopped at Lupe's station and thanked her for the coffee.

Lupe leaned toward her and whispered conspiratorially, "Did you slip one past him?"

Carla pretended surprise and then winked. "What would be the point of coming to work if I didn't? Are we on for lunch today?"

"I wouldn't miss it for the world."

CHAPTER 8

Atlangatepec, Tlaxcala, Mexico

The first faint rays of dawn painted the eastern sky with orange and pink. On the horizon, a line of plum-colored clouds darkened where the peaks of the surrounding mountains jutted into the heavens like crooked teeth. Lieutenant Fernando Briones peered through a pair of binoculars from his hiding place behind a barn a quarter mile away from the edge of a dirt airstrip, his radio volume turned low, the engine of his Ford Lobo truck idling. He checked his watch impatiently and glanced at the officer in the passenger seat, who, like Briones, wore a dark blue bulletproof vest with *Federales* stenciled in white across the back, and clutched an M16 assault rifle with nervous fingers.

"Still no sign of anyone," Briones murmured. The stakeout, in a rural agricultural area fifty miles from Mexico City, had been mounted in response to a tip about an inbound shipment of methamphetamines that was supposed to arrive at dawn in the hold of a private plane. It was to be picked up by members of the Knights Templar cartel and distributed in the capital's *barrios*, where the cheap drug's consumption had reached epidemic proportions along with a steep rise in associated violent crime. Under ordinary circumstances, the shantytowns that housed the untouchables of Mexico were as dangerous as any in the country, but since the cartels had begun distributing meth to the poor there, bloodshed had exploded and now rivaled the most infamous favelas of Brazil.

"Here comes the welcome committee," the officer said, watching two Cadillac Escalades bounce down a dirt track that led to the far end of the rutted runway.

Briones whispered into his radio. There were four other federal police trucks behind the barn with him, each with a complement of heavily armed men in the truck beds, wearing full assault gear including helmets and facemasks, and another half dozen vans and trucks on the other side of the runway behind a complex of storage sheds.

The narco-traffickers' SUVs coasted to a stop in a cloud of dust, headlights illuminated, and the doors swung wide. Eight men emerged, four with submachine guns, and surveyed their surroundings as they stood by the vehicles.

Briones' radio chirped back confirmation that his officers were ready to move, and he returned his full attention to the gunmen. The shipment tip had come anonymously, no doubt from a rival gang trying to make life miserable for their competitors, but Briones didn't care. If he could stop one day's flow of meth, he'd be happy. Too many were paying with their lives for the damage the drug did, and it was now the number one problem for the anti-cartel task force in Mexico City, heroin and cocaine having fallen out of favor as the cheaper synthetic took hold.

The air smelled of freshly turned soil and freshly cut grass, and the pasture next to the airstrip glistened with dew as the sun rose into the sky like an angry Aztec god. Briones cocked his head, ears perked, as the faint hum of an approaching plane droned from the south. He swung his binoculars toward the sound and spotted the outline of a Beech Baron 58 twin-engine prop plane against the brightening sky.

"This is it. Right on schedule. At least they're punctual," Briones said and passed the alert on to his men. "Nobody move until I give the signal. We'll wait until they're busy unloading the plane. Hold your fire unless they shoot first, in which case, take them down hard."

The radio crackled as his squad leaders confirmed, and they waited as the small plane drifted toward the runway. It seemed to hover in the still air, and then its wheels struck the red dirt strip and it slowed as it rolled toward the two Cadillacs.

If the information was correct, there were four hundred kilos of meth stashed in the plane, produced in a Honduran jungle lab. The airplane was a regular commuter, transporting thousands of kilos north every month, and always landed at different rural airstrips to evade detection. Four hundred kilos was a substantial haul by any measure, and the task force had scrambled to get into position with only five hours' notice. Briones' cell phone had awakened him in the middle of the night, and he'd raced to headquarters, assembled an interception squad, and then traveled to the airstrip under cover of darkness. They'd carefully draped tarps over the vehicles so they wouldn't attract attention from the air, and now they were only moments from game time.

No matter how many raids Briones participated in, his pulse always quickened in the seconds before launching into action. The same thought always occurred to him as he did his final mental check: this might be the time where his luck ran out and he ended the day in a body bag. The chance of death was a constant on the task force, but even so, a live operation always put his existence into perspective. He adjusted his vest as his eyes followed the plane's progress toward the waiting SUVs.

The four arrivals who weren't toting weapons began offloading white plastic-wrapped packages and stacking them into the back of the nearest Escalade. Briones gave the signal and gunned the big truck, leading the way from the barn to the airstrip. The gunmen froze at the sight of the vehicles bearing down on them, and Briones' voice boomed over the Ford's public address system.

"Federal Police. Drop your weapons. You're surrounded."

Submachine gunfire greeted his warning, and he swerved as a row of bullets blew dirt fountains into the air to his right. Briones cursed and gave the go-ahead over the radio as he skidded to a halt, twisting the wheel as he braked, positioning the truck so that its side provided cover from the cartel gunmen. His men were already shooting as the dust settled around them. He dragged himself across the seat and out the passenger door while the police sharpshooters returned fire.

Slugs thumped into the side of the truck, and one of the tires popped when a round hit it, but the cartel gunmen were badly outmatched, and the police made short work of them. The entire exchange was over in under a minute. The two surviving cartel members surrendered along with the pilot, their colleagues dead on the ground in pools of blood.

The police approached the men cautiously and wasted no time in cuffing the survivors before loading them into one of the vans. Briones placed a call on his cell phone and gave a terse update – they'd managed to avoid any police casualties, a rarity for this type of operation, and only one of his men was wounded superficially.

Half an hour later they'd inventoried the drug shipment, photographed the crime scene, and Briones left his men to mop up as he returned to Mexico City with a van full of meth. He took a final glance at the bodies of the gunmen already bloating in the morning sun, waved away several flies, and grunted to the driver, who eased forward down the dirt track escorted by two trucks loaded with grim-faced officers, and a second van containing the prisoners.

~ ~ ~

Cruz glanced around the task force floor as he made his way to his office, a cup of coffee in one hand and his briefcase in the other. As always, the area was controlled pandemonium, made more so by the recent spate of kidnappings in Mexico City. The anti-cartel task force was theoretically focused on narcotics trafficking since that was the cartels' primary activity, but some of the criminal networks had expanded into murder-for-hire and kidnapping to augment flagging marijuana sales. The entrepreneurial spirit being what it was, the cartels had taken to snatching high-net-worth targets and pocketing easy money for a few hours of work, resulting in a dramatic and highly visible increase in kidnappings throughout the capital.

His secretary wasn't at her desk, so he picked up his messages from a stack on her blotter and pushed through the door, set his briefcase on his conference table, and switched on the lights. His inbox had miraculously filled since last night with a small mountain of paperwork – the bane of his existence and the biggest part of his job running the largest police operation in the nation. Cruz checked his emails, listened to his voice messages, and was preparing to place a call when Briones tapped softly on his door, his face drawn, a smudge of dirt on his cheek.

"Come in," Cruz called out, hanging up.

"Good morning, sir. You wanted to see me?"

"Yes. Come, grab a seat," Cruz invited as he rounded his desk and joined the younger man at the small round conference table. "Congratulations on a job well done this morning. A big score."

Briones shrugged. "I wish they all went so smoothly."

Cruz nodded. "Enjoy it when one does. It's certainly rare enough." Cruz hesitated as he studied the dark circles under Briones' eyes. "I want to discuss an opportunity with you. A promotion."

Briones looked surprised. "A promotion?"

"Yes, from second lieutenant to first. Pay raise, the whole deal."

"That's…I don't know what to say."

"Wait until you hear me out. One of the requirements of the new job is that you spend a significant amount of your time in the office instead of in the field. At least six months, if not more. You'll need to delegate most of your active investigations."

Briones eyed Cruz's stack of paperwork. "May I infer that this has something to do with the change in the orientation of the task force to include kidnapping?"

"Not really. It's just that as we've grown, I've been dealing with all the documentation, and it's now a twelve-hour day just signing and stamping and reading. I need help. You're the only one qualified, so you were the first name I put into the hat. The only name, actually."

Briones hesitated, doubt written across his face. "I do enjoy being in the field," he said, his tone cautious as he considered the ramifications of being desk-bound.

"So do I. But if you're going to move up, you have to change with the times." Cruz sighed. "The alternative is I promote Damario or Felix, and then you'll be answering to one of them."

Briones' look of distaste required no explanation.

Cruz smiled. "I thought so. Then it's decided. The good news is that you'll get an office, too. And longer hours for very little additional pay, of course."

"I would expect nothing less."

"Congratulations. I'm sure you'll adapt without too much trouble. Now let's move on to other matters. The meth bust is a success; the survivors are being processed... What have you dug up on the Galo kidnapping?" Cruz asked. Two nights earlier the daughter of a prominent government minister had been kidnapped at gunpoint from outside one of Mexico City's most exclusive nightclubs. Her date had been pistol-whipped by the perpetrators and was in guarded condition at Hospital Angeles Pedregal.

Briones closed his eyes for a moment, recalling the details. "The father was contacted yesterday morning from an internet telephone that was bounced through multiple IP addresses, so untraceable. The kidnappers demanded five million dollars within twenty-four hours. The father doesn't have that kind of money liquid and negotiated it to two million within forty-eight."

Cruz shook his head. "Any idea which gang is behind it?"

"The kidnapping was organized and efficient. The boyfriend said the perps were wearing balaclavas, so he can't identify them, but based on the M.O. and the level of information they seemed to have had, I'd suspect Los Zetas as the most likely."

"Four, right? Kidnappers?"

"Correct. Plus the van driver."

"Anything on the vehicle?"

"Stolen plates. We tracked them on the traffic cams, but you know how that goes. They stop working once out of the city center, so we lost them five minutes later."

"Witnesses?"

"Six people. Everyone's story is the same, so nothing there."

"How's the family holding up?"

"As you might expect. The mother's a basket case, and the father's scrambling to round up money from his brothers."

"I had a message when I came in this morning from his uncle. It wasn't pleasant. He was acting like I was personally responsible. I was just getting ready to return his call when you saved me the grief, but it sounds like I can't put that off. Do we have any leads?"

"We're rousting all the usual street sources, but so far, nothing. Which is the same pattern we've been seeing. They're keeping their drug network separate, so nobody knows anything."

"Smart. But it makes our life harder." The solve rate on kidnappings was at an all-time low, and the accepted wisdom was to simply pay the ransom and move on. Victims were usually returned unharmed, making the prospects of cooperation between the families and the police unlikely. Cruz couldn't fault the thinking – if he had a child, he wasn't sure he'd roll the dice with their lives by bringing the authorities in. To do so changed the game, and the first condition kidnappers insisted upon was always no police involvement, on pain of death. The only reason they'd been alerted was because Cruz had promised not to make a move without consulting the father. But now that his uncle, one of the top heavyweights in the president's party, was involved, the situation was even more precarious, and Cruz was dreading the report he'd have to deliver along with the recommendation: pay the ransom.

It ran counter to everything he stood for, but there was no other way to ensure the girl's safety, so that was their best option. Kidnappers wanted the money, not a nationwide manhunt on murder charges, so in all likelihood half an hour after making the exchange she'd materialize in some alley, dazed but unhurt. Exceptions were rare, but those were usually when amateurs were involved, and from the description of the crime, they were hardly dealing with neophytes.

Cruz's life was even more difficult of late after a sensational series of reports on suspected police involvement with the kidnapping gangs. Long on innuendo and short on facts, they had nonetheless been successful in convincing the public that the cartels were operating with official involvement – a conclusion that Cruz publicly dismissed, but privately believed was probably correct. His task force was clean, but the Federal Police were notoriously corrupt, their larceny only exceeded by that of the local Mexico City force, some of whom had been recently charged with organizing their own extortion and kidnapping rings as sidelines to their formal duties.

"What are the chances of cooperation on the handoff?" Cruz asked.

"You can float that, but I'd say unless we can guarantee no screwups, the father's not going to play ball. Do you blame him?"

Cruz didn't. Several times the families had allowed the police to try to set up stings, and those had invariably backfired, resulting in either increased ransom demands or dead victims.

"Well, that's not how I was hoping to start the day. What else?"

Briones took him through the other active cases – a suspected drug lab location in one of the *barrios*; rumors of a large arriving shipment of cocaine in the warehouse district; seven kidnappings; and three bodies found beheaded in a dumpster outside a chain restaurant downtown, one of them a teenage girl who'd been helping her boyfriend skim drug profits from his street-dealing operation, the other two the boyfriend and his seventeen-year-old brother. In other words, standard fare in the largest city in North America.

Cruz tried not to let the sense of futility get to him, but every day brought a relentless tide of brutality that sapped his will. The cartels were infinitely better funded, were unbound by any legal constraints, and could afford to co-opt politicians and police alike with a tsunami of cash that rolled in from the U.S. drug trade. What twenty years ago had been a handful of regional players, unsophisticated thugs with little but guns and violence as assets, were now transnational criminal networks that banked at some of the largest firms and washed their cash through the stock and real estate markets, in addition to a web of hotels, retail outlets, casinos, and nightclubs around the world.

It was an unwinnable war that nobody had any real desire to fight, but for appearances the Mexican and U.S. governments went through the motions, and Cruz was part of that effort, regardless of his personal feelings. Even if the larger battle couldn't be won, he could make a difference at a smaller level, which was where he focused.

"Close the door behind you," Cruz said as Briones rose, his report finished. "I'll call you later once I dig out."

"Yes, sir."

Cruz moved back to his desk and sat heavily, staring at the phone for a few moments before reaching out and making the call he'd been dreading to the uncle, who was every bit as dirty as any of the cartel kingpins. It was the nature of the beast, and the man would want to throw his weight around now that his family was on the receiving end of the lawlessness he silently profited from. Cruz's job would be to listen, sympathize, and make assurances neither of them would believe.

He dialed the number and waited as the phone rang, counting the minutes until he'd be able to have Briones take over some of these noxious tasks. Not a minute too soon, he thought as the uncle's abrasive rasp grated over the line and the unpleasant dance began, one of an endless string of encounters in a day wholly absent of meaning or satisfaction, as obligatory as prayer and, ultimately, as useful.

CHAPTER 9

Sunlight streamed through the blinds and washed across the hardwood floor of the condo *El Rey* leased in one of the upscale Mexico City districts. Privacy and safety were his primary concerns – not so much out of fear for himself as for the attendant drama that would accompany his dealing with any burglary attempts. He kept to himself, but not so much so that it would arouse the attention of his neighbors, whom he'd met and who thought he had some sort of web design or technical support consulting company that he ran from home.

He rubbed a hand across the dusting of stubble on his jaw as he studied the image on the computer monitor: Rene Bolivar, the archbishop of Tijuana. *El Rey* studied the man's face – distinguished, at forty-six relatively young for so prominent an ecclesiastic position, a full head of curly hair, and a worldly air that seemed to jump off the screen.

Bolivar had been the top church official in Baja for four years, during which time nothing of note had transpired on his watch, other than a near miss during a savage outbreak of cartel violence close to the cathedral, when his car had been caught in the crossfire as two gangs had shot it out. Fortunately neither he nor his driver had been hurt, but there had been three bullet holes in the Chrysler sedan to show the press, who had declared his escaping unscathed from the attack a minor miracle. *El Rey* smiled as he read one of the accounts – it would have been a greater miracle if the bishop had progressed another block before the shooting had started and thus avoided any exposure to danger, but that wasn't how the newspapers worked.

The good news was that he had negligible security and would be the easiest of the targets. The admiral was still in intensive care due to his wounds and, per CISEN's poached military hospital records, was likely to remain there for some time, his age and his precarious cardiovascular condition complicating his recovery. But unfortunately he was being guarded like a head of state, the botched attack having been all the warning the navy had required, so getting to him would require considerably greater skill and planning than the cleric or, hopefully, the actor.

El Rey had quickly prioritized the two easiest, saving the admiral for last. Based on the physician's reports, there was a better-than-even chance he would expire on his own, not requiring the assassin's help to cross over to his eternal reward, so for the time being *El Rey* would concentrate on the younger targets.

Figuring out how to end their lives was a challenge, but well within his abilities. Creating the appearance of accidental deaths would be harder than a straight kill, but only marginally so.

The only part of his research to give him pause was that nothing in Bolivar's background even hinted at involvement in anything but doing the Lord's work. A member of the clergy since a young man, one of nine siblings, three of whom had been drawn to the cloth, his official record had been distinguished by piety and devotion through a series of appointments that had culminated in his present position, an unexpected upset within the Church, but a concession to its loss of influence and relevance among the younger generations. Bolivar was moderate in his views compared to the prior archbishop, whose stance had been only slightly softer than that of the Inquisition – and whose legacy had been one of alienation and separation from the flock as he'd grown increasingly reclusive and reluctant to appear in public before ultimately being called back to Rome to serve out his final years in study and introspection.

If this was a man who was moving tonnage of methamphetamines through Tijuana as CISEN had asserted, he was more deserving of an academy award than the American, Robert Perry, a vain, arrogant playboy with the slouching swagger and perennial sneer of the twenty-something slackers who idolized his mediocre performances.

Perry fit with CISEN's assessment of a U.S. distribution mastermind. The nephew of a prominent actress who'd had a long career in films and later on two popular dramatic television series, he'd never done an honest day's work in his life, having won early forgettable roles due to his aunt's contacts. A breakthrough supporting role had blossomed into his current box office celebrity due to a paucity of genuine talents for Hollywood to market as well as his smarmy good looks, which mainly consisted of a habitual smirk, chiseled abs, and the airheaded blue-eyed stare of an underwear model coupled with a bad boy reputation underscored by a mildly stoned demeanor.

A young single actor with a taste for the wild life and the time and contacts to move tonnage of drugs wasn't a stretch, but a priest whose most controversial feature was arguing for a more reasoned stance on difficult topics of interest to his congregation? *El Rey* didn't see it. That was the genius of hiding in plain sight, he supposed. Who would suspect him? And more importantly, who would dare prosecute him without ironclad proof?

The actor lived in Malibu, in a twelve-million-dollar beach house with its own gym, security system, maid, and groundskeeper. He was routinely photographed on the beach with a steady stream of eligible bachelorettes in various stages of undress, and several of the tabloids had enjoyed record sales due to his DUI offenses and scrapes with the law. Apparently young Perry wasn't shy about his chemical fortification, nor was he one to back down from a fight, which ensured that when he wasn't on the set, lavishing the camera with his brooding pout and monotone delivery, he was in the papers or on the news, growling 'no comment' or offering a middle finger to an adoring media that found his every utterance as fascinating as the discovery of a new gospel.

Freeing him from his mortal coil would be tricky but ultimately satisfying for *El Rey*, in that the world would be no poorer for the actor's departure, but the priest made him hesitate and question his mission. He'd contacted Tovar twice more since receiving the access codes to verify CISEN's intel on Bolivar, and Tovar had been irritable but adamant. Bolivar was the right man and was to be eliminated as soon as possible.

El Rey had long ago purged any moral or ethical concerns from his lexicon upon embarking on his career, and had executed enough miscreants to lose count. He'd learned long ago that there were no true innocents, and that when a professional of his stature was brought in, the target had earned his end, one way or another. Politicians were inevitably corrupt, cartel members were brutal animals, and all tended to drink at the same polluted watering holes from the same toxic sluice. If CISEN insisted that the admiral was dirty, he had no difficulty believing it, and even less imagining the American as bent; but the priest seemed a genuinely blameless man. The hit didn't sit well with him, but in the end, his job wasn't to play judge, simply executioner, and if CISEN wanted the archbishop terminated, it was out of *El Rey*'s hands to question it.

After an afternoon studying the archbishop's schedule and the layout of the rectory where he spent his nights, *El Rey* had developed a plan that would ensure the church stifled any in-depth investigation of his untimely death. He made a mental list of the items he would need and, after showering and affixing a goatee, went in search of the materials that would condemn the priest upon their discovery in his possession. Finding them was child's play for *El Rey*, who knew the seedy underbelly of Mexico City like the lines on his own hands, and by nightfall he was back and packing a bag.

He'd carry out the first assassination within the next forty-eight hours and then, with any luck, make his way into the U.S., where he'd have a date with Hollywood in a week's time in as unlikely a location as any he could imagine.

CHAPTER 10

Beatriz smiled at the two security guards in the lobby of CISEN headquarters, a nondescript building in downtown Mexico City with nothing to alert the casual observer that the nation's intelligence agency was located there other than an array of microwave transmitters on the roof. There were no signs, no external indications of the edifice's importance in the government framework, only steel and glass entry doors that a close inspection would have revealed as unusually thick, and a dearth of windows ascribable to poor design by an architect unconcerned with aesthetics or sensible ventilation.

The stouter of the pair held one of the twin doors open for her, and she offered demure thanks as she stepped onto the sidewalk, the quiet tree-lined side street still after the lunch rush had died. Beatriz took her time as she ambled to the corner and looked around as if uncertain of her destination and then darted across the larger boulevard during a lull in the steady procession of vehicles.

She wandered to the middle of the block and stopped abruptly in front of a shoe store featuring a big sale. She peered from behind her sunglasses at her reflection in the display window to ensure she wasn't being tailed while she appeared to consider the shop's selection. Satisfied she was clean, she continued down the block and disappeared around the far corner, picking up her pace as she did so, and hailed a passing taxi once she was out of sight.

Beatriz kept her eye on the side mirror as the driver negotiated the busy streets and regaled her with acerbic commentary about the mental deficiencies of the other motorists. She pressed a few folded peso notes into his hand when he rolled to a stop outside her destination and was out of the car before he had a chance to thank her for her generous tip.

As a senior aide at CISEN she had top security clearances, but her activity was confined to clerical functions. The agency, like all Mexican bureaucracies, was a patriarchy, where all the meaningful positions went to men, usually from prominent families, while the women got coffee or fetched documents. She'd been employed there for a decade and was used to it, practically invisible now, her once-remarkable looks faded from the years and her clothing demure, as befitted a serious woman of maturity.

She watched the taxi pull away into traffic before she continued past the restaurant and entered one of the countless small internet cafés that lined the downtown streets. She walked to the rear of the shop, where an ancient pay phone hung from the wall, deposited a coin into the slot, and dialed a number from memory.

"Hola," Carla Vega answered, her voice musical even over the telephone.

"Carla. Hi. What number should I call you at?"

Carla's voice quieted to a whisper. "Just a second." Beatriz heard muffled rustling, and then Carla returned and gave her a number. "In three minutes, okay?"

Beatriz hung up, eyed her watch as the minutes seemed to take forever to wind around, and then dialed. Carla picked up after one ring.

"I need to make this fast," Beatriz said.

"I understand." Carla hesitated. "Is everything okay?"

"Oh, yes, it's fine. I just don't want to be gone too long and arouse suspicion."

"Is that really an issue?"

"Probably not, but I'd rather not take any chances."

"Fine. What do you have?"

"It...it doesn't make much sense. I was asked to pull a file on the archbishop of Tijuana."

"Really? That's odd. Were you able to piece together why?"

"No, but it was the same section that's interested in the admiral and that actor."

"And you don't have anything more on them?"

"No. I've told you all I know."

"Which doesn't add up to a lot."

"I'll keep my eyes open and call if I find out anything more. That's all I can do."

Carla paused. "I appreciate it – I'm just frustrated that I'm not finding any connection so far. I'll...I'll see you next month, okay?"

"Sure. I have to go."

"All right. Ciao."

"Adios."

Carla replaced the handset of the pay phone at the hotel next door to the network building and stared off into space. Her cousin Beatriz had first approached her about irregularities at CISEN a month earlier, when she'd gotten a bad feeling after being asked to pull up data on Admiral Torreon – an unusual request considering his reputation of scrupulous honesty.

Carla had promised her cousin she'd dig around to see if there were any irregularities surrounding the admiral. When she did, she'd come up empty, which surprised her. Everyone had at least some dirt on them once they ascended to a certain level, and the military was no different.

Beatriz's next call had brought Carla the actor. Why would CISEN have any interest in a celebrity whose only connection to Mexico was a Mexican father – Arturo Perez – which the son had anglicized to Perry as soon as he'd been of age, and who described his deceased parent as 'Spanish,' obviously ashamed of his Mexican heritage? It made no sense.

And now a priest? Not just any priest, either. One of the more prominent figures in the Mexican Church.

Perhaps it was all meaningless, but Carla had good instincts, and her alarms had been clamoring ever since the admiral had stonewalled her. Most movers and shakers dreamed of an interview with the charming and beautiful reporter, even the corrupt and the obviously guilty.

The attack had driven home that there was more going on than was superficially evident, and if there was a connection between the actor and the admiral, she intended to discover what it was.

Beatriz's insistence on hyper-security bordering on paranoia would have been funny if she hadn't known precisely what the intelligence agency was capable of in terms of eavesdropping. She'd hinted that the phones at the network were monitored as a matter of course, and had warned Carla that cell phones were laughably easy to tap. She'd also told Carla after a few too many cocktails several years earlier that the Americans were listening in on everything, everywhere – something that had seemed delusional until the NSA was revealed to be spying on the entire planet.

Now Carla didn't know what to think, but she had a good nose for a story, and her gut was telling her there was something here – she just needed to figure out what.

CHAPTER 11

Assistant Director Rodriguez entered the conference room for his weekly staff meeting with a scowl on his face, and moved to the head of the table, obviously preoccupied. His quick eyes scanned the nine men in the room without any trace of good humor, and he began by asking the section heads general questions about their projects. The answers were expected to be short, informational, and on-point: Rodriguez had little tolerance for the typical polite waffling that constituted most governmental meetings.

As CISEN's assistant director, Rodriguez effectively ran the intelligence service. The director was, as in many countries, a political appointee, a figurehead with little or no relevant experience. Rodriguez, on the other hand, had spent his entire career with CISEN and had risen from being a field agent to an analyst and then into management. When the last shakeup had occurred, he'd been thrust into his current position, where he'd thrived on the long hours and constant intellectual demands.

Pedro Ybarra finished his report on several operations that were ongoing in Guatemala, and Rodriguez shifted his attention to Manuel Bernardo, who ran the agency's clandestine ops division – in charge of offensives that involved violence or assassination.

"What do we know about the attack on Admiral Torreon?" Rodriguez snapped after the preliminaries were over.

"We believe that the attempt was a cartel trying to eliminate him. He's done a remarkably good job in slowing the inflow of cocaine through the Pacific coast ports, and it's obvious that someone wants him out of the picture."

"Which cartel?"

"Unknown at this time. We have our ear to the ground, but so far nothing definitive."

"Keep me informed. I have a meeting tomorrow with the president's people, and that's going to be one of the subjects. It would be nice to have something other than a shoulder shrug to offer."

Bernardo nodded and made a small note on his pad.

"What about Hammer?" Rodriguez asked. Hammer was the code name CISEN had given *El Rey*.

"Nothing new to report. Up for another booster shot."

"He's been behaving?"

"As far as we can tell."

Rodriguez turned to the next section head. "Gabriel, tell us how we're going to stop the flow of guns from the U.S."

The meeting continued for another hour, and when it broke up, Rodriguez left without comment, his head pounding from another long night with little sleep. Once in his office, he dry swallowed two painkillers and poured himself his sixth cup of coffee of the day and, after taking a seat behind his desk, reached for the phone.

~ ~ ~

El Rey smiled at the ticket agent behind the Aeroméxico counter at Benito Juárez airport as she glanced at his driver's license and printed out his boarding pass. He'd been outfitted with several identities by CISEN and now carried both a set of new Mexican papers as well as a passport and American green card identifying him as an El Salvadorian cleared to work in the United States. That ID would come into play after he'd dispatched the archbishop.

The flight from Mexico City to Tijuana was smooth, and as the plane completed its final approach, he peered through his window at the border city's gray-brown sprawl. Shantytowns, little more than collections of pallets with tar paper nailed over them, clung to the sides of the hills within shouting distance of the United States' prosperity and boundless opportunity. The infamous wall stretched to the Pacific Ocean, with green and white Border Patrol trucks cruising along dirt tracks that ran along the no-man's-land between the state of California's southernmost reach and Baja California's northernmost.

A pall of smog hung over Tijuana as the plane dropped toward the airport, and *El Rey* contrasted the distant gleam of San Diego's chrome and glass skyline with the impoverished *barrios* that comprised most of Tijuana. It wasn't hard for him to understand the frustration the poor felt gazing at the riches only a few miles away from their shacks, where rudiments like potable water were a luxury and rivulets of sewage coursed down dirt streets, souring the atmosphere as toddlers played in the toxic dirt.

El Rey exited the terminal and eyed the border fence across the boulevard. Scores of multicolored coffins and crosses mounted to the steel siding commemorated the thousands who'd died attempting crossings. He waited in line for a taxi as vehicles raced by on the frontage artery, junkers that were more Bondo than metal jockeying for position between Mercedes and Audis. The trip to the district where the archdiocese was located took fifteen minutes in traffic, and *El Rey* had the driver drop him off near the municipal government building a block away from the church.

He ambled along the avenue, pausing to admire the bronze effigy of Miguel Hidalgo jutting from the roundabout at the junction of Avenida Independencia and Paseo Centenario Tijuana, and then settled in for lunch at a small sidewalk café across from the archdiocese, its tables deserted post-lunch hour. CISEN had provided blueprints of the cathedral and associated buildings, and *El Rey* had already decided on his preferred method of entry to the bishop's quarters. He had everything he required in his bag and now wanted to soak up the local environment – often, blueprints didn't capture important nuances about a target, and he'd learned to spend time at the sites of his missions before taking action.

His leisurely lunch took over an hour, and once he'd paid and walked around the block to verify the position of the traffic cameras, he walked to a moderately priced hotel a quarter mile from the archdiocese that catered to tourists. After suffering through an elevator ride with three American men in town for a bachelor party, their corpulent forms stinking of beer, tequila, and cigarettes, he made his way to his room, where he spent the late afternoon catching up on his sleep in preparation for a preliminary prowl around the archdiocese that evening.

CHAPTER 12

Mexico City, Mexico

Cruz rolled over and groped for his screeching cell phone on the night table next to the bed. Dinah groaned as he rose and padded to the bathroom, muted the ring, and answered as he pulled the door closed behind him.

"Yes?"

"*Capitan*, it's Briones."

"Yes, Lieutenant. I recognize your number. What can I do for you at…3:47 in the morning?"

"I'm sorry to call at this hour, but you wanted to be notified if there was another high-profile kidnapping."

"Don't tell me."

"It's bad, but could have been worse. This time there was a gun battle between the bodyguards and the kidnappers. The kidnappers were all killed except for the getaway driver, who crashed as he was leaving the scene. The bodyguards held him until the metropolitan police arrived, and then we got the call."

Cruz was wide awake now. "Where did all this transpire?"

"Club Vampiro. It's down on—"

"I know where it is," Cruz snapped. "Where are you?"

"On my way there right now."

"Can you pick me up in…ten minutes?"

"That's one of the reasons I'm calling."

"I'll see you downstairs. Oh, what about the driver? Where was he taken?"

"The local police turned him over to us. He's at headquarters in a holding cell. A doctor's with him right now – apparently he's got some bruises and contusions, but the airbag and his seat belt saved him from worse."

"I'll see you shortly," Cruz said and hung up. He dressed quickly and whispered to Dinah as he was opening the bedroom door.

"I'm sorry, *mi amor*. I have to go."

Dinah grunted, pulled the covers over herself, waved a limp hand, and was asleep again before Cruz made it to the condo entry. He struggled into his shoulder holster, donned a black windbreaker, and slipped his badge and wallet into a pocket before making his way downstairs. Two uniformed *Federales* sat in the lobby, his round-the-clock security team, a mandatory precaution ever since he'd been kidnapped by the head of the Sinaloa cartel for an impromptu meeting. The men stiffened when Cruz emerged from the elevator, and then scrambled to their feet.

Cruz exited the building and waited on the deserted sidewalk, framed by his security men, only the distant rumble of a car passing on the main boulevard for company.

Briones' Dodge Charger rolled to the curb a minute later, and Cruz got in. Briones handed him a cup of coffee and pulled back onto the street, cheerfully ignoring the speed limit as he accelerated and blew through a red light.

"Maybe you should hit the emergency lights," Cruz suggested, and Briones flipped a dashboard switch. Flashing blue illuminated the car interior from the bar bolted across the upper windshield. "Fill me in on what you know."

"The shoot-out occurred an hour ago. The target of the kidnapping was Romeo Saldado, the son of the beer magnate. He was at the club with several friends and two ex-marine bodyguards. When he left the club, four masked gunmen jumped out of a nearby van and tried to force him into the vehicle, but he fought them, which bought enough time for the guards to get their guns out. The kidnappers were armed with pistols, and there was a shoot-out. One of the guards took bullets in the chest and leg, but between the two of them they killed all the kidnappers. The unharmed guard emptied his weapon into the van as it took off, and a delivery truck slammed into it as it was crossing the intersection."

"Sounds like the same MO as the other recent attacks, doesn't it? Van, four men, a nightclub…"

"You'd think these kids would figure out that getting laid isn't worth the risk of being snatched, or worse," Briones said, ignoring that he was only five or six years older than the youths he was castigating.

"Any ID on the perps?" Cruz asked.

"Negative, but three of the four had tattoos that looked military. We're running prints."

"Military?"

"You know the kind. Flags, crossed rifles, that sort of thing. Oh, and one of the men had a scar from a gunshot wound. Not recent, but it might help get a fix on him."

"Anyone besides the bodyguard hurt?"

"No, by the grace of God. There were some close calls, but everyone ran inside once the shooting started. We got lucky."

"Sounds like it. A survivor, and the kidnappers didn't open up with AKs and spray the street." Cruz took a cautious sip from his cup. "And the coffee isn't bad, either. Thanks, by the way."

Briones smiled. "OXXO," he said, mentioning the ubiquitous convenience stores that had spread like cancer recently. "What did we ever do before there was one on every corner?"

Cruz eyed him. "How much sleep did you get?"

"Four hours. I'm fine."

"Are you up for the interrogation after we see the crime scene?"

"Try keeping me away."

"That's the spirit." Cruz gave him a tired grin. "You see, even if you're a desk jockey, you'll still get hauled into the field in the dead of night. So it's not all reports and meetings – there's a little excitement to be had."

"Nice to know."

The club was chaos, with almost a thousand partygoers emptying out in waves through side doors as police vehicles blocked the street.

A coroner's van sat near the entrance, where a dozen uniformed police were standing around, exchanging jokes or complaints as they waited for the cleanup to conclude.

Cruz and Briones approached the area where the forensics technicians were working on the corpses. Cruz shook hands with the metropolitan police sergeant in charge of the scene, who gave them the rundown on what had transpired, finishing with his estimation that the techs would need another hour to finish their job and haul the dead away.

"We got statements from the two guards, the victim, and his girlfriends."

"Plural?" Cruz said, an eyebrow raised.

"It's a different world than I grew up in," the sergeant observed. "As to the witnesses, everyone's story is the same. It's a classic grab that would have gone perfectly if the abductee hadn't kneed one of them in the groin and kicked another in the stomach."

"Really? That was aggressive."

"He told me he does martial arts. I guess even half in the bag, the practice came to good use."

"It could have gone the other way."

"I know," the sergeant agreed. "He's very lucky he didn't get a bullet to the head for his trouble. I told him."

"Where is he?"

"Sitting in that Suburban with his bodyguard and the two girls." The sergeant indicated a dark gray SUV with several police officers leaning against it. "The ambulance already took the other bodyguard to the hospital."

Briones went to see what he could glean from the victims as Cruz inspected the bodies and asked a pointed question here and there. After fifteen minutes it was obvious that their presence at the scene wasn't yielding any new information, so they thanked the sergeant and then made their way to headquarters.

The interrogation didn't provide any breakthroughs. The driver knew very little, other than that he'd been hired by one of the dead men, who he believed was cartel-related. He'd been paid five thousand pesos for the night – the equivalent of three hundred and fifty dollars – with another five thousand promised upon the successful completion of the abduction. Cruz shook his head at the stupidity of the transaction. The man would spend at least ten years in prison for a total possible payday of seven hundred dollars.

Only one thing the driver said gave them pause: that the man who'd hired him had indicated that if he did a good job on this one, there would be plenty more work, because they were targeting more rich kids, the next grab to occur at a rave the following weekend outside of Mexico City. The driver had gotten the impression that the kidnapping ring was larger than the four dead men, but who else was involved he couldn't guess, nor did he know any details about the coming attempt. He'd been picked up outside his tenement earlier that night, and he had no idea whether the kidnappers had a headquarters or, if so, where it was.

Briones accompanied Cruz to the elevators that led from the basement holding cell, moving slowly, fatigue obvious in his stride.

"What an idiot. His whole life thrown away…for what?"

"Not our problem. He chose his future," Cruz said, his tone glum.

"I'm not sure what we do with the information about the rave. I'll check to see what we have on upcoming events, but those are underground deals, with invitations strictly word of mouth."

"We might think about leaking it to the papers."

"True, but then what? The bad guys just change their plan, and we've accomplished nothing," Briones said, frustration in his every syllable.

They waited for the elevator to arrive in silence, and Cruz turned to Briones. "Sounds like a big group, doesn't it? Not a backyard outfit."

Briones nodded. "It definitely has cartel written all over it. Way too organized for one of the local gangs."

"I agree. Hopefully one of the dead men can be identified and we'll better understand who we're dealing with." He paused. "The girl still hasn't been returned. They paid the ransom last night, but so far, nothing."

"You think it's the same group?"

"Too early to say. But the fact that she hasn't shown up yet is troubling. You know we'll take the heat if they kill her."

"But we weren't involved. The parents deliberately kept us out of it."

"I know. But that won't matter if she shows up dead. There'll be press conferences and angry demands by the media. They'll be looking for someone to fry, and we're it." Cruz sighed. "Go home and get a couple of hours of sleep. That's an order."

"I told you, I'm fine."

"And I told you to go rest. Be back at ten. No arguments."

The door slid open, and they stepped into the elevator, Briones silently grateful for being ordered home in spite of his protestations, Cruz could tell. Between the prior night's mission at the airfield and now this, he was running on empty.

The elevator stopped at the main floor, and Briones got out. "Ten o'clock," he confirmed, and Cruz watched with a trace of envy for his relative youth and resilience as he signed out at the security desk. Cruz considered taking his own advice, but knew that he wouldn't be able to sleep, so he resigned himself to another long slog through the never-ending river of paperwork while he waited for the computers to cough out names to put with the kidnappers' faces. He swallowed the acid that rose in his gorge, a combination of anxiety and coffee, and offered a silent prayer that at least the kidnapped girl would be returned alive.

CHAPTER 13

Tijuana, Mexico

Archbishop Rene Bolivar thanked his guests – a group of society wives who were instrumental in the Church's charity drive to raise money for orphans – for coming, and shook hands with each as they left the rectory hall, where he'd hosted a dinner in appreciation of their tireless efforts. When the last woman had departed, he waved to Sister Catalina and wished her a good night. The cleaning staff was already at work clearing the tables and bussing dishes. He snagged a half-full glass of cabernet, a donation from one of the local wineries in the nearby Guadalupe Valley, and trudged wearily to his quarters on the second floor – an expansive suite of rooms by any measure, certainly compared to his prior Spartan digs when he was but a humble priest.

Bolivar was a hard worker, a hands-on administrator who was convinced he could make a difference in the community, changing attitudes about important issues like corruption, domestic violence, and abuse of property rights, all of which were greeted with apathy at present. Mexico's history was one of constant corruption at every level of government, from the local police to the presidency, and his flock no more expected honesty from its public servants than it expected levitation. Likewise, spousal and child abuse were considered off-limits for discussion, dirty secrets best left unexplored, which ensured that they thrived through fear, ignorance, and ambivalence – or at best, quiet condemnation.

Property rights were his pet issue, due to the amount of land in Baja that had been sold to moneyed interests under questionable circumstances. His latest crusade was against unlawful restriction of beach access, which was guaranteed by law for the population – but which was routinely violated by resorts that paid off the local officials to turn a blind eye. And huge tracts of land had been stolen from their rightful owners by corrupt regimes that ignored legitimate deeds, preferring to write new ones for their cronies while the rightful owners spent decades in a court system that was as easily purchased as a dancing girl's charms.

He'd managed to make progress on some things and was happy to see an increase in prosecutions against domestic violence, usually inflicted by alcoholic boyfriends or husbands while their mates cowered, afraid to tell anyone. There was also a slow increase in public outcry against corruption, although he had a long way to go on that one. In southern Baja's most prosperous metropolitan area, Cabo San Lucas, the papers had leaked that over thirty million dollars had gone missing under the new mayor's stewardship – not surprising given that his brother was in prison awaiting trial for embezzlement from his own term as the previous mayor.

Mexicans didn't share the naïve beliefs of their northern neighbors and were under no illusions that prosperous men ran for office in order to become tireless public servants. The only reason any politician ran for anything was so he could get elected and steal everything that wasn't bolted down, handing out sweetheart contracts for bridges to nowhere and misappropriating or otherwise absconding with the tax receipts while avoiding anything resembling actual work. That was how it had always been, and despite elevated rhetoric about change and a new era, nobody believed it would ever be any different in a society where votes were purchased for a few pesos and even the watchdogs were as corrupt as an Ecuadorian customs inspector.

Bolivar pushed his door open and took a long sip of the magnificent cabernet, grateful that another demanding day had drawn to a close. Unlike his predecessor, who had spent most of his time avoiding his responsibilities, Bolivar believed that it was his duty to work long and hard, and that if he didn't want to, he shouldn't have the job of being a an opinion leader. But in spite of his commitment and religious enthusiasm, some days the size of the task seemed overwhelming. This was one of those days.

Bolivar removed his clothes, taking care to fold them carefully and place them over the back of a chair, and treated himself to a long, hot shower – his first real opportunity to relax since launching into action early that morning. He took his time and was toweling off when he heard a rustle from his office.

"Hello?" he said, his head cocked as he listened.

Nothing.

"Hello…" he called again as he tied the towel around his waist. He tried to remember whether he'd opened his office window that morning, but couldn't. Perhaps he had, or his housekeeper had, and the wind from the ocean was rustling his papers.

He walked into the office, but nothing was out of place, and the window was closed. He peered at the vines outside, making a mental note to have the gardener cut them back, and returned to his bedroom and the glass of wine. He drained it in three swallows, the dregs tasting bitter to him, and returned to the bathroom to brush his teeth. By the time he was done, his eyes were so heavy he was barely able to stand, and he almost didn't make it to the bed before he passed out.

El Rey stepped from behind the armoire, wearing a priest's cassock, his bag slung over his shoulder. The 30 mg of zolpidem he'd put into the priest's wine was enough to knock out a pony, rendering the archbishop unconscious for the final moments of his life.

The assassin glanced around the room and opened his bag. He retrieved three DVD cases and slipped them under the desk blotter near the priest's computer, and slid one of the disks into the CD player so it would be found in the morning. Pornography was widely available, but deviant porn of this type was rarely seen, the bestiality, violence, and other offensive content so disturbing that even if it had been legal, it would have been frowned upon by most.

The dossier CISEN had provided indicated that the bishop was a pervert of the most extreme sort, his tastes running far beyond what might be considered normal in even the most liberal interpretations.

El Rey had no doubt that when the good father was found and the contents of the DVDs reviewed, the church would ensure the case was closed before it even opened.

He removed a length of black silk rope from his satchel and secured it to the lamp fixture over the desk area, pausing to test it with his weight. Satisfied, he moved to the priest and lifted him. The cleric's thin form was relatively light, and in five minutes he'd finished setting the scene, a package with six Ambien still unconsumed in the bathroom and one of the CDs looping on the computer. He glanced at the dead priest without expression and then slipped out the way he'd come, leaving the bishop to be found in the morning, naked and suspended from the ceiling, the victim of a deadly drug-and-alcohol-fueled bout of autoerotic asphyxiation gone wrong in pursuit of the ultimate climax.

CHAPTER 14

Tepuche, Sinaloa, Mexico

Serpentine waves of gentle breezes from the nearby mountains washed across the tall grass, the field undulating like the surface of a stormy sea. Indalecio Arellano eyed the approaching clouds with a wary eye.

The pigs had gotten loose again, and he was out looking for them, hoping to find them before they got really lost or a less-than-charitable neighbor got his hands on one and decided to have bacon for breakfast. As industrious as any animal when it came to escape, his freedom-loving swine were highly intelligent and possessed of a fierce independent streak. And now he was paying for their newly acquired liberty with sore feet from hours of marching through the grass.

The sound of motors reached his ears, and he squinted against the high afternoon sun. Two pickup trucks were racing up the dirt road that led to his property, trailing a dust cloud that lingered like beige smoke. Indalecio lived in a rural area of Sinaloa, far from the bustle of Culiacán, the capital city, and rarely had visitors on his large farm, where he grew lush harvests of tomatoes and organic vegetables as his forefathers had for centuries.

He watched the trucks slow at the gate and roll across the cattle guard. Whoever it was seemed in a hurry, which was unusual – nobody was in a rush in Sinaloa, least of all on a farm, where each day blended into the next and the passage of time was measured in seasons rather than hours. He removed his hat and wiped his brow with a soiled red bandana, resolved to abandoning the pig hunt for the time being as he turned and retraced his steps to the ranch house in the distance, where he lived alone, save for his hand, Ruiz, who'd been with him for six years – ever since his wife had died from a fever that had blazed out of control in spite of the best efforts of the local physicians.

Indalecio was sixty-four but looked a decade younger, mostly due to a rigorous regimen of exercise tending to his farm and a diet that was primarily vegetables he grew himself. The truth was that he hadn't had the heart to butcher any of his pigs for as long as he could remember, having named each one and gotten familiar with their personalities, which were as distinct as any human's, and which he generally preferred to his fellow man's company. He'd read somewhere that a pig had the intellect of a four-year-old human child, and ever since that time he'd been unable to bring himself to eat them, incurring regular ribbing from Ruiz, who didn't share his idealistic philosophical idiosyncrasies. Still, Indalecio had made it clear to his hand that the pigs were off-limits, and he doted on them like they were his children, which in many ways they were.

"Frigging pigs will be the death of me yet. Fine. Go run free and see what it gets you. You'll be back before nightfall, begging for slop. Let that be a lesson to you," he muttered under his breath as he trudged toward his ranch.

Ranch. A grandiose term for his sixty acres of land for which he fought a constant battle against the encroachment of the surrounding wilds. Only a third of it was really suited to farming, and the rest was more of a nuisance than an asset most of the year. Still, it was his, and he viewed himself more as custodian than owner, still thinking of it as his father's land, even after these many years had passed since the elder Arellano had gone to his reward.

A mockingbird flitted from one of the perimeter trees, and Indalecio watched its flight, wondering what had startled it from its perch. Then he saw – six men carrying assault rifles were clubbing Ruiz with their weapon butts as he tried to regain his footing. Blood streamed down his face onto his soiled white shirt, and now Indalecio could hear the blows, like truncheons, the wet smacks of wood on flesh, skin splitting with each smack.

Indalecio stood, horrified, frozen in his tracks. He was unarmed, and the only ones with assault rifles in Sinaloa were the cartels and the police – and these weren't police. What the cartel wanted with a simple farmer escaped him, but the rifles were real enough.

One of the men screamed at Ruiz so loudly that Indalecio could hear him even at that distance.

"Where is he? Come on, old man. You don't want to die to protect him."

Indalecio couldn't hear Ruiz's response, but he didn't want to learn the limits of the man's loyalty – if Indalecio had been in his place, he would have told the assailants whatever they wanted to know already, and it was only human nature that Ruiz would do so sooner than later.

He turned and began running, his legs pumping beneath him, the muscles ropey and taut as he put distance between himself and the house. He flinched when a burst of automatic weapon fire sounded from where he'd abandoned Ruiz, but he kept moving, not needing to look back for confirmation of his worst fears.

Sweat streamed down his face as he reached the edge of the clearing and plunged into the trees, following a trail that led to a stream, the water source for his precious tomatoes. A quarter mile away, if he could make it, was a shed where he had some supplies and a couple of tired burros that hung around to eat their fill of the sweet grass and plants that surrounded the water. Where they'd come from, he never questioned, just as he didn't question most things in his life. If providence had chosen to favor him with hoofed visitors, then who was he to be inhospitable to his land's bounty?

Depending upon how skilled the gunmen were, he had anywhere from fifteen minutes to half an hour lead on them. With any luck he could disappear into the foothills and wait them out while figuring out how to deal with the latest wrinkle fate had thrown at him. He didn't question why they'd killed Ruiz, nor why they were after him. It could have been anything.

Or could it?

Was it possible that this was the retribution he'd long feared because of his lawsuit?

No. That was a title dispute over *ejido* land, communal property that belonged to agricultural collectives – farmers, like him. Farmers didn't drive fancy trucks and kill innocents in broad daylight. No, that smacked of the cartel.

The cartel operated according to its own logic, and it could be anything from an imagined slight to one of the new breed wanting Indalecio's property to grow marijuana or opium poppies – something he'd been approached to do numerous times over his lifetime, but he'd always politely declined. The older leaders of the cartel tended to have respect for the old ways and had honored his wishes, but these new ones…who knew what they were capable of?

It was best to slip away and contrive a strategy from a safe distance rather than die a meaningless death today. He was not without means, having saved the lion's share of his earnings every year and having sold several worthless patches of land along the edges of his property to speculators a decade earlier.

He'd get away and then seek out the police – the trick being finding some that weren't in the cartel's pocket. Finding an honest cop in Sinaloa was as easy as finding a virgin in a whorehouse, so the saying went, and he, like most Mexicans, avoided anyone in uniform or in a position of authority like the plague, not wanting to invite the attention of parasites who wanted nothing more than to suck honest folk dry.

But still. A cold-blooded murder on his property would not go unpunished, and he'd find someone to investigate. He had an attorney in Mazatlán he could call. Perhaps he'd know how to proceed.

Indalecio reached the shack and swung the door open, relieved to see that nothing had been disturbed. He gathered the bare essentials he could comfortably carry and filled two canteens from the stream and then went in search of the burros, hoping he could coax one into returning his generosity by transporting him into the hills, far away from the danger that was working its way up the rise to find him.

Chapter 15

Tijuana, Mexico

A thermal layer had settled over the city, the cool temperatures from the ocean meeting the heat rising off the land to create a thick, low overcast that blanketed the area and blocked any light from the full moon or the stars. The streets that wound through the industrial district of Otay Mesa, near the border crossing of the same name, were deserted at three a.m., the only life an occasional stray dog or a brave seagull on a nocturnal foraging expedition far from the shore. A semi-rig groaned along the road that led south, on its way to Baja loaded with freight, its engine roar dulled by the cloud cover.

El Rey stood with several dozen other men and women near a paint supply warehouse, hidden from view behind the gates, waiting for the escort who would get them across the border to the U.S., where, depending on how much they'd paid, they would either be ferried into San Diego and dropped off downtown, driven north to Los Angeles, or in *El Rey*'s case, handed the keys to a car.

CISEN had offered to handle getting *El Rey* into the United States, but he had decided to trust it to the professionals – the cartels that trafficked drugs and human cargo in one direction and weapons and cash in the other, through a network of tunnels that propagated weekly beneath the supposedly impenetrable border. He'd contacted one of the top coyote organizations that worked with the Tijuana cartel and negotiated a platinum-level package: guaranteed crossing via a tunnel, a Ford economy sedan on the U.S. side with current registration and decent tires, and no questions asked. The entire bundle came to twenty-five thousand dollars, but it was CISEN's money, not his, so he wasn't price sensitive.

For all his interaction with CISEN, he didn't trust the intelligence service, and the less he depended on them for anything besides info and cash, the better. When he'd asked, they'd proposed getting him in using a diplomatic passport, but that would leave a trail he didn't want. Instead he'd made his own arrangements through a set of contacts he'd developed over the years, which was how he found himself shifting from foot to foot in the chill, his bag over his shoulder, amidst a group of tired-looking fellow travelers from Mexico, El Salvador, and Guatemala.

The Tijuana tunnels were the surest but most expensive route north for those wishing to try for a new life in the land of promise. There were approaches for every budget, varying from stowing away in hidden compartments of northbound freight trucks to night crossings in the high desert east of Tecate to the longer and more treacherous route that began in the Sonora desert and ended in Arizona. All had their risks, but *El Rey* liked his odds with the tunnels. Barring a cave-in or a raid, which the cartels usually knew about well in advance, they were a safe bet, with none of the danger of the other approaches: that their guides might execute them and take their belongings, or leave them to cook in a van in the middle of nowhere, or that they'd be apprehended by an increasingly trigger-happy border patrol.

A forest green nineties-era Lincoln Town Car pulled up, and two men got out. The car backed away and disappeared into the night as the pair approached the iron gate, opened it, and moved to the waiting group. *El Rey* dressed to blend into American life, wearing a No Fear T-shirt, a black hoodie, ratty beige cargo shorts, and a pair of new hundred-dollar Nike running shoes. To anyone studying him, he looked like a typical twenty-something slacker – that is, except for his eyes, which were as flat and dead as a shark's.

The taller of the two men cleared his throat and spoke in a low rasp.

"Everyone knows what to expect, right? It should have been explained. We'll be in the tunnel for half an hour, and there's no reason to be concerned about ventilation or cave-ins, so I don't want any freaking out. I'll warn you all that it can be claustrophobic, but once we're in, there's no going back, so take a pill or have a last drink or whatever you need to do, because this is a one-way ride. You don't need to bring a bunch of survival crap like food or water, so leave anything you have here – toss it in the dumpster. We've got water on the other side, and the neighborhoods where we'll be taking you are a hundred percent Latino, right down to the street signs in Spanish – you can get tamales just like mama used to make within a block of the drop-off points, and they probably take pesos. So lighten your loads and get ready. We'll go down in five minutes." The speaker looked around. "Which one of you is Pablo?"

El Rey stepped forward. "That's me."

"Okay. Stay close to the front. Once we're on the other side, you have your deal. Everyone else goes into a pair of vans."

"Works for me."

Three of the younger men in the group lit up a joint and nervously passed it among them. *El Rey* watched them for a moment, and then his eyes moved to a pregnant woman who looked ready to pop. It was common to make a run for the border in the final weeks of pregnancy so that the baby would be born with American citizenship and the mother would be able to avail herself of free health care and a social support infrastructure, whereas in Mexico there was nothing but the social security hospital. He guessed that her parents had scraped together the ten grand to get her across, hoping for a better life for their daughter than they'd had.

"All right. Follow me," called their guide, and the group trailed him to one of the outbuildings. He unlocked a padlock and swung open the iron door. Inside it was pitch black, but he knew the way and in a few seconds had switched on a single low-wattage bulb.

"From this point on, no talking. Not even a whisper, do you understand? The border patrol has been using listening technology lately, and I don't want to risk it. Any questions?"

Everyone shook their heads, and he nodded. His companion moved to a pallet, pushed it aside, and opened a steel hatch in the concrete floor. "This way," he said, motioning for the pregnant woman to go immediately after him, and then he dropped into the darkness. *El Rey* could hear him scrambling down the rungs of a ladder. Light flickered to life below, and the woman eased herself down next, her face determined even as she struggled to avoid straining herself.

El Rey went next and found himself in a long shaft with support struts in place the entire two-story length. Once at the bottom he gazed around – more shoring, wood beams holding the earth above in place, and a chamber that was larger than he'd expected, at least twenty by twenty. A string of LED lights illuminated the area, and he eyed the steel door on the far end, triple-bolted on the cement wall.

Once everyone was in the room, the lead guide moved to the steel door, slipped the bolts free, and opened it. He flicked a switch, and more lights glowed into nothingness down a ten-foot-wide shaft. *El Rey* noted rails running along the floor, no doubt to make the efficient, silent transport of drugs or cargo possible. A ventilation fan hummed above his head, and he could feel a stirring from air being blown into the shaft, which receded as far as his eye could see.

The trip was anticlimactic given his expectations, nothing more than a third of a mile walk below ground. He was used to spending days in caves, so for him it was unremarkable, but he could smell the fear from the others as they forged deeper into the earth.

When they ascended a ladder that was the twin of the one on the Mexican side, *El Rey* helped the pregnant woman up the first rungs, for which he received a frightened but grateful glance. He amended his prior guess about her age – she was nothing more than a girl, perhaps sixteen or seventeen. This was probably the furthest she had ever been from home, headed into an uncertain future in a country she only knew from rumors. He allowed her to make her way at her own pace and then followed her up, anxious to be on the road.

When they emerged into the still night, two vans were waiting by the rear of the warehouse. The guide motioned to *El Rey*, and the assassin followed him through a gate to the street, where the promised vehicle sat under a streetlight. *El Rey* inspected the license plate, confirming that the tags were current, and after starting the engine and listening to it for several seconds, handed over the remaining ten thousand dollars.

"There's a map in the glove compartment," the man said and then left the assassin to make his own way. *El Rey* belted himself in and pulled away, glancing at the gas gauge showing full, and within minutes pulled onto the 905 freeway headed north. As he accelerated to cruising speed, he checked his watch and did a quick calculation – he could be in Sedona by late afternoon, at which point he would find a motel and get some rest before embarking on the next stage of his mission.

The archbishop had been found, as expected, that morning, and the evening news had been filled with vague accounts of the tragic death of a beloved community leader. As *El Rey* had expected, the Church had ensured that any embarrassing details were kept confidential, and the only things he saw were glowing testimonials and expressions of sadness at having lost such a fine holy man. He wondered what the average reader would have thought if they'd had access to the information in the CISEN dossier, but decided it didn't matter. That was one out of three down, without a hitch.

Hopefully the next one would go as smoothly.

CHAPTER 16

Sedona, Arizona

The old Indian sat down heavily at the bar of the honky-tonk roadhouse and ordered a beer and a sidecar of cheap bourbon. A country western quartet was plodding through a Hank Williams standard with all the enthusiasm of cattle on the way to slaughter. The saloon was barely a quarter full at 10:00 p.m. He looked around the darkened room at his fellow celebrants – sixties throwback hippies with long thinning gray hair and rainbow-colored Grateful Dead T-shirts, scrawny biker chicks with leathery faces wearing knee-high moccasins and faded jeans, truckers in flannel shirts and grimy baseball hats, ex-cons and future inmates standing around a battered pool table at the back of the main room – the sort of detritus one expected to see hanging around a third-rate carnival or a soup kitchen.

The seat to his left swiveled, and a young man with refined features and longish black hair sat and ordered a draft beer, his English accented with the cadence of a native Spanish speaker. The bartender brought his drink, and the young man slid two dollars to him before taking a long pull and sighing contentedly.

"Boy, does that taste good," *El Rey* said, a lopsided grin on his face.

The Indian clinked his glass against *El Rey*'s and nodded. "Been a dry one."

"That it has." *El Rey* eyed the Indian's glass. "You look about done. Next one's on me."

The Indian shook his head. "You don't have to do that."

"No problem. Gotta spend it on something."

79

El Rey waited until the bartender brought the man another round and then extended his hand. "Name's Domingo."

"Sam." They shook and returned to drinking, both having pushed their customary level of interaction to the limits.

Three hours later Sam and *El Rey* staggered out of the bar into the gravel parking lot. "You sure you can drive?" *El Rey* asked the bleary-eyed Sam.

"Yup. Done it a million times. Hey, and I'm serious about the job. You want to come watch the ceremony a couple of times, if you think it's something you can do, I'll put in a good word for you. I've been looking for a replacement for a while."

"No takers, huh?"

"It's not exactly a growth business," Sam slurred, and burped loudly.

Both men laughed. "Well, like I said, I'm not doing much right now. I was planning to see about getting a landscaping job, but your thing sounds interesting."

"All you gotta do is look Indian and mysterious. Rich *gringos* don't know the difference between a red and a brown man. You'll see."

"I'll come by tomorrow. What time again?" *El Rey* asked.

"Six. We usually start it at around seven and go till eight or so. Sometimes later. I'm telling you, it's the easiest money you'll ever make." Sam squinted at him. "You got your work papers?"

"Sure."

"Then leave the rest to me." Sam burped again. "Shit. I shouldn'ta drunk so much."

"I can give you a ride if you want."

Sam considered the offer, stared at his old pickup, and then grimaced. "Maybe that's a good idea. I don't feel so hot."

"All right. Come on. Just tell me where to go. I'm right over here," *El Rey* said, leading him to the Ford, which was parked in the shadows.

"Cool. Thanks again, Dom."

El Rey popped the lock and swung the passenger door open for his new friend. "No problem. Hell, if you're going to get me a cush gig like that, it's the least I can do."

Sam struggled to focus as *El Rey* followed his mumbled directions to his house, a run-down single-story ranch that looked like it had been through a flood. When they arrived, it took Sam three tries at the door handle to get it open, and *El Rey* watched him weave and stumble to the entryway, bleary from the six shots and matching beers he'd put down while regaling the assassin with his dismal life story: growing up on the reservation, then working a variety of menial jobs in between bouts on government assistance, which had culminated in his current role as a faux shaman for a boutique hotel that specialized in new age soul-searching.

Old Sam had a taste for the sauce, that was clear, and *El Rey* smiled to himself as he waved and rolled away. This was going to be easier than he'd hoped.

The following afternoon he returned to Sam's house, which looked even worse in the cold light of day, and gave him a ride back to his vehicle. The old pickup started with a belch of blue smoke, and *El Rey* followed it into the nearby hills until they reached the entryway to the Golden Meridian Lodge, where Sam worked.

The lodge turned out to be a series of small cottages arranged in a semicircle near Oak Creek, with breathtaking views of the nearby striated red mountains. They parked in a gravel lot, and Sam gave him a tour of the grounds, explaining the layout and the philosophy of the development: charging insane prices to privileged white people so they could commune with nature, which in this case meant buying expensive native art and jewelry, eating organic food, and cleansing themselves with a host of pseudoscientific rituals. This was where Sam came in, as the official lodge shaman – a role he'd grown into over the years as he'd proposed attractions like the Indigenous People's nature walks and, his specialty, the sweat lodge.

Sam's job was taking tourists for long hikes and acting as a quasi-mystical guide: divining what the guests' spirit guide animals were; offering holistic healing advice for their inevitable eating disorders, sleeping problems, and arthritis; and immersing them in the lodge's specialized three-day detoxification and purification ritual, which concluded each evening with an hour in the sweat lodge.

"I'm not bullshitting you. People will pay, like, five hundred to a thousand bucks a day for a third-rate massage, a hike, some liquefied crap I wouldn't feed my dog, what we call 'American Indian yoga,' and an hour or two in a glorified sauna," Sam explained. "It's pure genius, and the lady that owns the place has made millions from it."

"I don't understand. Who buys into this? American Indian yoga?"

"Anyone with the popular new money social disease of white man's guilt. They think that if they live for a few days like they think we did before they took our land away from us, they'll be reborn, or at least, be less guilty. I don't bother pointing out that our life expectancy two centuries ago was about half of what it is now, back when we were running around in buckskins in this supposedly magical wonderland and dying from stuff you can take a pill for today." Sam shook his head. "Throw in some crystals, some New Age philosophy, some copper bracelets, and it's perfect."

El Rey studied his face, which could have been hewn from the red mountain rock. "And how do I help you relieve them of their money?"

"I'll teach you what you need to know to help me out. Basically, it involves heating stones and tending to the sweat lodge, learning a few Indian terms, mastering the stuff I sling at them on our hikes, and a lot of penetrating gazes and cryptic comments. Once you've got it down, I'll introduce you as my protégé to the lady who runs the place. That sounds suitably important, doesn't it?"

El Rey's eyes widened. "That's it?"

Sam laughed. "Yup. Now I have to get cleaned up for tonight's ceremony. You can start off your training session by going down the road to the market and getting a few cold ones to take the edge off. Wouldn't hurt if a pint of Jack made it into the bag, either."

El Rey nodded. He wasn't surprised that Sam's head felt like a punching bag. The assassin had forced himself to vomit twice in the bar bathroom, clearing most of the alcohol out of his system as the night had worn on, but Sam had enthusiastically poisoned himself until he could barely walk.

He headed back to the car, noting the wind chimes and the faint odor of incense drifting from the pool area, happy that the first part of his plan was coming together so nicely. He had a few days to gain Sam's full trust, which he intuited could be easily won with more firewater and offers to do anything resembling actual work, and he intended to make himself indispensable during that time so that when the actor arrived for his cleansing, he would be Sam's constant companion and alcoholic support system.

CHAPTER 17

Mexico City, Mexico

Cruz walked across the task force floor to Briones' new office and stood in the doorway, watching as he sorted through piles of reports with a look of concentration on his face. Cruz allowed himself a small smile and cleared his throat.

"Looks like you'll fit right in, Lieutenant. Congratulations again on your meteoric rise. I trust this office will be suitable?" Cruz teased.

Briones cocked an eyebrow. "It's about twice as big as the cubbyhole I had before, and even has a window, so yes, it's more than adequate."

"It will feel a lot smaller once you get more file cabinets in."

"How did all this get processed before it came to me?" Briones asked, gesturing at the stacks of documents.

"Now you know what I do from sunup to sundown. This is only half the load. I'm still fielding the other half."

Briones shook his head. "Amazing. I honestly had no idea. Two days of this and I'm already drowning."

"Makes being shot at by cartel baddies almost appealing, doesn't it? Don't worry. It gets better. You'll devise a system that works."

"Is that what you did?"

Cruz grinned. "Absolutely. I promoted you to do some of it."

Briones gave him a glum look. "I had my staff meeting this morning. We have a lead on that rave that's happening in a few days. It's going to be at a big warehouse in Tepotzotlán. Outside of the metro area, in an industrial section where there won't be any noise complaints. It's supposed to be a big deal. There's a lot of buzz on the street already."

"What do we know about the organizers?"

"Couple of wealthy kids, entrepreneurs. This is all they do – throw a big party every month."

"There's a living in that?"

"A hundred fifty pesos a head, that's around twelve dollars U.S. If they see a couple thousand attendees, it adds up. Even after paying for rent, security, portable toilets, and some DJs and light systems, they'll probably walk away with ten thousand dollars apiece."

"Not bad for a night's work, is it? I need a new career."

Briones considered Cruz and returned to his paperwork. "You might be a little mature for the rave scene, sir."

Cruz snorted. "Story of my life. What have we heard about the kidnappers?"

"Not a word."

Cruz shut Briones' door. "The girl was finally returned to her parents, but there's a disturbing wrinkle. She claims to have been raped by one of the kidnappers, and her physical examination bears that out."

Briones' eyes narrowed. "That's a first. They usually don't harm the victim…"

"I know. You can imagine the heat I'm taking. The parents want their heads on a platter, and that's translating into a lot of angry calls from the uncle. He wants this group found and exterminated. That was the word he used."

"Exterminated. Can't say as the world would shed any tears."

"Agreed. But there is that whole idea of making arrests and bringing them to justice."

"Perhaps. Anyway, it's a moot point. We've got nothing. The getaway driver clammed up after our discussion, and now he's in the system being processed. Even if he knew anything, he's out of our hands."

"I didn't get that impression, though, did you?"

"No."

"And there's nothing on the street? No rumors? No snitches wanting to improve their finances in return for a little information?"

"Not a word. The plainclothes guys say that whenever they ask, their sources clam up tight."

"That's consistent with it being a cartel operation."

Briones nodded. "No question. But knowing that doesn't get us any closer to shutting them down."

Cruz sighed. "Let's plan on mounting surveillance at the rave. That's our best lead so far."

"It will have to be a big operation. The area around the warehouse grounds is pretty large."

"Whatever it takes. This has been prioritized as our most important issue. The brass wants results and wants them quickly. So whatever you need, fill out a requisition, and I'll make it happen."

Briones nodded again. "Yes, sir. And can I take it that I'll be unchained from this desk to run the operation?"

"I think we can make an exception this time, don't you? But you'll find that the paperwork keeps flowing whether you're here or not, so don't get too excited. I've learned it just means a couple of even longer days after I get back to catch up."

"I don't suppose I can just shred every third file, can I?"

Cruz opened the door. "Glad to see you're getting acclimated. That's the spirit."

Briones watched his superior walk back across the floor and rubbed a hand over his face as he wondered what he'd signed up for. Maybe getting shot at wasn't so bad after all.

CHAPTER 18

Sedona, Arizona

Carla Vega stretched her long bronze legs as she lay by the Golden Meridian Lodge pool, her black bikini providing scant coverage of her toned body. She'd arrived that morning, sending her cameraman on to Los Angeles for the award ceremony in three days, and had checked in and taken advantage of the hot stone massage after a long lunch, her cares melting away now that she was soaking up the sun.

A white SUV rolled up the drive, and she watched from behind her Dolce & Gabbana sunglasses as a striking man sporting a fedora and a dusting of beard got out of the passenger seat while the driver moved to the cargo door for the luggage. One of the white-clad service staff shouldered a rucksack, and they strode up the small rise to the main building to check in.

Robert Perry was instantly recognizable even from a distance, Carla thought as she sprayed a light film of suntan oil onto her skin. If her information was correct, he'd be there for two days, giving her more than enough time to contrive a meeting and see what she could ferret out in the low-key setting.

Perry was six years younger than Carla but looked the same age or older, his hard-driving lifestyle, habits, and constant sun exposure from his surfing hobby having taken its toll, she knew from her research and his most recent photographs. A good-looking man, no question, but not her style. She preferred grown men, not boys, and everything she'd learned about Perry pointed to a playboy with an adolescent ego, a narcissist wholly concerned with his own gratification and nothing else.

But she wasn't in Arizona to find love, or even lust. Perry was somehow connected to the admiral and the archbishop – ex-archbishop, she thought, having seen the coverage of his untimely demise amidst cloudy circumstances. It hadn't escaped her that so soon after the attack on the admiral one of the other names Beatriz had dug up had met with disaster, but from what she could gather, there was nothing suspicious about it – the bishop had taken his own life, a sad event, but hardly on par with a helicopter attack in front of several thousand bystanders.

Still, a part of Carla had cringed when she'd seen the news. She didn't believe in coincidences, and while she wasn't ready to go full-blown conspiracy theory, one dead man and another in a hospital bed gave her pause.

And of course, there was Perry, presumably here to clean his system out before the awards – one of his regular haunts, she'd learned, on a semiannual visitation schedule, a concession to his body's protestations at the constant abuse to which he subjected it.

Carla closed her eyes and breathed in the clean, clear air, devoid of the taint of pollution that was a constant in Mexico City. She drifted off and started awake when a lounge chair scraped nearby. She cracked an eye open and found herself staring into Robert Perry's baby blues.

He smiled at her as he reclined. "Gorgeous day for it, that's for sure," he said in his famous laconic drawl.

"Beautiful," she agreed.

"I love it. One of my favorite places," Perry said.

"It's a nice break from the rat race," she agreed.

"You look familiar."

Carla sighed. "I'm a television journalist. But I'm here incognito."

"I love your accent."

"Thanks."

"I'm here on the QT as well. I'm an actor."

"Ah. I thought I recognized your face."

He grinned infectiously, and Carla had to admit there was considerable magnetism in his smile, even if he was little more than an unruly schoolboy. "Robert Perry, at your service."

"Carla Vega. Nice to meet you," Carla said, raising her water bottle in a toast.

"Likewise."

They made small talk, he about the Hollywood scene he was escaping, she pretending interest. Carla had long ago developed the skill of making any man she was speaking with feel like he was fascinating, which had helped her enormously in her career. Any questions directed at her she laughed off or gave superficial answers to, preferring to hear more about Perry's riveting life.

After longer than she'd thought it would take, he finally got around to asking her where she was from.

She gave him a beaming white smile. "Mexico."

"Really," he said, having not thought through a follow-up line – typical, given how self-involved he'd been so far.

"Yes. Have you ever been?"

"Oh, yeah, a few times."

"What part?"

"Baja. Surfing, mostly. I did a few road trips down the peninsula a few years ago, and I fly to San José del Cabo every now and then. It's a good weekend getaway. Only a couple of hours from Los Angeles."

"Yes, I hear it's quite popular. I haven't been in forever," she said.

"You should go. It's really pretty."

Carla turned over, giving him a good view of one of her most famous assets. "Are you going to be at the awards ceremony next week?"

"Which one? People's Choice? Yeah, I suppose so. I've been nominated for a few."

"Oh, well, then maybe I'll get a chance to interview you for my station. On the red carpet?"

Perry looked less interested now that the discussion had turned to business. "Uh, sure. If I see you. But I don't speak Spanish."

"Really? I got the impression from something I read that you were part Mexican."

"Um, no. Spanish, but we never spoke it at home."

"Ah." She paused. "So you like Baja. Do you ever get to Tijuana?"

He shook his head. "Not since high school. It was kind of a shithole then. I haven't had any reason to go back."

"It definitely has its low spots. Did they cover the death of Archbishop Bolivar in the American press?" she asked, watching his face for any trace of a reaction.

"Who?" His disinterest wasn't faked. Perry had never heard of him.

"Oh, the head of the Church in Baja."

"Mmm, no. I don't read the papers much, though."

Of course not. As the bright star in his universe, he wouldn't. What could possibly be more interesting than the events in his own life?

"Well, Mexico can be a very hospitable place, Mr. Perry. You should try to spend more time there." Carla's smile could have powered a small city, her flirtation unmistakable.

Forty-five minutes went by, during which she learned little she didn't already know. He was returning to Los Angeles on Monday morning, his schedule packed: the show on Tuesday; a charity dinner on Wednesday before flying to Australia on Thursday for preproduction on an independent film – a favor to one of his buddies, he said. Perry seemed nice enough and invited her to dinner, but she declined, not wanting to seem too eager to spend time with him.

"Maybe a cocktail after, if you're around," she suggested.

"I'm only supposed to be drinking celery juice or whatever this weekend. All part of the detox thing."

"Oh, I didn't realize. I'm just here because it's exclusive and peaceful."

"I do the whole program. You should really check it out. You'll feel like a million bucks after two days of hikes and dieting and everything."

"That's good to know. Ah, well. I'm getting a little tender from the sun. If I see you this evening, I'll buy you a juice," she said, collecting her things. By the way he was devouring her with his eyes, she was confident she'd be running into him later.

"That's the best invitation I've had all day."

She slipped on her sandals and pulled a cover-up over her thong bikini and then gave the young actor a long, contemplative look.

"I'll be at the bar around nine."

CHAPTER 19

Mexico City, Mexico

The fair-haired man meandered down the sidewalk in the historical district, unremarkable amongst thousands of other pedestrians, his jeans, green soccer jersey and five o'clock shadow a kind of ubiquitous uniform for the city's young males. Only his hair color might have stuck out, but it was tucked under the brim of a black baseball cap featuring the logo of an American sports team.

Vendors clogged the gutters, their carts laden with bags of nuts and candy, blissfully unconcerned by the dust thrown up by traffic. A squat woman with a surgical mask flipped hot dogs on a portable grill as customers waited, money in hand. The air was filled with the smell of cooking and exhaust as he turned a corner and moved onto a smaller side street. The pavement underfoot changed to cobblestones as he made his way toward the coffee shop, its sign already lit to compensate for the crepuscular glow in the sky, where he was certain his rendezvous would be waiting.

He pushed through the doors and saw his man sitting in a corner, looking like he'd been drinking battery acid. He approached and sat down across from him, the café empty at the late hour. A waitress appeared by his side, and he ordered a cappuccino, and the two men stared at each other wordlessly until she returned with the coffee and set it in front of the newcomer.

The fair-haired man took a cautious sip and set the cup down. "Delicious," he pronounced softly.

"I'm glad you're enjoying this," the other man grumbled.

"When God gives you lemons…" He eyed the cup. "But perhaps you're right. Let's get to it. Give me an update."

92

"The assassin's in play. You saw the news about the archbishop's regrettable accident. I'm confident that the other two names will be dispatched shortly."

"Yes, we were amused by the creativity of the hit. Several of the smaller papers carried a few of the more lurid details before they were throttled by the archdiocese. Well done on that one."

A pained smile. "I told you he was the best."

"Let's hope he continues to live up to your description of his skills. You've managed to keep the entire affair compartmentalized so far?"

"Of course. I'm the only one that knows this isn't an official op. But as I said before, no secret remains hidden indefinitely, and the more time that goes on, the harder it will be to keep it quiet."

The fair-haired man took another sip of his drink. "Given the paranoid nature of your organization, I'd think that this little adventure would stay confidential in perpetuity. Silent as the confessional, as it were." He cleared his throat. "There's no easy way to say this. While we're happy with your performance so far, I'm afraid I have some less than good news."

"What now?"

"There's another name we'll need help with."

A long pause. "Absolutely not. We had a deal."

The fair-haired man waited a few beats. "Yes, we did. But may I remind you that deals can change, just as this one now has. Don't worry. We'll compensate you for it."

"You know I'm not doing this for the money. Don't insult me."

"Still, a quarter million dollars per sanction takes the sting out of it."

"That money will do me no good if I get caught."

"Then don't get caught." The fair-haired man studied his companion, taking in the stress showing around his mouth and the tightness of the skin below his eyes. "It's regrettable, but you're a victim of your own success."

"Who is it?"

The fair-haired man whispered a name and title. The other sat back, an expression of shock on his face. "You're insane. I know this man. He's one of the most protected in the city. It's impossible."

"Seems your fellow specializes in the impossible. Before you get too upset, I'd remind you that it's not I who has such a regrettable liking for…the little ones." The fair-haired man sat back, his face impassive. They'd discovered that their CISEN contact had a large collection of child pornography on his home computer, which even in Mexico would land him in prison for a long time, given that much of it was homemade over a period spanning years and featured his unmistakable features in the lion's share of the shots.

"You miserable shit."

"Yes, well, that's hardly news. And remember that your family's lives hang in the balance." He'd been instructed to increase their leverage by not only threatening to expose his perversions, but if he took his own life, as was a distinct possibility to avoid the fallout, that his nine-year-old daughter and his wife would be killed.

"How could I forget? You bastards have ruined me."

"Hardly, with a cool million in an account in the Caymans." He finished his coffee and settled back in his chair. "Relax. You look a little green. I'll get you the details on the new target once your man's finished up his little errands. Any idea on timing for the remaining two?"

"He indicated that it should be done by the end of the week, if all goes well."

The fair-haired man stood and flipped a two-hundred-peso note onto the table. After looking around the small café a final time, he fixed the other with a cold stare. "Then you'd better hope it all goes well."

He moved to the door and disappeared onto the darkening street, leaving his reluctant companion staring at the bitter dregs of his coffee, now cold, the hand holding the cup trembling slightly as he watched the younger man depart.

Madness. The entire thing was madness.

And at the rate things were going, he'd be lucky to get out intact.

Why had he kept the photographs? Why had he taken them in the first place? To memorialize his compulsions? All the children had been prostitutes, slaves to the underworld predators that preyed on society and catered to the most deplorable perversions, but nobody would care about their backgrounds if the photos were made public. It had been a stupid oversight – one that had placed him in an impossible position with his new master. The phone call had come out of the blue, on an afternoon like any other, the whispered words demanding a meeting like a knife to the heart.

How could they have known? How did they find out? It had to be the pimps, he'd realized too late. He was too well known in certain seedy circles, too regular in his urgency. He'd handed his enemies the weapon with which to destroy him through his own carelessness, and the irony was not lost on him. He stood, his legs shaky, and squared his shoulders. He was a tenured member of the intelligence community, a veteran with an impeccable record. There was a good chance that if he continued to do as directed, the whole sordid affair would pass with nobody the wiser. The fair-haired man was right about the tight control of information within the agency – there was every likelihood that neither his nor *El Rey*'s role in the mess would ever come to light.

But this new name changed everything, worsening those odds considerably.

His footsteps echoed off the colonial façades as he strode toward the larger street, lost in thought, brain churning furiously to find a way out of the trap his desires had placed him in. He didn't even register the woman who took up after him, maintaining a discreet distance from the far curb, just another shadow as the last of the sun's glow faded and the busy metropolis was overtaken by night.

CHAPTER 20

Sedona, Arizona

El Rey helped Sam with the stones he'd heated in the fire and carted them into the sweat lodge, taking care to place them in the central pit exactly as Sam indicated. He and the old man had bonded again at the bar the prior evening. Sam had regaled him with stories, many likely invented or heavily embellished, all the while knocking back drinks, and tonight he was still hungover – not surprising given his age or the amount he'd put away. Today's nature hike had been a Bataan death march for the Indian, and *El Rey* had been hard-pressed not to smile as he'd watched the man sweat eighty proof as he directed the tourists along trails and told tall tales about the eagle's watchful eye and the power of the wild creature's spirit.

Upon their return, *El Rey* had done a run to the market and returned with a pint bottle of whiskey to help Sam fend off the worst of the shakes as the sweat lodge ceremony approached. The bottle's level had steadily dropped as the afternoon stretched on, and a second had been deemed necessary for the proper ceremonial spirit to flow.

El Rey returned with the half pint as Sam settled onto one of the logs that had been carved into benches by the fire and, after taking a seat nearby, had told him about their night's guest.

"He's some hot-shit actor. We've done this deal together a half dozen times over the years. Big tipper, so be nice."

"He's the only one tonight?"

Sam nodded. "He likes his privacy. I had no idea who he was, which I think was part of the appeal – he told me once that he couldn't go anywhere without being recognized, and he liked that I wasn't impressed. Which is pretty easy considering I don't own a TV and haven't been to a movie since John Wayne was alive."

"You haven't missed anything."

"Have you got that second bottle?"

"Yeah. Hey, is that our boy?" *El Rey* asked, nodding in the direction of an approaching figure swaddled in a white cotton terry-cloth robe.

"Yup. You have everything ready?"

"Just like you showed me last night. The peace pipe's a nice touch."

Sam smirked. "Powerful wampum in these hills."

They chuckled, and Sam struggled to his feet. The embroidered figures on his ornate cloak danced in the darkness as the fire crackled and flickered. *El Rey* glanced down at the robe he was wearing, one of Sam's extras, and hoped he looked convincing.

The actor drew near and smiled. "Well, you ready to do this? I need some purging and cleansing, Sam. I've been a very bad boy since you last saw me."

Sam could have been carved from wood. "Your magic is strong. A young buck needs room to roam."

"Damn if we don't agree on that." Perry sniffed. "You guys been sharing a cocktail while you waited for me?"

Sam ignored the question. "Come. The moon will be up soon. It is a good night for this. A powerful night."

Sam led the actor into the sweat lodge, *El Rey* trailing them with the long wooden pipe in hand and a satchel with shrubs Sam had selected for the occasion. Perry took a seat on the wooden bench that ringed the interior of the lodge and fidgeted with his robe. Sam chanted for a half minute, reciting what could have been his recipe for a Bloody Mary for all either the assassin or Perry could tell, and then bowed slightly from the waist and motioned for *El Rey* to draw near. He removed a handful of vegetation from the bag and tossed it onto the stones while humming an atonal dirge, and the small chamber filled with the pungent scent of smoldering leaves. Sam then poured water onto the stones from an earthenware pitcher by the door, and steam filled the space.

El Rey's final act was to light the pipe, filled with a special blend Sam had provided, and hand it to Perry, who took long drags, held the smoke in his lungs as long as he could, and then exhaled noisily. When the pipe had gone out, Sam led the assassin to the wood plank door and peered in the dim light at the actor.

"Enjoy. I'll be right outside if you need anything," Sam assured him.

Perry waved at him with a limp hand and leaned his head back against the clay wall.

Sam closed the door behind him and moved to the fire. "That's three hundred of the easiest bucks this place will ever see. He usually tips me a hundred, so tonight I'm buying." Sam coughed and spit on the dirt. "Now where's that damned bottle you've been holding out on me?"

Five minutes later Sam was slumbering by the fire, the zolpidem *El Rey* had dissolved in the whiskey having done its job. He'd wake up still drowsy within a few hours and be out of it for a while, but *El Rey* suspected that wasn't an altogether new feeling for him.

The pipe had been filled with Sam's special blend – and the addition of a liberal dosing of liquid PCP the assassin had brought with him across the border. In higher doses it would knock a bull elephant out, enabling *El Rey* to carry out the business end of his plan – suffocating Perry with heat.

El Rey darted to the nearby building where the electrical panel was housed, and after slipping on a pair of surgical gloves, pulled the fuse for the ventilation fan and sensor that ensured the temperature didn't rise to dangerous levels, and then returned to the lodge. Perry was already comatose from the fast action of the PCP. *El Rey* removed the actor's room key from where it was hanging from a rubber lanyard around his wrist and poured an extra measure of water on the stones to ensure the steam continued to build. Satisfied by the stifling cloud filling the chamber, he retreated, closed the door, and checked his watch. By his calculations, Perry would be dead inside of an hour, possibly sooner; and now all he had to do was attend to one last chore.

He slipped into the actor's room and removed several cigarettes from a pack he'd bought at the bar the prior night, which he'd partially soaked in PCP. Anyone investigating the incident would draw the obvious conclusion: another spoiled Hollywood brat with everything to live for had overestimated his tolerance for his drug of choice and taken his last hallucinogenic trip to the cosmic plane.

El Rey returned to the fire and sat beside Sam's slumped form, listening to the night creatures in the trees. It really was beautiful, he thought – he could see why the wealthy would enjoy the seclusion. He felt somewhat bad for Sam, but the old man would weather the storm – the PCP would show up on a blood scan but would be accounted for as self-administered, and after a period of heightened concern over the safety of sweat lodges and hysteria at how drugs were ruining America, things would return to normal, with business quite possibly better than ever as curiosity seekers came to visit the lodge to tread the same ground as one of the fallen greats.

He checked his watch, and after forty-five minutes returned to the sweat lodge. The heat hit him in the face when he moved through the door, and a quick pulse check confirmed that the actor was no longer alive. He wound the key back around Perry's wrist, taking care to wipe it off on the robe, and repeated the wipe-down on the door handle as he exited the lodge.

Replacing the fuse took longer than he'd hoped in the darkness, the moon having yet to have risen above the mountains. As he was leaving the building, he spotted a flash of color at the pool bar in the distance. He squinted and saw what had caught his eye – a stunning woman in a bright red miniskirt, long auburn hair cascading down her back. She looked familiar to him, but he couldn't place her, and after another glance at the time, he returned his attention to his task.

He elbowed Sam awake after the fan had cleared most of the heat from the lodge. Sam was predictably disoriented but came to quickly enough and groped for the bottle *El Rey* had replaced the drugged one with.

"I don't know if that's a great idea, Sam. Your client's been in there for an hour. Didn't you say that was about the limit?"

"What? Damn. I must have dozed off."

"Not a problem. Nothing happened – nobody came by."

"Yeah, but it's a good idea to pour some more water on the stones after about half an hour. The lodge is really a sauna, and you don't want it to get too dry or it loses its effect." Sam rose unsteadily to his feet. "I'll get him. Might want to hide that bottle for later."

"You bet," *El Rey* said, slipping it into his pocket beneath the robe.

Sam's cry sounded muffled inside the lodge, and *El Rey* waited a few seconds before going to him.

"What is it, Sam?"

The older man's face was ashen as he looked up at the assassin. "He's…he's dead."

"Dead? You're kidding."

Sam shook his head. "No. There's no pulse."

El Rey straightened, concern written across his face. "Sam…what do we do?"

"I…I've got to go tell the manager. Shit. His heart must have stopped or something. Poor bastard."

El Rey glanced around. "Sam, don't take this the wrong way, but I'd just as soon not be here when the police show up. I…well, I've had some brushes with the law I'd rather not revisit."

Sam didn't appear to hear him and then hunched his shoulders. "I kind of figured you might be in some kinda trouble. Don't worry, kid. Your being here or not isn't going to bring him back."

"You sure? I mean, I'll stay if you need me to."

"No. Go on. Get outta here. I'll see you at the bar tonight. If not, tomorrow."

"I'll definitely be buying the first round."

Sam stared at the fire, his look as bleak as a prisoner going to death row, and grunted. "No point delaying this. He isn't going to get any fresher. See you around, Slim."

"You too, Sam. Good luck."

CHAPTER 21

Tepotzotlán, Mexico

"Can you believe this? It's insane. There must be five thousand people here already," Briones said to Cruz, watching more cars arrive and park in one of the three fields being used for the rave. They'd been in position for two hours in a surveillance van set up as the field headquarters for the operation. A loose cordon of *Federales* was stationed along the perimeter of the warehouse district.

"If we're lucky, the police presence will scare any kidnappers off," Cruz said as a sedan with six scantily clad young women emptied out across the street from their position. The new arrivals laughed as they passed a bottle back and forth while making their way to the warehouse. "You ready to get going?"

"Sure. Everyone's in place. I'll stay in constant communication," Briones said, seating his earbud more snugly. He was wearing a pair of loose jeans and a vertically striped polo jersey that covered the compact automatic pistol at the small of his back. A reversed baseball cap completed his disguise, and to Cruz's eye he looked more like a twenty-something slacker than a hardened veteran of the cartel wars.

"Let's hope we dodge a bullet tonight," Cruz said. "This is twice the crowd we anticipated, and I'm not convinced we have it locked down."

"All right. I'm going in." Briones opened the rear door of the van and stepped out, his civilian clothes no different from those of countless other young males heading to the warehouse. The dull thump of a hypnotic beat boomed from the building, and the distinctive smell of marijuana drifted on the light breeze. Laughter sounded from his right, and he peered into the darkness where three youths stood in the moonlight drinking beer and puffing on a joint. Briones wondered how they would react if he pulled his badge, but decided to forego the theatrics in favor of getting into the rave.

He knew from the first undercover agent who'd gone into the cavernous space that there was no security check at the door, so he wasn't worried about his gun. He stood in line with at least a hundred of Mexico City's most beautiful people, the women wearing miniskirts and five-inch heels in spite of the brisk night air, the men with the smug sense of entitlement fostered by being young and wealthy and sure you were going to live forever. Four girls in front of him flirted as they shuffled forward, and by the time he was at the entry handing over his money, he was convinced that the chances of stopping a determined kidnapping were slim given the number of people.

Inside the building the music was loud enough to strip the enamel off his teeth. A girl with streaks of phosphorescent paint on her face materialized from the crowd and handed him a glow stick before moving to the next person. Half the females in attendance had their faces painted, some with sunflowers or the Mexican flag, others with a few stripes in a psychedelic homage to their Indian forefathers, all glowing neon when they moved within range of one of the plentiful black lights. At least seventy percent of the mammoth building was a dance floor, with the throng bouncing and grinding to the trance beat, purple and pink and lime green lamps blinking in time with the bass as mini-spotlights strobed over the dancers' heads.

The smell of marijuana was powerful and cloying. A girl, probably no older than sixteen and obviously high, wearing a halter top and hip-hugger jeans, her bare midriff tanned and cut, her navel piercing glinting in the light, danced up to Briones with vacant eyes. She opened her mouth and offered a white dot on her tongue, which he momentarily mistook for a piercing before he realized it was a pill. Her gaze invited him to kiss her, and he shook his head. She smiled and moved to the youth behind him, no doubt more amenable to taking unspecified drugs from total strangers, and Briones pushed toward the closest wall in an effort to get his bearings.

A tall young man with long black hair and a perennial smirk approached three girls near the DJ booth and offered the one he'd exchanged glances with a cocktail he'd bought from the illegal bar. Set up on one side of the warehouse, it was dispensing rum-infused punch and plastic bottles of water, the latter in great demand – the ecstasy that was the drug of choice in the rave crowd caused pronounced dehydration. The girl ran a hand through her long hair and smiled – it was far too loud to attempt conversation. The man toasted her with his punch and closed his eyes as his head bobbed to the robotic rhythm. Her friends giggled and returned to their flirtations with the DJ and his assistant, whom they'd agreed were total babes.

The man offered the group a joint, and they passed it around, taking in the smoke in greedy gulps and blowing clouds at the rafters, and the long-haired girl moved closer to the man, who leaned in and said something to her. She flashed brilliant white teeth, her flawless caramel skin accentuating their luminescence in the dim light, and rolled her head dreamily, the marijuana already hitting. They stood together, lost in the music, and the song changed and then changed again, the tunes interchangeable with no discernible start or finish. When she'd drunk half her punch, she grabbed one of her friends' shoulders and yelled something, and the friend nodded after taking another glance at the grinning man.

He offered his hand. She took it and followed him outside to where the portable toilets were set up, sipping her drink. He escorted her to the line for the facilities, and they chatted, her mild slur becoming more pronounced as they inched forward. By the time she was three-quarters of the way to the porta-potties, she was barely able to stand, and the young man slipped his arm around her and guided her along the side of the warehouse to a darkened area near a stack of pallets.

A security man stopped them, his flashlight on her face. "Is she okay?"

"Yeah. She just overdid the punch and all. I think she's going to be sick. I got it."

The guard considered her fluttering eyes and slack face and nodded. "Let me know if you need any help. There are a lot of kids throwing up. Lightweights," he said with a roll of his eyes, and the young man nodded in agreement.

He reached the area with the pallets, and after glancing back at the guard, who'd moved along to the toilets, he ducked with the girl, who was barely conscious from the Rohypnol he'd dropped in her punch.

"What…I need to…go…" she slurred, her voice dreamy from the effect of the roofie.

"I know. But it's gross there. This is better," he said, leading her along the pallets to another cleared area.

"I…where's the toilet?" she asked, her words barely distinguishable under the thumping music emanating from inside.

Her eyes widened as the man moved closer to her, and then another pair of hands reached around from behind her and clamped over her mouth so she couldn't scream. A third man approached with a syringe.

The girl was too narcotized to struggle much, and her eyes rolled back into her head sixty seconds after the injection hit her system. Her escort and his accomplices manhandled her to a container and wedged her inside and then placed a board over her and filled the area above her with cellophane-wrapped confections.

The young man turned to the others. "See you at the truck in fifteen. Good luck."

"I'm glad we got the heads-up about the cops. It would have been a shame to call this off." The kidnappers had been tipped off by one of their contacts at the *Federales* about the heightened security and the likelihood of departing vehicles being searched, and had improvised a solution they'd all agreed bordered on genius.

"They'll never suspect a thing."

Two squad cars partially blocked the small side street, one of four roads that ran along the edge of the warehouse. Few cars were leaving the rave at the relatively early hour, it being only midnight, but the police had three vehicles pulled over and were questioning the occupants, checking IDs, and searching the trunks while a pair of officers looked on.

A tinkle sounded on the road – a cow bell – and a vendor appeared pushing a cart with churros and other treats hanging from a frame. "Good evening, officers. Churros?" he asked, his voice a rasp.

The vendor found a willing clientele for his wares and, after making several sales, continued on his way as the policemen munched on their snacks while searching the vehicles.

Briones was tired by four a.m. Tired of dancing stoners, tired of the never-ending monotonous beat, tired of the theatrically forced feeling of the event. He was getting ready to call it a night when his earbud chirped and Cruz's voice came over the comm channel.

"We just got a call. There's been a kidnapping at the rave. It's puzzling because she's not from a particularly wealthy family – but the friend she was with is. We think they might have grabbed the wrong girl, but that's speculation."

Briones cupped his hand over his mouth and glanced down. "What? Aren't the streets sealed? They have to still be here."

"Yes, they're closed off. I want to shut down the party and search every vehicle. Every one, no exceptions."

"That's going to take hours."

"I agree. But it's the only way."

"What do you want me to do?"

"Go to the entrance and wait for us to arrive. We're coming in heavy."

The rave quickly became pandemonium when the *Federales* arrived and the music stopped. When the lights went on, the crowd lost its magical allure and became mostly scared kids, many of whom were struggling with varying stages of intoxication.

By dawn, the last of the cars had cleared the fields, and Cruz was pacing anxiously, talking on his cell phone. When he hung up, he glowered at Briones and the sergeants who were in charge of the roadblocks.

"Let's take this one more time. Every vehicle was searched since the beginning of the evening?"

"Yes, sir. Nothing made it past us. I'm a hundred percent sure – we had all exits covered," Gustavo, a twenty-year veteran of the force, assured Cruz.

Briones' eyes narrowed. "What about pedestrians?"

Doubt flitted across Gustavo's face before his expression returned to normal. "There were only a few every hour. Individuals or groups of two or three. But nothing suspicious."

"Did you ID them?" Briones pressed.

"No. Those weren't the orders. The orders were to stop every car leaving the rave. Which is what we did."

Cruz frowned. "Then how the hell did they get by us? We know they're not here. We've searched every inch of the warehouse and the grounds." He stalked off to the edge of the field and stared into the distance. When he returned, he was on the phone again. He terminated the call and shook his head.

"The family of the victim's wealthy friend just got a ransom call. The kidnappers apparently believed they had the daughter, who's now home, safe. They didn't respond well to being told that they had someone else." Cruz paused. "At least the family notified us."

"We need to contact the other parents. They're next," Briones said.

"I'm already ahead of you." Cruz sighed. "I just don't understand how they slipped through. You men were on duty the entire time?"

"Yes, sir, as ordered. Not a single vehicle made it past us without a thorough search and the occupants ID'd. No exceptions."

Briones stepped forward. "It had to be the pedestrians. That's the only answer. They must have walked her out, maybe holding a gun on her."

"Seems pretty risky to me," Gustavo said, shaking his head. "Besides, we didn't see anyone suspicious, and you'd think we would have noticed someone being marched through our lines at gunpoint. Or carried."

Cruz shook his head and eyed Briones. "Come on. Let's get over to the victim's house. We're not getting anywhere here."

The two men walked to the surveillance van, shoulders sagging, the entire effort for naught – somewhere there was a girl who'd been abducted right under their noses, in spite of a heavily armed police presence. The press would have a field day with that, and he knew the calls would start coming in soon as outraged lawmakers and his superiors called Cruz onto the carpet, his string of successes with the cartels quickly forgotten in light of this debacle. The van dropped them off at Briones' cruiser parked a few blocks outside of the cordon, and as the rising sun colored the washed-out sky with tangerine and red, neither noticed the churro cart abandoned in one corner of the dirt lot near an overflowing dumpster.

CHAPTER 22

Ensenada, Mexico

El Rey sat at a sidewalk café, drinking a cup of coffee. Off in the distance the huge Mexican flag that was a city landmark fluttered in the sea breeze, beyond which he could see a towering American cruise ship making its way from the harbor, bound for points south. A motor scooter narrowly missed colliding with a taxi only footsteps in front of him, and the blare of the horn made him wince.

He'd made it back into Mexico by simply walking across the border in Tijuana, leaving the car in a lot on the U.S. side. There had been no checks, even though he'd been prepared with his newly minted identity, but apparently Mexico wasn't worried about being overrun by *gringos*, and the U.S. only cared about arrivals.

The trip from Arizona had been as uneventful as the drive to Sedona, a monotonous blur of fast-food restaurants, strip malls, and shuddering semi-rigs. Once back in California the Highway Patrol had been everywhere, and he'd taken care to keep his speed down so as not to attract unwanted attention on the final leg of his journey.

He'd picked up a newspaper in San Diego and read the coverage on Perry's death, which was being treated as accidental, a sad reminder of the perils of substance abuse among the entertainment set, with a long list of overdoses from just the last few years. *El Rey* smiled when he saw the article – two for two, and nobody the wiser.

But now, sitting in Ensenada, the problem of the admiral was thornier. He was being treated at the naval base hospital, which was behind fortified walls and guarded gates. The assassin had toyed with the idea of posing as a naval officer to gain entry, but once the admiral died, a phantom officer would be a natural red flag to anyone investigating – and he had no doubt it would receive considerably closer scrutiny in the wake of the bungled helicopter attack.

He flagged down the waiter and paid the check and then headed down the waterfront sidewalk. Tall palm trees swayed in the late afternoon sky, emerald green fronds flapping from gusts of balmy wind. When he arrived at a small seafood restaurant across the boulevard from the base, little more than a gaudily painted cinderblock shack with a half dozen plastic tables stuffed beneath weather-beaten *palapas*, he paused and chatted up the young waitress, asking offhand questions about traffic from the base and when she was busiest. After promising to return for dinner, he continued south, eying the main gate, which, as he'd expected, was guarded by six rifle-toting marines.

He looped back around and entered the private marina north of the docks and, after verifying the scant security there, continued north to his modest hotel, where he contacted Tovar and told him what he required. The CISEN man listened and repeated the items back to him.

"The map of the base and the sewer blueprint should be in the email inbox in…an hour, at most," Tovar concluded.

"Very well. I'll touch base when I've figured out how I'm going to do it. No doubt I'll have other requirements."

The layout documents arrived, and he studied them using a laptop he'd purchased that afternoon at an office superstore. He preferred to jettison anything that could leave a trail once he left each location, including computers and cell phones, opting to buy new ones rather than risk being caught with anything incriminating.

The base hospital was located just off the main entry road, in what appeared to be a clear line of sight of the armed contingent at the gate. The sewer schematic showed promise, with a central artery leading from the street and running beneath the base, and smaller branches stretching from the administrative and housing buildings. But a note from CISEN warning of an overhaul of the security systems four years earlier referenced work done below ground.

He spent the evening at the seafood shack, charming the waitress while watching the base. By the time he returned to the hotel, he was ready for bed, but no closer to figuring out how to get at the admiral, who, according to the latest reports, was still in precarious condition due to his age, blood loss, and complications arising from high blood pressure, diabetes, and cardiovascular disease.

He spent the next morning shopping, and by afternoon he'd assembled everything he needed for an exploration of the sewers: a crowbar, tire iron, various other tools, a backpack, waterproof fishing overalls that came to his chest, an army surplus gas mask, and a headband-mounted halogen reading lamp.

Once it got dark he set out for the entry to the sewer system he'd chosen, a block and a half from the base – a manhole in the middle of a small street in an industrial area that would be deserted after business hours. His pry bar made short work of the cover, and within seconds he'd slid the heavy disk aside, climbed down the iron rungs, and dragged it back overhead.

The sewer was as foul as any he'd been in, and he was thankful for the gas mask as he eyed the coagulating river of goo swirling around his thighs. He checked his bearings on the map he'd drafted and made his way west. Even inside his mask his eyes watered at the noxious seepage as the beam of his light roamed over the crumbling brick of the tunnel. At a junction that marked the near side of the boulevard, beyond which lay the base, the lamp reflected off a metal grate halfway down the destination passage.

He stopped and studied the barrier – newish, heavy gauge stainless steel showing none of the rusting of the other metal elements he'd passed. He approached it and noted the heavy lock, and looked beyond it at the unmistakable shape of a motion detector and camera suspended from the tunnel ceiling.

The assassin slowly backed away and followed the lateral passageway until he reached a smaller tributary that led to the base, and saw the same thing – CISEN's report about heightened security hadn't been exaggerated, and even if he could somehow get past the barrier, the motion detector and camera made it a moot point. If he disabled them, the technical problem would be noted, and in light of the admiral's demise it wouldn't be viewed as an ordinary glitch.

El Rey retraced his steps to the main road and climbed back up to the street, where he quickly stripped off the filthy waders, his nose wrinkling at the stench. After shifting the iron disk back into place, he hiked to a line of warehouses three blocks away and tossed the gear into different dumpsters overflowing with garbage.

He spent the remainder of his evening prowling the waterfront, and when he returned to his hotel, he sent CISEN another list of requirements. Unless there was something the new documentation revealed, some weakness in the security measures, he might have to rely on CISEN's doctored identification to gain access to the base.

When he received the information he'd requested, he spent several hours studying it, but his eyes grew heavy, and he realized he wasn't focusing. He decided to continue studying his options in the morning, and after taking a long shower, he lay on the bed and stared at the orbiting ceiling fan before drifting off.

Four hours later he sat up abruptly, his heart racing, and returned to his computer, where he went through CISEN's list of security electronics and the timing of the guard patrols.

It could work. It wasn't foolproof, and there would certainly be risk involved, but it might be viable. He'd return to the waterfront at first light and evaluate the approach, and if it looked positive, would source the requisite equipment locally and have CISEN send him anything he couldn't procure in town.

When he closed his eyes again, he had a slight smile on his face, and this time when he slept it was the untroubled slumber of the innocent.

CHAPTER 23

Guadalajara, Mexico

The dark-haired man frowned as he read the report, obviously unhappy with the news it contained. When he put it aside and stared at his young, fair-haired companion, his scowl creased new lines into his annoyed face.

"I suppose we could just assume that this Carla Vega being at both the admiral's press conference and the actor's secluded hotel is some sort of bizarre coincidence?" he asked, the question dripping with sarcasm.

"That would be one option."

"What do we know about her?"

"I have our network collecting information." He pointed at the report. "She's currently in Los Angeles for the awards show and will return the day after tomorrow."

The dark-haired man's eyes narrowed. "What do you think?"

"It's troubling. I just don't know whether it means anything."

"Yes, well, that's the problem, isn't it? Says that she has a reputation for her investigative stuff. Need I remind that the word 'investigative' and anything we're associated with is disastrous?"

"I'm clear on that. We have someone internal at the network who's going to look around in her system and see what she's working on. Which, of course, assumes that she keeps documentation on her active cases. Depending upon how secretive she is…"

"I don't think we can chance it. Her discovering anything."

The fair-haired man studied the older man's face for any tics or indications that he was cracking under the pressure. He looked as calm as a choirboy.

"She's an extremely visible public figure."

"That hasn't stopped us so far."

"True, but there's a practical limit to how many people we can…how many obstacles can be surmounted using the CISEN asset."

The dark-haired man waved the objection away. "One more shouldn't be an issue. That's the business this fellow's in, isn't it? What's one more?"

"I received considerable resistance over the last one."

"Do whatever it takes, but I'm of the opinion that one of the nation's top investigative reporters sniffing around is about as bad as it gets, and we need to take preemptive action immediately."

"It absolutely has to appear accidental," the fair-haired man said quietly, as if talking to himself.

"Yes. It's a dangerous world. Perhaps a hit and run?"

"Let me set up a meeting. I'll see what our liaison thinks." He paused. "We may have to up the compensation for this one."

The dark-haired man made a vague gesture towards his companion and flicked a piece of lint off his trousers. "See to it."

~ ~ ~

The moon beamed a shimmering silver path on the surface of Ensenada harbor as the last of the downtown bars closed, the din of their music fading as 3:00 a.m. neared. The occasional hot rod or muffler-free clunker rolled down the deserted frontage road, keeping the roving dogs and wharf rats company.

A ripple played along the water adjacent to the concrete jetty where the naval ships were docked, resembling the wake made by one of the plentiful seals that called the harbor home. An ebony-swathed head emerged from the water, all metal areas of the dive mask and rebreathing apparatus blacked out. *El Rey* glanced around to ensure that there were no guards before hoisting himself onto the boulders next to the jetty and shrugging out of his gear, keenly aware that he only had ten minutes between patrols, the last one having gone by three minutes earlier.

He hoped CISEN's intelligence on the security system was accurate. The motion detectors along the wharf had been disabled shortly after installation, when it was discovered that sea birds and the odd seal would trigger them – an unforeseen complication the company who'd designed the hi-tech base defenses hadn't predicted, but one that had created an opportunity for him to get onto the grounds undetected. Once he was out of the oversized wetsuit, he unpacked a waterproof pouch, removing a set of green surgical scrubs and a pair of black running shoes. He donned them and checked his watch. Two minutes until the guards would round the corner and patrol along the water again. After a final check to ensure that none of his equipment was visible, he slipped the pouch into a gap in the rocks, taking care to extract the final item from the case and slide it into his pocket.

The area was quiet, the only sound the groan from the huge dock lines that secured the ships to the jetty and the occasional truck roaring by on the highway. Condensation beaded every metal surface, and the cement walkway was slick from the moisture. He spotted the twin sets of boot prints from the marines on guard duty, still fresh.

El Rey darted along a row of hedges, sticking to the shadows, avoiding any of the areas lit by the streetlights around the perimeter. The hospital was dark except for the dim glow of a lamp at the main nurses' station, and he edged to the rear entrance, which the report had indicated would be unlocked.

The lever turned easily. The hallway was shrouded in gloom, the tile floor shining from a slim shaft of reflected light emanating from the far end of the corridor, where the night nurse was stationed around the corner, out of sight. A cart with towels, bedding, and toilet paper sat midway down the passage on the right – near the room where the admiral was recuperating, hopefully fast asleep.

Air hissed from the overhead vents, the climate control keeping the interior at sixty-nine degrees, masking any sound he made as he crept toward the room door. He edged forward, senses alert, but detected no threat.

His rubber soles were silent on the tile, and he was almost at the admiral's room when he heard muffled laughter from the ward – at least two men. He froze, waiting. Another murmur, more laughter, and then silence. He stood as if carved from granite, and when he heard nothing more from the nurse's station, he continued his approach with cautious steps.

He slipped into the room. Faint light traced through the blinds from outside, combining with the orange glow of the vital signs monitor next to the bed. The area was filled with muted beeping and the admiral's soft snores. *El Rey* stood just inside the door, wary of waking the old man up, allowing his eyes to adjust before he moved to the IV line and withdrew a syringe from the pocket of his scrubs. He stole a final glance at the admiral's darkened form and then unclipped the IV bag and emptied the syringe's contents into the line. Tovar had said the CISEN substance he'd sent to *El Rey* would take two minutes to kill, which left little time. He reconnected the line and made his way back to the door, listening for any signs of motion in the corridor.

Nothing.

He slipped into the hallway and retraced his steps, pulse hammering in his ears as he forced himself to maintain a measured pace to the exit. *El Rey* was confident that the admiral would be long dead by the time the sun rose that morning, and Tovar had assured him that any autopsy performed would show cardiac arrest due to unspecified causes – old age and the cumulative effects of his injuries being the likely culprits. All the assassin needed to do now was evade detection and make it past another armed patrol.

He was pushing through the exit door when the first ward alarm sounded, signaling that the admiral's heart rate had spiked through the roof. Several loping strides carried him back into the gloom, and he stopped at the row of hedges again and checked his watch – six minutes until the patrol returned, assuming they weren't early.

It would be just enough. He stripped off his shirt as he raced to the rocks, his breathing rapid as he covered the ground. Once at his gear, he stowed his shoes and clothes in the pack and set to work donning the wetsuit. He pulled on the vest with the rebreathing unit and slid the dive mask in place, fins in hand, pouch over his shoulder, and eased into the icy water just as the patrolling marines rounded the bend.

El Rey vanished into the depths without a sound as the men marched along, weapons dangling from slings, the routine duty as boring as any on the base, there having been exactly zero incidences of anyone trying to breach the fortifications in its peacetime history.

The assassin drove himself through the water with powerful strokes seven feet beneath the surface, guided by his compass, leaving no bubble trail due to the miracle of the rebreather, which filtered out the carbon dioxide from his breath in a closed system and trickled in pure oxygen, enabling him to remain submerged in the darkness without a trace. Visibility was negligible, but he trusted his instruments, and fifteen minutes later he was hoisting himself onto shore on the far side of the private marina where the black nylon bag with his street clothes was stashed.

He knew from his reconnaissance of the marina security that there was only one guard, who spent most of the night in his shack by the gate watching a portable television. *El Rey* removed his fins and moved to the sack with his clothes, which he'd left beneath the overhang of the boardwalk. He was out of the dive gear in a few minutes and making his way along the deserted sidewalk, a lone figure on the *malecón* in the quiet hours after the town shut down.

He was back at his hotel ten minutes later, would be on a bus to Mexicali at dawn, and with any luck back in Mexico City in time for a late lunch, his obligation to CISEN discharged. As reward for doing the agency's dirty work, he would get the semiannual booster shot of the antidote he required to stay alive the following week, and if he was fortunate, six months later his blood would be completely clear of the toxin he'd been injected with, and he could disappear to pursue whatever interested him, his stint of questionable government service over forever.

CHAPTER 24

The faces of *El Rey*'s fellow passengers were drawn and tense as the jet dropped through the clouds toward Toluca Airport, the plane shuddering as trees of lightning seared the sky around it. The woman next to him drew in a sharp intake of breath as the aircraft jolted its way through a series of air pockets, slamming from side to side like a child's toy in a hurricane. The pilot's voice came over the public address system and warned that everyone should remain buckled up for final descent as a worried stewardess with a smile frozen in place made her way along the aisle, checking to ensure that her precious cargo was strapped in.

The jets roared as the pilot juiced the throttle and banked to avoid the worst of a black thunderhead. *El Rey* closed his eyes, shutting out the anxiety and fear radiating from his seatmates as the plane pitched and yawed. Another drop, another slam, and then the clouds broke and he could see the gray outline of Toluca, the afternoon drizzle obscuring Mexico City's skyline in the distance.

Nervous applause broke out in the cabin when the plane's wheels touched down. The jet slowed as it neared the runway's end as the sky exploded with flashes of lightning, and *El Rey* offered the woman beside him a small smile. Five minutes later he was trudging in single file through the fuselage door and up the Jetway, with only a small overnight bag for luggage. He made his way through the arrivals terminal, approached the long taxi line, and waited as an attendant waved a car forward. *El Rey* slipped a few coins to the man and tossed his bag onto the back seat, then slid in and gave the driver an address in Mexico City several blocks from the condo he rented by the month.

Traffic was a snarl, and the twenty-five-mile freeway run to Mexico City took twice as long as normal. Sheets of rain blew across the road as the car entered the western reaches of the metropolis, and rivers of runoff clogged the streets as the driver threaded through the parade of vehicles clogging the avenues. The downpour stopped as they neared *El Rey*'s building, and he was grateful that only a light drizzle remained when he got out of the cab.

The air in the condo was stale and dank, and he opened two windows, careful to avoid framing himself where anyone could see him, more out of habit than genuine concern he was being watched. He walked through the living room as the fresh breeze from the passing storm wafted through, pausing to set his bag down in his bedroom and retrieve his phone and charger.

He plugged it in and powered it on, and was surprised when the phone buzzed in his hand, signaling that he had a message in his blind email account. It was Tovar, six hours earlier, asking him to call as soon as possible. The hair on *El Rey*'s arms stood on end as he read the innocuous code phrase, and he debated ignoring it until the following day and instead getting some solid hours of sleep. After a brief internal struggle, he dialed the CISEN man's number.

"You got my message," Tovar said by way of greeting.

"Obviously."

"We need to meet. I can be at Cambalache Restaurant in an hour. I'll pick you up."

"I just got into town. Can it wait until tomorrow?"

"I'm afraid not. One hour."

Tovar disconnected, both men knowing better than to say anything on an unsecure line, and *El Rey* cursed CISEN, Tovar, and the weather, for good measure. He was unaccustomed to having terms dictated to him, and the man's tone was always dangerously close to outright insulting with an undeniable undercurrent of contempt in his words.

He shook off his annoyance. It was unlike him   a product of inadequate sleep. Instead of bemoaning his fate or trying to second-guess what Tovar wanted, he opted for a hot shower and fresh clothes. There was no way the CISEN man could have known it, but *El Rey*'s latest condo was only a ten-minute walk from the restaurant, and after a half hour of isometric exercises and a few moments checking the headlines on the web, he set out for Cambalache.

Tovar undoubtedly had plentiful faults, but a lack of punctuality wasn't one of them, and in exactly one hour his car pulled to the curb on Avenida Presidente Masaryk. The rear door swung open, and Tovar peered out of the interior and then sat back, waiting for *El Rey*.

When they were underway, Tovar's eyes narrowed as he studied the assassin's tired face.

"Nice work on the admiral," Tovar said.

"No complications, I trust."

"None. He wasn't a young man. Everything's perfect."

"Great. Then I get my injection next week, and our business is concluded for the time being."

Tovar's eyes flitted to the side. "In a perfect world…"

"Which you're about to tell me it isn't," *El Rey* stated flatly.

"Unfortunately, no. As part of the same assignment, we have another set of targets that must be neutralized, and time is of the essence."

"That wasn't our arrangement."

"Arrangements are subject to change."

"Why didn't you just give me the whole list in the first place?"

Tovar lifted his hands almost apologetically. "Need to know. That decision was made above my pay grade." He handed the assassin a folder with three more dossiers in it.

El Rey took it with a sigh and opened it. He flipped through the photographs and the reports, his face betraying nothing. The car bounced along as he read more slowly on his second pass, and when he closed it and handed it back to Tovar, his expression was as flat as a professional gambler's.

"Why?"

"I beg your pardon?"

"I need to know why these three. Two of them are extremely high profile, and one, I know for a fact, is unreachable."

"As I said, it's part of the same case. These are the last, by the way."

"That's not an answer."

"It's the only answer I have." Tovar appeared to choose his words carefully. "They also need to appear to be accidental deaths, and are urgent."

El Rey shook his head. "That's not how I work. If I don't know everything, I don't have to take an assignment. You're holding out on me, so find somebody else."

Tovar's expression took on an ugly cast. "I'd suggest that you rethink your position, given that you're up for an injection in a week. It would be nice if all three were dealt with before you receive it."

"I just told you, I'm not taking these."

"Perhaps I wasn't clear. If you want your injection, you'll do as you're told."

"I have a signed letter from the president, you little worm."

"Yes, well, that's all well and good, but that signed letter can't keep a vial from being broken or getting misplaced. These things can happen. It's Mexico, after all."

El Rey debated snapping Tovar's neck then and there, but decided that the momentary satisfaction wasn't worth the fallout. They rode along in silence for two blocks, and then he leaned forward.

"You're playing an extremely dangerous game with the wrong man, and believe me, I'll remember this. You may think you have me over a barrel, but by threatening to withhold the antidote shot, you've crossed an important line."

"It wasn't my intention to do so. Wouldn't it be easier if you simply attended to these errands and then went back to doing whatever it is you do, in peace, having received the shot, as planned? Why force my hand in this?"

El Rey's voice was so soft when he next spoke that Tovar had to strain to make out the words. "I'll need the dossiers in my inbox today. And anything I ask for is to be supplied, immediately and without question. Do you understand?"

Tovar pressed his hands together. "Of course."

The assassin eyed the tiny beads of sweat on the CISEN man's forehead and took the folder from him. "What does a pig farmer have in common with these others?"

"They'll all be dead inside of a week. Isn't that enough?"

El Rey gazed at the farmer's photograph and then flipped to a headshot of the startlingly beautiful woman whose name he recognized from her numerous appearances in the news: Carla Vega. He thumbed through a dozen more photos of her from every angle, many from celebrity events, and then turned to the final file.

"You do understand that the level of difficulty in trying to take out someone of this man's stature makes everything I've done pale by comparison, right? I mean, even if I had a month, it's almost certainly impossible, but in the time I have before the next injection's due?" The assassin shook his head. "Like I said. Impossible."

"I've come to believe that nothing is beyond your abilities. I have complete faith you'll succeed."

"For the record, you're refusing to tell me why CISEN wants me to execute the most visible law enforcement official in Mexico along with one of its most beloved celebrities."

"I've told you all I know, and all I've been authorized to. I appreciate that this isn't how you'd hoped things would go, and believe me, if I had any other options…"

"Right. But you don't. And I don't suppose that Rodriguez or your boss will talk to me."

"All due respect, you're a bit of a hot potato at present. You'll find that nobody can afford that discussion."

El Rey returned his attention to the dossier he was holding. Smoldering eyes burned from the page with quiet intensity in the official photograph. It had to be at least four or five years old by now, judging by the man's countenance, which *El Rey* knew was thinner and harder than the photo showed, any trace of good humor seared away by the demands of the job. It had been half a year since he'd last seen him, but the assassin was willing to bet that the passage of time hadn't been kind to *Capitan* Romero Cruz, a man who owed *El Rey* a favor he could never adequately repay.

CHAPTER 25

El Oso Negro was the kind of working man's bar that tourists to Mexico City never saw. Tucked away on a side street on the edge of an industrial district, the façade was run-down. A hand-painted caricature of a rampaging grizzly bear with a frothing mug of beer in one paw as it swatted at white-clad villagers with the other glared from a rusting steel billboard over the entrance, the pair of red lights that served as its eyes blinking on and off in either invitation or warning.

Briones pushed through a pair of worn saloon-style half doors and peered around the gloomy interior, which continued the bear motif on two of the walls. The interior was as sorry as any he'd seen, and the clientele was largely in worse shape: middle-aged men with nothing to say, their drinking silent and committed. A stereo blared seventies-era banda music through a pair of partially blown speakers, the tuba that served as the bass reduced to a crackling woof. The floor was bare concrete, stained gray-brown, and had seen more than its share of sucker punches and spilt blood.

Briones moved to the bar and sat down next to Cruz, who had a half-empty shot glass in front of him and an amber bottle of Indio beer sweating beside it. A bartender with pasty skin queried him with a glance, and Briones pointed at Cruz's drinks and held up two fingers.

The tequila was El Jimador Reposado, cheap and strong, a smoky caramel that promised damnation and salvation in the same glass. The first bite burned his throat as he threw it back, and his eyes immediately brimmed as he reached for the cold comfort of the beer. When he'd taken two large swallows and had caught his breath, he turned to Cruz, who hadn't said anything.

"I guess you heard the news."

Cruz grunted and downed the remainder of his shot, his movements deliberate and wooden. The bartender raised an eyebrow, and Cruz held the glass up and gave a curt nod. Another serving of tequila arrived, and Cruz paused as he reached for it, as if only now hearing Briones' words.

"Yeah. Coroner's preliminary report said she'd been raped and sodomized repeatedly before they killed her. That the burns were likely inflicted while she was still alive. As was the butchering. Did you see the pictures?"

Briones shook his head. "No."

"Good. You don't want to. After they were done with her, they tossed her in a dumpster like yesterday's garbage. She'd been there for at least twenty-four hours." Cruz gazed bleakly at his reflection in the mirror, seeing an unfamiliar face twisted by disgust and the mirror's imperfections. "The rats had gotten to her."

"I heard."

"Some things you never forget. That's one of them," Cruz said and drained his shot.

It was Briones' turn to grunt.

Cruz looked at the younger man. "How did you find me?"

"Dinah."

"Ah. She gave me up, did she?"

"She's worried. Said you sounded…distant…when you called."

Cruz gazed at a nonexistent spot on the wall. "You didn't look at the pictures, did you?"

"No." Briones hesitated, took a pull on his beer, set it back on the weathered bar top, and ran a blunt thumb across a burn scar left over from the days when smoking was permitted indoors. Someone had used a cigarette, or perhaps a knife and a lighter, to leave their mark. Briones swallowed hard before he continued. "I was hoping we could grab something to eat and head home. When you're done with your beer."

This was the tipping point. The moment when the car ran out of gas and someone suggested that the party was over. Briones knew it could go either way, and he held his breath as he waited for Cruz to respond. The captain was a smart and serious officer, but he also had demons large enough to bury ten men, and it was debatable who was sitting on the barstool next to the lieutenant.

A phlegmy cough echoed from down the bar – a wet, ugly sound, the result of decades of inhaling dust at construction sites, end-stage lung disease as common as cockroaches with laborers by the time they hit forty. Cruz closed one eye and glared at the mirror behind the bar with the other, and then his face seemed to collapse, like wax before a flame.

"What kind of animals would kill a sixteen-year-old honor student because her parents aren't millionaires – would rape her and cut her nose and ears off? Who does that?"

Briones had no answer. The tequila had begun to warm him, and he more than understood the flight into oblivion that his superior was seeking. But that had never been his way, and he hadn't come to be a drinking partner.

"We'll find them, and when we do, we'll return the favor."

"It's just so…senseless," Cruz muttered, his voice quiet, the consonants surprisingly well pronounced. "I mean, with the cartels, it's about drugs, power, territory. Nothing surprises me with their atrocities. It's like junkyard dogs fighting for dominance. I completely get that. But this? What was this about? She was just a child." Cruz took a long breath. "Her mother was hysterical on her last phone call with the kidnappers. We were taping it. She offered herself, to sell the house, whatever they had to do to get her baby back. Didn't do any good, did it? Burner cell phone. She was crying, begging for her child's life, offering everything they had in exchange. I listened to her. The kidnapper laughed." Cruz groped for his beer, missed with clumsy fingers, got it on the second try. "I heard him. The bastard laughed. Like it was a game. Funny in some way."

Briones waved at the bartender and motioned for the check. Cruz stared dully at his bottle, eyes only partially focused, the whites bloodshot, the skin around them sallow and slack. For a moment Briones was afraid Cruz was going to fight him about leaving, with the drunken belligerence that was particular to tequila and mescal, but he just sat quietly, clutching his beer, the stylized green and gold image of an Aztec warrior staring into eternity from the label.

Briones didn't need to see the size of the tab to know that Cruz would be suffering tomorrow. He paid with a wad of pesos as the banda song wound down, the singer's croon ending the tune with a promise of eternal love. When the bartender arrived with his change, he doled out a tip and pushed back from the bar, glad he'd decided to only have one shot.

"You about ready? I'm hungry. And Dinah…she loves you and wants you home."

Cruz slid the beer away from him and stood, blinking mechanically, like a prizefighter trying to get off the mat after a knockout punch knocked his legs from under him. He gazed around the dingy room; the other patrons ignored him, immersed in their own dramas. Another song began blaring from the stereo, the accordion screeching like a wounded eagle from blown tweeters, the tempo downbeat, like a New Orleans funeral march without the swing.

Briones took his arm to steady him, and Cruz leaned in, his breath a thousand-proof wheeze, the sour taint of perspiration strong as he sweated alcohol.

"You didn't look at the pictures, did you?"

CHAPTER 26

Dinah pushed through the bedroom door, holding two steaming mugs of strong coffee. Cruz struggled to sit up in bed and rubbed his hand across the stubble on his chin, wincing from the morning sunlight streaming through the window.

"What time is it?" he croaked.

"Ten o'clock. I decided to let you sleep late," she said, sitting next to him and handing him the cup. He took it and sipped at it gratefully, and then his eyes widened.

"Damn. Ten? I have to get dressed."

Dinah smiled, her eyes dancing in the sun. "It's Sunday, *Capitan*. Even the great Cruz can rest on Sunday."

"Is it? God. I completely lost track. Every day seems to blur into the next..."

"I wouldn't lie to you." She regarded him. "How do you feel?"

"Like somebody put me in a sack and dragged me behind a truck." He closed his eyes. "I'll never drink again."

"Yes, well, we'll see about that. In the meantime, you owe Fernando a thank-you for driving you home. You weren't making a lot of sense when he brought you to the door."

"It was that bad?"

She nodded. "Oh, yeah. That and more."

"I didn't...do anything embarrassing, did I?"

"No more than usual."

They sat together, comfortable, drinking coffee, neither feeling any compulsion to speak. Cruz finished his cup and took her hand. "I don't deserve you. I'm sorry about last night."

"I'll exact my punishment when you're more up to it. This morning you look like something the dog ate."

"We don't have a dog."

"I know. That's another thing we need to talk about."

After a long shower, Cruz dressed as he checked his messages on his cell phone. There were dozens in his email inbox, all work related, nothing that couldn't wait until the following day. His head felt like his blood pressure was through the roof, a by-product of a world-class hangover, one of only the first in a litany of tortures his aging body had in store for him as payment for his excesses. The screen of his phone seemed to blur in and out, and he gave up trying to read in favor of finding a bottle of aspirin in the bathroom cabinet.

Dinah had prepared a large meal by the time he made it out of the bedroom, and he sat down to another cup of coffee and a liter of water as she spooned out heaping portions of chicken, cheese, and tortilla chips slathered in a spicy red sauce – her breakfast specialty, *chilaquiles*. At first he thought his appetite had deserted him, but after forcing a few mouthfuls he managed to clean his plate and convince her to give him seconds. When he was done, he sat back and patted his belly.

"This sounds terrible, but all I can think of is going back to sleep for a few hours."

She gave him a skeptical look. "Little early for a *siesta* at eleven, don't you think?"

"Can I plead extenuating circumstances?"

She shook her head and handed him a short list. "I have needs."

He read it. "Really? Groceries?"

"They don't buy themselves. We're short a few things, and the walk will do you good."

"Nothing will be open."

"Of course it will. Don't procrastinate. When you're done, then it's *siesta* time."

Cruz knew Dinah well enough to understand that he'd never win this battle, so he slipped on shoes and his shoulder-holstered Glock, donned a light jacket and a baseball cap, and after swigging another half-liter of water and pocketing the list, kissed her and let himself out the door.

The day was blustery, partially overcast with a new storm blowing in, but he still put on his sunglasses as he exited the building after telling his men to stand down. A two-block trip to the market didn't require an escort. They nodded wordlessly, and Cruz wondered whether their night-shift peers had shared the story of him being drunk the prior evening, and then decided he didn't care.

There were only a few pedestrians on the wide sidewalk – a man leading a golden retriever, a pair of teenage girls giggling as they strolled arm-in-arm, a middle-aged woman chatting on her cell phone as she ambled by. Cruz set out for the market, the sunlight like daggers on his visual cortex, and wondered to himself whether the entire day was going to be spent suffering.

He rounded the corner and picked up his pace, determined to will some life into his step, and had about convinced himself that things might steady out when a familiar voice from behind him chilled his blood.

"Just keep walking. Don't turn around. Up at the metro stop, go down the stairs, and buy a ticket on the northbound route. I'll meet you there."

"What's this about?" Cruz demanded, not turning.

"Don't say anything more."

Cruz kept walking, his mind racing. He hadn't heard that voice in half a year, but it was the kind of thing you never forgot – and he knew he was one of the very few still alive who would recognize it. He debated continuing past the metro to the market, but decided that if something had drawn *El Rey* out of hiding and warranted making contact, he'd do his best to find out why.

He paused at the metro station and checked his watch and then took the stairs down into the depths of the city, where he inserted some coins into a machine and purchased a ticket. As he neared the turnstile, a street urchin ran up, startling him. The little boy's face was coated in a layer of grime. His clothes were little more than rags, and his hands were filthy. Wary of the city's young pickpockets, Cruz's hand automatically drifted to his wallet.

"*Señor.* Chiclets?" the child offered, his voice a whine.

129

"No. Thanks anyway."

"Come on. Only two pesos."

"I said no. Now get out of here," Cruz snapped, his headache and the odd circumstances he found himself in fraying his nerves.

"What a dick. Here you go," the little boy said and pressed a crumpled ball of paper into Cruz's hand before running off between the legs of the other travelers. Cruz didn't know what to make of the scene, but after several seconds realization dawned, and he unfurled the wadded note. He read the neat handwriting and pocketed it and then slid his ticket into the turnstile and pushed through the barrier.

The next train arrived in five minutes, and once aboard Cruz didn't bother to sit down. The cars were almost empty on a weekend, and he eyed the few fellow passengers, none of whom showed the faintest interest in him. He'd been the only passenger to get on at the previous station and was the only one to get off at the next stop, other than an ancient woman with a stooped back who was muttering to herself.

When he arrived at the street level, he proceeded half a block, rounded the corner, and then turned right in the alley. He made for the street at the end and continued to a restaurant with a sign featuring a charging bull, named, appropriately, Olé Olé!

Inside, a tall man with a grim countenance looked up from where he was sorting receipts at a podium. Cruz took in the colorful interior festooned with red ribbons and photographs of famous bullfighters as the man eyed him like he was a bill collector.

"We're closed."

"I was told you have a private dining room."

The man didn't blink. "Up the stairs, first door on the right. It's open."

The dining room door opened with a creak. Cruz entered the garishly painted space and took a seat at the rustic wooden table set for six. He looked at his watch again and wiped a bead of sweat from his brow. The room was quiet except for the sound of traffic outside, the roar of a bus, an occasional horn honk or the buzz-saw whine of a motorcycle. He was growing increasingly irritable when the door opened and the assassin stood in the doorway, barely recognizable in baggy jean shorts, high-top Nike tennis shoes, and a blue basketball jersey, his flat-brimmed baseball cap twisted to the side. *El Rey* studied him wordlessly as he closed the door behind him and took the seat opposite Cruz, his face giving away nothing.

"You weren't tailed. That's positive," he said in his distinctive soft voice.

"Should I be worried about being tailed?"

El Rey gave a small smile. "You should be worried about everything."

"I'll bear that in mind." He hesitated, afraid to ask his question, the assassin's parting words to him as vivid in his mind as though he'd just spoken them: "Remember your promise." He swallowed, his mouth suddenly dry. "To what do I owe the pleasure?"

"I have some information for you, and I need your help."

"I see. What can I do for you?"

"It's not what you can do for me, so much, at least not right now. It's more about what I can do for you."

Cruz leaned forward, his face puzzled. "I'm afraid I don't understand."

"Someone's going to try to kill you, and I need to find out why."

Cruz's eyes widened. "Kill me? Good luck. I move around constantly, and I'm surrounded by police, even at home."

"Didn't stop me from finding you, did it? I could have taken you out any of a dozen ways when you left your building. An ice pick to the spine. A slip in front of a truck. A needle stick with curare."

Cruz grunted. "How did you know where I live?"

El Rey's expressionless face shifted slightly. "I was told."

"Told? What the hell are you talking about, told? Nobody knows where I live."

"Wrong. And the reason I was told..." The assassin paused. "You don't look so good. You want some water or something?"

Cruz shook his head. "No. I won't be staying long. Anyway, you were saying you were told...?"

El Rey tried to keep the impatience out of his voice. "That's right. By the same people who want you dead."

"Want me dead," Cruz repeated slowly.

The assassin sighed, annoyed, and looked at Cruz like he was addled, taking care to over-enunciate each word so the older man wouldn't miss anything.

"Right. They contracted me to kill you."

CHAPTER 27

Cruz's gaze held *El Rey*'s for a long moment before he looked away. "I thought you were out of the game. That's the official story, isn't it? No longer a hired gun?"

"Right. But there was one exception, if you recall."

"For CISEN. I remember." Cruz's eyes narrowed. "Wait. Are you telling me…?"

"You owe me a favor. You promised to do whatever needed to be done. Do you remember?"

"Of course I do. But I'm not going to lie down and die, if that's what you're after."

"Again, if I wanted to kill you, you'd be dead already, and I'd be eating brunch."

"Then what?"

"I need you to die and then help me figure out why CISEN wants you killed."

"Back up, and let's cover the part where I die again. It all sounded good until that bit."

"Not literally die. But you need to appear to die, or I won't get my booster shot, and that would put me in a very cranky mood. So you need to go to your reward sooner than later, and it has to appear to be accidental or of natural causes."

"Accidental."

"Right, but the problem there is the *corpus delicti*. If there's a body, you can be identified or, rather, whoever died will be identified as not you. So it'll be a little tricky. Fortunately, I have some ideas."

Cruz sighed. "I want that water now."

El Rey stood. "Sure you don't want something stronger? You look a little green."

"Just water."

"You aren't thinking about running out on me, are you?"

"And do what? Get hit by a train? Have a piano fall on me? Just hurry up. My wife thinks I'm at the market."

El Rey returned in sixty seconds with two plastic bottles. He placed one in front of Cruz, cracked his own open and took a sip. Cruz twisted the top off and drank half the bottle and then paused. "You could have put poison in this, couldn't you?"

"Don't be paranoid."

"Says the man who's here to kill me."

"Final time. I'm not here to kill you; I'm here to help you stay alive."

"By killing me. Faking my death."

"Now you've got it. If we can do it tonight or tomorrow, so much the better. They won't give me my shot until you're dead. And I need to get it next week."

"This is the antidote you told me about?"

"No, it's a flu vaccine. What do you think it is?"

Cruz exhaled noisily. "Okay, let's say I play along. Start at the beginning, and tell me what's going on. You mentioned CISEN and killing me…"

El Rey stood and paced while he spoke. "Correct. But I have no idea why. Or why they had me kill the others."

"The *others*? Killed, as in past tense?" Cruz asked.

"That's right."

"Anyone I know?"

El Rey told him the whole story. When he was finished, Cruz closed his eyes.

"How likely do you think it is that all of them were somehow involved in a drug operation?" he asked.

"Slightly less likely than that CISEN decided to terminate people for no reason."

"We're missing a connection. I mean, we know I'm not involved in smuggling meth to the U.S. So that doesn't wash."

"It gets worse. There are two other names on the list that I have to terminate. One of them is Carla Vega."

"The TV star?"

"She'd probably prefer 'television journalist.'"

"Right. Because there's so much journalism involved." Cruz paused. "What's the other name?"

"Indalecio Arellano."

Cruz grunted. "Never heard of him."

"He's a farmer in Sinaloa."

"And all this doesn't sound crazy?"

"Of course it does. That's why I'm here. But first things first. We need to get you out of the crosshairs while we can."

Cruz shook his head. "I'll go to the president."

"And tell him that his intelligence service is committing mass murder of random dignitaries and foreign citizens? Oh, and pig farmers."

"He'll take it seriously from me."

"Maybe. I mean, you'll have proof that those were all murders, right?"

"I'll have you to back me up."

"Here's the problem. We don't really know what this is all about. So we don't know who's involved or what the real objective is. What I do know is that if I go live with the fact that I terminated these people, I'm dead meat. There's no way I walk away from that – either my injection mysteriously fails to work this time, or someone takes me out while I'm walking down the street. In the meantime, CISEN simply shrugs its shoulders and says that one of the side effects of the agent I was injected with is vivid hallucinations, that I invented the entire story because I'm delusional, that of course they had nothing to do with it and there's nothing to support my contention those were executions…and then it's my word against theirs. Who do you think they're going to believe? The national intelligence agency or a former hit man?"

"You have no reason to lie."

"Right. Except I'm nuts. Which will be their story. And they'll smear you with the same brush – how could you buy into my paranoid ramblings? You can see how that plays. And then one day, maybe soon, you die, either in one of your tactical operations or choking on a bone or from an unexpected heart attack." *El Rey* let his words sink in. "Or maybe it's both you and your wife in a car crash. Those happen all the time. The point is, you'll still be in jeopardy, I'll be exposed, and we'll have done nothing to stop whatever this is and find whoever's accountable."

"What about Rodriguez? We can go to him."

"Which assumes he didn't order it. He's the second highest-ranking man in CISEN – the director's an appointed figurehead. There are very few people in the organization that could order the termination of high-ranking Mexican officials and not risk having their subordinates go over their heads. He's one of the few. If I were him, I'd deny everything, express sadness that my 'treatment' has taken this delusional turn for the worse, and that would be it. Again, with no proof, it's my word against his."

"What if it's one of his subordinates?"

"Then we discover who. That's not my biggest worry – have you stopped to think about the alternative? That this is an official op that'll be denied at every level the instant it comes out, and then we'll be dealt with at their own speed?" *El Rey* took another drink of water. "The history of intelligence agencies is doing really ugly things and then denying everything when they're caught. You think the Americans invented that?"

"I'm not going to debate the honesty of governments with you."

"That's probably wise. We're wasting time we don't have. We need to figure out how to kill you and make it look like an accident but leave no body."

A thought occurred to Cruz. "What about Dinah?"

"She won't be in danger. You'll be dead."

"Wait. I'm not supposed to tell her I'm alive?"

"So if she's drugged and interrogated, she'll be able to blow it for you, and kill both of us in the process as well as herself?" *El Rey* studied Cruz. "Are you usually this slow on the uptake? No wonder the cartels run the country."

"That's uncalled for."

"Then stop asking stupid questions, and start figuring out how we can get rid of you."

They considered a car crash and discarded it – no matter how bad, there would be a body to check dental records against. Ditto for an operation gone wrong or a cartel hit. As they went through their options, it became readily apparent that faking a death in a convincing way that left no traces was nearly impossible. Cruz was getting increasingly anxious as they discussed possibilities, and after twenty minutes, they hadn't come up with anything that would work, and his head was buzzing like a beehive.

Cruz slid his chair back and rose. "I have to get to the market. Let me think about this some. How do I get ahold of you?"

El Rey handed him a burner cell phone. "I programmed my number into speed dial. It's the only one."

Cruz took the phone and slid it into his breast pocket. "You're sure I can't just disappear until we figure this out?"

"Only if I want you to sign my death warrant. You go missing without being dead, the game's over. These are not stupid people. So forget that. It's not an option."

"I'll call later."

"Do that. Leave the phone on. In the meantime I'll keep thinking."

Cruz finished his water and tossed the bottle into a trash bin. "And I thought my day couldn't get any worse."

"It could have. I could have decided to fulfill the sanction."

Cruz took in the assassin's emotionless stare. "Why didn't you?"

"If I kill you, how do I collect on the debt of gratitude you owe me? It's bad business."

Cruz tried to tell whether the younger man was kidding or not, but gave up. The assassin was unreadable, and there were some things Cruz would never know. He left the room and made his way back down the stairs, where the host was nowhere in evidence. As Cruz stepped out onto the sidewalk, a chill ran up his spine, and he had to choke down a spurt of stomach acid that accompanied his thought.

Maybe the assassin was playing him in some way, and getting him to fake his death was part of a larger design.

The idea roiled in his guts like a twisted knife, and his entire body broke out into a sweat. He looked around and saw the approaching roof light of a vacant taxi. With a final glance at his watch, he hailed the car, unwilling to try to find his way to the market from where he was and unsure that he was thinking clearly enough to do so if he wanted to.

An hour later he was back at the condo, lost in thought as he watched Dinah put away the groceries. She eyed him as she did so and then cracked a Modelo beer, poured it into a mug along with some tomato juice, half a lime and some Worcestershire sauce, and then brought it to him.

"All right, *caballero*. You've done enough penance. Drink that and go take a *siesta*. You'll feel better in no time."

He sniffed at the drink, caution playing across his face, and drained the glass without pausing. When he set it back down on the table, he took a deep breath, his eyes watering, and offered a pained smile.

"*Gracias.*"

"Go on. Get some sleep. The world will still be here when you get up."

She was right. He returned to the bedroom and shed his clothes, pausing to set the burner phone on the nightstand next to the bed, alongside his Glock. He was just drifting off to sleep when the little phone trilled.

"Hello?"

El Rey's voice was barely a whisper. "I have an idea."

CHAPTER 28

A tangerine moon drifted from behind high clouds as a black Cadillac Escalade pulled up to the valet parking area of the Four Seasons hotel in Mexico City. The driver waited as a young woman teetering on impossibly high heels, wearing a white one-piece miniskirt that melded to her body like a second skin, hugged another similarly clad young woman near the palatial entrance, their voices loud, martini glasses in their hands. Four suited men with short haircuts and chiseled features waited nearby; their square shoulders and military bearings identified them as bodyguards.

The shorter of the two ferreted in her purse, withdrew a cigarette case, and offered her companion a smoke. She lit both with a Dunhill lighter and blew a cloud at the glimmering stars, the overcast clearing now that the front had blown through the valley. She continued telling her story in a loud bray and glared at her purse when her iPhone warbled. Emptying her glass with a single swig, she retrieved the phone with a shrugged apology to her friend and, after answering, erupted in laughter, her momentary irritation at the interruption forgotten.

The taller woman busied herself with her own phone, checking her Facebook page for responses to the photos she'd taken that evening and posted from the hotel nightclub where her cousin was having her eighteenth birthday celebration. Both women stood scant inches apart, discussing the party they'd left only moments before with their online friends, now on their way to an exclusive disco in the penthouse of one of Mexico City's high-rises.

The first woman hung up with a final titter and returned her attention to her companion, who held up a finger and continued inputting her message before swaying toward the guards and handing the nearest one her empty glass.

"You want to ride with me or take two cars?" the first woman asked.

Her friend rolled her eyes. "You know how my parents would freak if I didn't take the dynamic duo over there with me, Isabel. Can we all fit in your car?"

Isabel eyed the Escalade, trying to calculate, and shook her head. "Not comfortably. When will yours be here?"

"Maybe three more minutes. I'll tell you what, I'll just hook up with you at the club, okay? Wait for me at the bar."

"What a pain. All right, then. See you in a few."

Isabel approached the gleaming SUV and waited while two of the bodyguards moved to the vehicle. The closest one held the rear door open for her as the other climbed into the passenger seat. She appeared to take no notice of them and was already reading something on her phone screen, back in her cyber-world as she slid her long legs into the vehicle.

The second bodyguard closed the door for her and then trotted around the rear of the SUV and got in beside her. The driver slipped the attendant a hundred-peso note and put the transmission in gear. The modified exhaust burbled as he inched to the end of the drive and signaled to pull into traffic. A sedan slowed and gave him an opening, and he gunned the gas, rear tires chirping as the big truck accelerated into the stream of cars.

Fifty yards behind, a van pulled into traffic, leaving six car lengths between it and the SUV. Late night traffic was sparse on a Sunday night, and the van varied its speed so as not to arouse suspicion. A second vehicle, a dark blue Chevrolet four-door with tinted windows, edged ahead of the Cadillac and settled in one car length ahead of it.

The seven blocks to the club went by in a blur as Isabel tweeted her impressions of the party to her coterie of followers. The Chevrolet made a right on the smaller street that fronted the destination building, and the SUV followed suit, its custom suspension smoothing the rough pavement.

Isabel's driver glanced in the rearview mirror at the van's headlights as it also made the turn, but thought nothing of it as he rolled to a stop at the curb. The two bodyguards got out, and one moved to the door of the high-rise where a uniformed doorman stood. Far above the street, neon red and blue lights flickered in the penthouse windows, where an elite crowd was dancing into the wee hours as the rest of the city slept.

None of this registered on Isabel as she dropped her phone into her gold clutch purse and emerged from the rear of the Escalade. She tossed her mane of thick hair, her two-hundred-dollar highlights catching the reflection of the van's headlights, and then the night exploded with gunfire as three masked shooters piled out of the Chevrolet and opened fire on the bodyguards.

Isabel froze as rounds thumped into the man who had only a second before been holding her door open. She gasped as he went down, and the driver's scream sounded like it was coming from a mile away.

"Jump in. Hurry," he yelled and then the top of his head blew against the windshield in a spray of blood and brains as a row of armor-piercing rounds punched through the bullet-resistant rear window.

Isabel screamed and tried to make it to the building, but her second bodyguard took two slugs to the chest and collapsed in the doorway. The doorman ducked into the shelter of the lobby, leaving her gasping near the dead guard as two masked assailants sprinted toward her from the van, brandishing pistols.

"Come on," the brawnier of the pair growled as he grabbed her arm. She resisted, and he slammed the butt of his pistol into her head, dazing her. The other man caught her other arm as her legs buckled, and together they dragged her to the van.

Less than thirty seconds had passed from the first gunshot to when the two vehicles roared off, leaving three dead men and one three-hundred-dollar pump perched like a trophy on the sidewalk, its tiny buckles twinkling in the faint moonlight.

CHAPTER 29

Tres Marías, Mexico

Cruz coasted to a stop at the end of the gravel drive and got out of the unmarked Dodge Charger he'd signed out of the *Federales* pool, wondering what the hell he was doing. He'd picked a fight with Dinah as *El Rey* had suggested, and had told her that he intended to take a day or two away from everything to clear his head at the rustic cabin he owned on the road to Cuernavaca in the hills just outside of the small town of Tres Marías. The hurt and lack of comprehension in her eyes had been like a dagger to his heart, but he hadn't faltered, even though his self-loathing had blossomed with every step toward the condo door.

El Rey had been adamant that he couldn't even hint at what was to come, and that any foreshadowing would be a death warrant if she were questioned. It had been one of the hardest things he'd ever done, and he'd slipped at the last minute, hugging her and sobbing as he held her in his arms, which he hoped would be viewed, in retrospect, as evidence of his precarious mental state – distracted and unbalanced.

He retrieved a flashlight from the glove compartment and moved around the exterior of the house to the thousand-liter propane tank, which he'd filled the last time he'd been there with Dinah seven weeks earlier. It would play a critical role in the night's ugly work, and he felt a tug of nostalgia as he eyed the humble little cabin, which soon enough would be vaporized by the explosion when the propane ignited.

The interior of the dwelling was as simple as the exterior – one large room at ground level and a loft above up a rickety set of wooden stairs with a bed that featured in many happy memories. The cabin, like most in the area, had been built from local timber and brick, and was perfect for long weekend getaways of stargazing and hiking.

Cruz flipped a light switch, and the lamp over the dining room table illuminated. He set the bottle of tequila down and removed his jacket and then his Glock. The assassin had been clear – everything would have to point to a man drunk out of his mind, who had passed out with the gas stove on, perhaps intending to commit suicide, perhaps just incoherent. Whatever the explanation, what happened next would be self-evident. The flame had gone out on the stove, either intentionally or from a gust of wind, and then a spark ignited the gas that had flooded the cabin. Boom. No more Cruz.

If bits of his weapon survived, so much the better. Likewise if the tequila bottle residue was found, although Cruz had bought two and left one in the car, still a quarter full, just in case. It told a story of despair and alcohol abuse – not an unfamiliar one among the *Federales*, just as with most police forces, where officers turned to the bottle to relieve the stress that accumulated over the years, and occasionally one ate his service pistol when the voices of the ghosts from his past made another day in the present unbearable.

It wasn't a perfect plan, but it was the best they had. The combination of the explosion and the resultant fire would obliterate everything in the cabin, and the likely cursory forensics investigation by the small-town police department would be as superficial as they could hope for, everyone eager to put the unpleasantness behind them, the evidence framing a sad end to a dignified career.

The pain it would cause Dinah was the one element he couldn't live with, but the assassin had been adamant. So his wife, the love of his life, would have to believe him dead, hopefully for only a short while as they worked to uncover what was behind the killings.

Cruz went into the bare-bones kitchen and got a shot glass. He returned to the dining room table, poured it to the rim, and stared at it for a good five minutes before tossing it back with a single swallow, a toast for the dying. He closed his eyes, remembering Dinah's face when she'd looked at him with surprise and fright as he'd fought with her over nothing, and took a deep breath, the tequila fumes making him want to retch.

The bottle shattered against the wall. The violent gesture relieved some of the tension that had accumulated like a steel band tightening around his chest, and he felt better for it. The alcohol no longer a temptation, he sat and waited with his eye on his watch for the assassin to arrive, his onetime mortal enemy the one to ease him across the threshold.

A vision drifted through his consciousness, one that he'd thought banished for good, now vivid as the morning sun in the haze of his memory. His original wife, Rosa, smiling as she pressed his hand against her belly to feel their unborn daughter kick. The corners of his mouth turned up at the image, but then it disintegrated into the stuff of his waking nightmares: Rosa's and Cassandra's heads in boxes, slaughtered by psychopaths, delivered to his office for effect.

The sound of a motor outside shook him out of his grim reverie, and he looked up as headlights brightened the windows. The assassin had arrived. *El Rey*, an explosives expert, would rig the cabin however he deemed appropriate while Cruz stood by. Then, in the dead of night, a fireball would soar into the heavens, and *Capitan* Romero Cruz of the *Federales* would cease to exist.

When *El Rey* opened the front door, he was all business, moving like a wraith on soundless feet. If he explained what he was doing, Cruz didn't register it. Cruz's last memory of the long night was the sight of the cabin fading in the rearview mirror of the assassin's car just before *El Rey* called the cell phone he'd left on the dining table, rigged to create the spark that would obliterate any trace of the cabin and the man trapped inside.

CHAPTER 30

Mexico City, Mexico

Briones groped for the telephone in the darkened bedroom, fumbling before answering it. "Hello?"

"Lieutenant Briones. This is Hiliberto at headquarters. Sorry to call you in the middle of the night."

Briones switched on the bedside lamp and looked at the clock: 4:18. If Hiliberto, the night supervisor at headquarters, was calling at that hour, it was important.

"No problem. What's the emergency?"

"You wanted me to alert you if there was another high-profile kidnapping."

Briones sat up, instantly fully awake. "And?"

"Isabel Cifuentes was abducted earlier this evening, downtown. Her two bodyguards and the driver were gunned down. All dead."

"Christ. Where did it happen?"

Hiliberto gave him the details. Briones frowned as he finished. "Isabel Cifuentes. That wouldn't be the daughter of Senator Cifuentes, would it?"

Hiliberto sighed. "It is."

Cifuentes was one of the most influential men in Mexico, representing the interests of some of the wealthiest industrialists in the country. If someone as prominent as he couldn't keep his offspring safe...

That there was going to be a firestorm in the wake of the attack was a given. The only positive was that, like most politicians, he had barrels of money, so a ransom wouldn't be a problem. It was the way the system worked. You went to your job as a humble public servant

145

and wound up with millions sticking to you, and nobody could explain how it happened. Very much like most governments, he supposed.

"Have you reached Cruz?"

"No. I tried calling, but his cell says he's out of service range."

"That's odd."

"Then I called his landline, and his wife said he'd taken tomorrow off and had gone to the mountains to relax. So that makes you the top dog until he gets back."

"Damn. All right, I'm on my way. I should be able to make it to the crime scene in half an hour." Briones paused. "Has anyone been in touch with the senator yet?"

"No, sir. I thought it would be best for either you or *Capitan* Cruz to handle that."

"I should do it in person. I'll add that to the list. Poor bastard probably doesn't even know yet. If the bodyguards were all killed, there's nobody to alert him except us…or the ransom call."

"Let's hope it isn't the same gang that killed the last one."

"I'll second the thought. Call me if anything else comes up."

"Yes, sir."

Briones hung up, his stomach churning. *How could this get any worse? No Cruz, one of the top men in the government in the firing line of kidnappers after a sensationally brutal kidnapping-turned-murder only days before…*

There was no point in belaboring his bad luck. Best to do what he could until his boss got back. Although he couldn't remember a time when Cruz had just taken off without telling anyone. He hadn't mentioned going to the mountains at the bar, and he'd given no indication he wouldn't be in on Monday – his staff meeting had still been posted on the board when Briones left the office on Saturday.

Maybe the pressure buildup had finally been too much for him and he'd snapped? God knew he had every right to. He worked Herculean hours, and now with the additional responsibility of high-profile kidnappings added to his already overflowing cartel task force plate, was it any wonder?

The streets were deserted, except for garbage trucks laboring along, emptying the heaping bins overflowing with the weekend's detritus. When he turned the corner onto the crime scene street, the darkness was transformed by the glare of portable work lights. A pair of forensics technicians worked on the bullet holes in the Cadillac while several others knelt by the dead bodyguards. Yellow tape draped the area. The doorman had retreated to the interior of the building after giving his statement and was herding departing partygoers out the building's rear exit so they wouldn't disturb the scene.

Briones parked in the middle of the street behind a line of Metropolitan police cars and approached the dark blue *Federales* van near the entrance. A muscular sergeant that Briones knew stood by the rear doors watching the technicians, a cup of coffee in one hand and his cell phone in the other.

"What have we got?" Briones asked.

"Three dead, one kidnapped. Looks like over thirty shots fired. But nothing indiscriminate, looking at the groupings. They were using automatic weapons, but they placed their shots carefully."

"So, professional."

"Absolutely. I'd say ex-military. These guys were organized, efficient, and from what the doorman says, were in and out within seconds. They knew exactly what they were doing."

"Any descriptions?" Briones asked halfheartedly.

"Two vehicles we already have an APB on, which we both know will turn up stripped in the *barrios* by tomorrow, if we find them at all. As to the shooters, they were wearing balaclavas."

"Just like we do."

"Exactly. Oh, and I should mention that they obviously knew that the victim was coming to this party, and probably followed her vehicle from the hotel where it picked her up. Which could mean an inside job."

"Maybe. Although these kids' entire lives are online to anyone with a computer."

The sergeant shook his head. "I've never understood that. Can you imagine? I mean, to make your info public and let people know what you're doing and where you are…it's insane."

"Still, we can't discount that they had advance notice from someone connected to the club or the party preparations. Plan on questioning everyone."

The sergeant lowered his eyes glumly. It was going to be a very long night. "I'll need backup."

"That's why I'm telling you. Call whoever you need in. Get a list. I don't want any of the staff leaving today until you're done."

"What about the party people? We've probably lost at least fifty of them already."

"In this building, a private party would be attended by some of the richest kids in the city. They're unlikely to be suspects, Sergeant."

Briones went inside to find the doorman. After twenty minutes of questioning him, Briones hadn't gleaned any new information, and any suspicion he'd harbored that the man had been involved in the kidnapping had been put to rest. He returned to the crime scene, where the techs were finishing up with the corpses as the coroner's van pulled alongside the Escalade. He spoke with the local cops for a few minutes, who knew about as much as the corner fire hydrant. When he approached the sergeant again, he felt five years older.

"Get any traffic camera footage and have it analyzed. It's a long shot that they didn't think of that, but every now and then we get lucky, so it's worth running it." Even as Briones spoke, a familiar sensation of futility washed over him. There would be no careless mistakes on this one, he was sure. The shooters had been disciplined and precise, every eventuality covered. Most criminals chose their careers because they were stupid. Whoever this was didn't fit that description.

That left the *Federales* with nothing but body bags and holding news conferences where hollow assurances of bringing the offenders to justice were offered by insincere spokespeople.

Briones left the scene and pulled onto the large boulevard that led to headquarters as the first faint trace of dawn brightened the eastern sky. Huddles of workers were already standing at the bus stops along the way, many making connections from the *colectivos* they'd caught hours earlier in the slums at the fringes of the city, their plodding reality one of four-hour commutes to clean toilets or scrub floors for ten dollars a day.

His cell jingled as he neared headquarters, so he slid the phone from his pocket as he slowed to enter the employee parking lot. The guard peered at him and then thumbed the barrier open as Briones held the cell to his ear.

"Briones."

"Lieutenant?" Hiliberto's voice sounded strained.

"Of course. Who else would answer my phone with my name?" Briones snapped.

"Where are you, sir?"

"Arriving at headquarters. I want to file a preliminary report before I go to see the senator."

"Oh, good. Then you'll be here shortly?"

"That's what I just said, isn't it? What's wrong, Hiliberto? You sound…odd."

"I…we just received a call from the local police in Cuernavaca."

"Cuernavaca? What do they want?"

"It's *Capitan* Cruz, sir."

Briones pulled into a slot near the building entrance and put the transmission into park. "What about him?"

"There was an explosion at a cabin in Tres Marías. They found his cruiser in the drive. There's…there's apparently not much left. They suggested we send someone down there to liaise with them."

The world seemed to tilt. Briones had the sensation of free-falling from a great height, disoriented by vertigo as his rational mind tried to process the words. "What are you talking about? What do you mean, there's not much left? Liaise? Liaise what?"

"It was the propane tank, sir. Took the house with it." Hiliberto's voice cracked on the last words. "*Capitan* Cruz is dead."

CHAPTER 31

Mazatlán, Mexico

Two *pangas* streaked from the harbor toward the leeward beach on Isla de Venados, kicking up gentle turquoise swells in the late morning. Indalecio Arellano walked down the beachfront road in the Golden Zone past the Hotel Emporio, his new jeans and dress shirt stiff, his crisp white Stetson hat unsoiled. When he arrived at a two-story commercial plaza, he climbed the stairs to the second level, pausing at the landing to look over the half-full parking lot, and then proceeded to the law offices at the end of the building.

Inside he was greeted by a twenty-something receptionist with a shy smile, almond skin and mahogany eyes, who took his name and lifted the telephone handset to her ear. She announced his arrival, and two minutes later another young woman emerged from the back and invited him to follow her.

Emilio Navarro rose from his executive chair and rounded his oversized desk, hand extended, a lawyer's smile on his debauched face.

"Indalecio, it's been too long. Let me get you something. Coffee? Water? Soda?" he asked, shaking the farmer's calloused hand.

"For me? No. I'm fine. Thank you," Indalecio said, eyeing the woman's trim dress and the way her pumps flattered her calves.

"You sure? Please. Sit. I'll have some coffee, Elma. The usual."

The woman left, closing the door behind her, and Indalecio seated himself in one of the overstuffed chocolate leather chairs while Navarro returned to his throne. The attorney studied the farmer's weathered features and deep tan, his newly trimmed hair and his

150

close shave, and smiled again. He leaned forward as if sharing a secret with a friend, his expression earnest.

"I'm sorry about the farm and your man. Savages."

"Is there any news?"

"The police are investigating, but you can imagine how that's going. I don't think there are many that aren't in the cartel's pocket."

They were interrupted by Elma's return with a porcelain cup filled with rich brew. She set it down in front of Navarro, affording Indalecio another chance to admire her, and then slipped wordlessly away.

"Then there's nothing new? These men tortured and executed my hand, and the police are powerless to do anything about it?"

"I won't say powerless so much as not particularly motivated to rock the boat. I took the liberty of hiring a detective out of Culiacán – one of the few honest investigators there – and he says that while nobody will talk on the record for fear of reprisals, the rumor is that it was the cartel."

"That's hardly fresh information. I could have told you that from the guns they had."

"He also has discovered there's a price on your head. A hundred thousand pesos for any leads on your whereabouts. Apparently it's been circulated all over Sinaloa."

Indalecio's eyes narrowed. "Am I safe here? I mean, you're on record as my attorney…"

"Of course – I represent hundreds of clients, not just you. But if you have any doubts, I can have Elma drive you wherever you want to go once our business is concluded. She's an expert in personal security."

"Why do I think you're exaggerating?"

Navarro spread his hands apart, palms up, and shrugged. "Perhaps a little. But she will be happy to drive you wherever you like. You can take the rear stairs when you leave."

"It's disturbing that there's a contract on me." He paused. "Did your man say why?"

Navarro shook his head. "It's a mystery. Again, nobody's talking."

"It must be something related to our suit. That's the only thing I can think of."

"Speculation. It's not like you're far from the action up in the hills. You must be surrounded by drug farms, no? Maybe it's as simple as they want your land, and because of your reputation, they know you'll never sell it."

The farmer considered Navarro's words as the lawyer tasted his coffee. "Where does that leave us?"

"I'll continue to dig around to see what I can discover. In the meantime, get as far from Sinaloa as you can. Or more importantly, as far from the influence of the Sinaloa cartel as possible."

"I can't hide forever."

"I'm not suggesting that you do. I'm simply advising you to take the most prudent course of action until I get a handle on what we're up against. If they want to buy your land, that's a different problem than if it's something more...complex."

"The farm's been in my family for six generations. They're right that I'll never sell."

"Unfortunately, if they're willing to kill you on sight to get it, holding onto it could be a fatal gesture."

"I understand." Indalecio paused. "Do you have the money?"

Navarro nodded. "Of course. Ten thousand American dollars and fifty thousand pesos, as you requested."

"I'm still in good shape financially, then?"

"The accounts have never been better." Navarro handled the farmer's finances in exchange for a small fee every year. It amounted to cutting a few dozen checks and rolling over the bulk of the money into a mutual fund that averaged five percent annual interest.

"At least that's something. Any suggestions on where I should go?"

"I'd say go east. Maybe Veracruz. Or the Yucatán. Someplace with a high turnover, like Cancún, which is rumored to be Los Zetas territory these days. It's pretty safe to assume there won't be any Sinaloa influence in one of their cities."

Indalecio thought about it as Navarro slid one of his drawers open and removed a small nylon laptop bag. "Here's your money. Just call when you need more. I can have it wired wherever you like."

"This should last a while. Hopefully this will all be cleared up before I run out. But one thing that disturbs me – how can you be so sure this isn't related to the suit?"

"It's been in the court system for…five years? Why suddenly would anyone want to eliminate you, and especially why the cartel? It makes no sense." Navarro shook his head. "No, the likelihood is that you have something they want, and the only thing you have is your land. A simple deduction on my part."

Indalecio took the bag and stood. "Very well, then. In light of my situation, I don't want to stay too long. I'll take you up on your generous offer of your assistant. Walking around with this much money makes me nervous. Can she take me to the bus station?"

"I'd rather she drove you to the airport. The cartel would expect you to take a bus. Watching an entire airport…well, it's not practical. Although if I could make a suggestion, you might want to shave your mustache and lose the hat. It does stand out among the tourists."

The farmer considered. "You mentioned some back stairs?"

"Yes. Come. I'll show you the way." Navarro dialed two digits, spoke rapidly, and stood again as he hung up. "Elma will be in a silver Corolla by the exit in two minutes. Have her stop at a barber shop or a pharmacy so you can trim the mustache."

Indalecio touched the salt-and-pepper bristles with his fingers. "I…I've had it for over thirty years."

"Yes, well, fortunately it will grow back. But that's also the reason it needs to go before you arrive at the airport." Navarro moved to the door, easily a foot taller than his client, his suit a sharp contrast to the farmer's rustic apparel. "Don't worry. We'll get this straightened out."

Indalecio fixed him with a penetrating stare, his eyes filled with intensity. "They killed Ruiz. Someone has to answer for that."

Navarro held out a hand placatingly. "Of course. But for now, I'll settle for you on a beach a thousand miles away."

"I won't let this go, Emilio. He was a good man. Loyal to the end."

Navarro opened the door and put his hand on the farmer's shoulder.

"I know you won't, Emilio. I know."

CHAPTER 32

Mexico City, Mexico

El Rey led the way to a small stand-alone house in the Iztapalapa neighborhood south of the international airport. Rusting iron bars adorned the windows on both stories. Its peach-colored paint had faded and was peeling off the mortar from acid rain. Colorful graffiti marked every inch of the high wall that protected the postage-stamp front yard and the one-car garage from the street. Coils of razor wire ringed the top along with bottle fragments that jutted from the mortar like broken teeth.

El Rey's twenty-year-old Ford Explorer had raised no eyebrows as it crawled through the empty streets in the predawn hours. The assassin led Cruz into the house, which smelled of ammonia and was simply appointed with cheap flea market furniture. Mexican blankets affixed to wooden rods over the windows served as curtains, muting the worst of the traffic noise.

A laptop computer sat on the square dining room table, its power indicator blinking in the darkness as Cruz followed the assassin into the living area. *El Rey* flipped a wall switch, and the lower floor was bathed in light. He gestured at the stairs and eyed Cruz.

"Bedrooms are up. Three. Take your pick of the two smaller ones. I've got the master."

"Fair enough. Is there anything in the refrigerator?"

El Rey nodded. "I stocked it yesterday evening. Water, beer, food, orange juice. Make yourself at home. I'm going to grab a few hours of sleep, and then I want to continue my research. I'm hoping you can help. I was focused on how to pull off your untimely demise.

Now that that's over, we can turn to figuring out what this is all about."

Cruz walked into the kitchen, got himself a water bottle, and then mounted the stairs. The entire house was no more than fifteen hundred square feet, a cinderblock cube laid out with all the charm of a prison, but the beds were clean and inviting, and within five minutes of lying down Cruz was snoring, fully clothed, dead to the world.

He tossed and turned, his sleep fitful, his dreams otherworldly renderings of his funeral, an empty casket carried by fellow officers in full dress uniforms before a small crowd of co-workers. There were only a few faces he would miss, the most obvious that of his beautiful wife, a black lace veil over her face, tears streaming as a cedar box symbolizing her husband was interred on a drizzling gray day, Briones next to her, his young face angry and sad.

A crash from downstairs jolted him awake, and for a moment he was lost, the room plunged in gloom, his surroundings unfamiliar. Then it all came back to him – the cabin, the explosion, the run from the mountains. He looked at his watch and was surprised to see that he'd managed to sleep five hours.

He rose and used the bathroom. His reflection showed an unshaven parody of his official self – hair askew, bloodshot eyes puffy, the lines creasing his face deeper after the last twenty-four hours. When he came downstairs, *El Rey* was cleaning the last of a broken plate off the tile floor, looking fit and energetic.

"Morning. Sorry about the noise," he said.

"No problem. I'm anxious to get going on figuring this out. You mentioned you had food?" Cruz asked, and then the aroma of coffee reached him.

"In the refrigerator. Help yourself. I made a pot, too. You're welcome to as much as you can drink."

"Thanks."

When they'd fed themselves, Cruz joined the assassin at the computer, where it was obvious he'd been up for hours working, judging by the pad next to it covered with lines of neatly printed notes.

"What do you have so far?" Cruz asked.

"I'm trying to figure out what the link is between the admiral, the archbishop, the actor…and you. Have you ever met any of them?"

"No."

"Were you investigating anything that could have involved them? A meth ring going through Tijuana?"

"Negative. Most of the meth I know of goes through Texas. So if someone was getting it into California, it would be a new one on me."

"Think. What about the newswoman and the farmer? Anything there?"

Cruz shook his head. "No. None of them have anything in common that I can see, and certainly nothing to do with me. The closest to a connection among any of them is Carla Vega and the actor because they're both in the entertainment business."

"There has to be something. We're missing it. But it's got to be there. They want you dead, which means you're somehow involved, even if you don't know how."

"Fine. I don't dispute that. Why don't we start with you bringing me up to date on the official dossiers on all the targets? That way we'll be on an even playing field, and I may catch something you missed."

El Rey squinted and waved in the direction of the coffee table. "I printed out everything. It's all in that file. Read through it, and tell me if you have any breakthroughs."

Cruz went to the sofa and began reading the materials as *El Rey* typed in Carla Vega's name and watched some of the videos of her on YouTube. She had a thriving following, based on the number of clips and the views she received, and he killed time watching Carla report on meaningless silliness, starting at her newest clip, shot at the People's Choice awards, and working backward in time.

Fifteen minutes later he called out to Cruz. "Come look at this."

Cruz was just finishing up the file on the archbishop. He left it open on the table and joined the assassin at the computer. "What is it?"

"The attack on the admiral in Ensenada."

"I saw it on the news."

"Guess who features prominently in this footage?"

El Rey pressed the play icon and the video began streaming. Carla Vega was framed against a blue sky, the superstructure of a naval ship in the background. She was finishing up an unenthusiastic description of the new pride of the navy when the roar of a helicopter drowned out her voice, and then the distinctive chatter of automatic weapons sounded from the water amidst panicked screams from the crowd.

They watched the attack on the boat, captured by the quick reactions of the cameraman, and *El Rey* paused the clip.

"You said she's a celebrity on Mexican television, right?" he asked.

"Absolutely. There's nobody bigger in the news game. Don't you watch TV?"

El Rey shook his head. "No. But if she's all that, what was she doing at a ship launching in Baja?"

Cruz tugged at his hair in thought. "Beats me. Maybe it was a slow news day in DF?"

"She was in Los Angeles at an awards show rubbing shoulders with movie stars, an interview in Mexico City before that with Carlos Slim on the deregulation of the telephone scheme…and a ship christening even the navy barely cares about? Doesn't that seem a little beneath her?"

"Maybe she doesn't get to choose her assignments."

El Rey stared at the image frozen on the screen and then sat back and snapped his fingers. "Damn. I can't be sure, but I think she was at the hotel in Arizona."

"What? Where's that on YouTube?"

"It isn't. I saw someone at the pool bar. But it was dark, and I was otherwise occupied. Only I remember seeing a woman who…who took my breath away. It looked a lot like Vega, now that I think about it."

For the first time that morning, Cruz spoke with animation. "If it was, then there's a connection between both the admiral and the actor. Tentative, but a connection. But what about me? I've never met her. I have nothing to do with her."

El Rey nodded, lost in thought, eyes unfocused. Cruz left him to his ruminations and got a second cup of coffee. When he returned, the assassin was typing furiously.

"What are you doing?"

"Pulling up everything I can find on *Señorita* Vega. Starting with the layout of her home."

"How do you know where she lives?"

"CISEN was kind enough to provide that."

"Ah. I haven't gotten that far in the files." Cruz frowned. "How can you pull up blueprints on a random address in Mexico City?"

"Through the building department. They've recently automated and scanned most of their files."

"How do you get into the building department?"

El Rey smiled. "If I told you, I'd have to kill you."

Cruz took a sip of coffee. "I thought you already did." He returned to the couch and finished reading the dossiers. When he was done, he closed the folder and stood. "I don't see anything you haven't already described. If there's a connection other than Vega, it's well hidden. So now what do we do?"

El Rey drummed his fingers on the tabletop as he studied a set of drawings on the screen. "I pay young Miss Vega a visit and see if she can clear any of this up."

Cruz's eyes widened. "You're not going to actually kill her, are you?"

"No. I want to talk to her."

"You think you'll be able to waltz into her home, past the inevitable security she'll have, and strike up a conversation with one of the highest profile celebrities in the city?"

El Rey ran a hand through his thick mop of hair and fixed Cruz with a flat stare. "I can be very persuasive."

"You'll have to be bulletproof and invisible, too."

The assassin gave the slightest of smiles and returned his attention to the screen.

"I've been known to be both."

CHAPTER 33

The skyscrapers along the Paseo de la Reforma gleamed in the midnight sky as *El Rey* made his way along the wide boulevard to the exclusive neighborhood Carla Vega called home, Cruz in the passenger seat beside him. A police car edged alongside at one of the intersection traffic lights, and he could feel the driver's eyes burning into his profile as he waited for the green. *El Rey* wasn't worried about being recognized – he had a get-out-of-jail card with the president's signature on it – but the last thing he needed was to get into an altercation with a bored cop who didn't like the look of his vehicle. The squad car surged ahead when the light turned green, and he let out a small breath of relief. There were both positives and negatives to driving a beater car, increased suspicion from law enforcement among the drawbacks.

The assassin turned down Vega's street, which boasted a stately mansion on the corner, and rolled along at a moderate pace, already confident about where he would park to avoid attracting attention. He'd walked the neighborhood that early evening, wearing the expensive slacks and fashionable jacket of a wealthy Mexican, and had singled out a number of likely candidate spots near the woman's home – one of a row of multimillion-dollar townhomes in the toniest area of the metropolis, home to captains of industry, politicians, celebrities, and successful criminals.

He pulled to the curb around the corner from Vega's townhouse and turned to Cruz. "If all goes well, I should be in and out in half an hour. Get a taco over at one of the late night restaurants on the boulevard, and I'll call you when I'm ready for a pickup."

Cruz nodded, the burner cell phone the assassin had given him seeming to pulse in his shirt pocket. "Will do."

El Rey got out, leaving the door open for Cruz, and hurried away, his all-black outfit blending with the shadows as he strode off. Cruz slid behind the wheel and adjusted the seat forward, then pulled away, eyes roving over the empty street.

El Rey slowed as he neared the townhouse next door to Vega's and eyed the light on in the downstairs room of her residence – the area that would be occupied by her bodyguards, who, according to the CISEN report, were with her round the clock when she was in Mexico City. The security was purely for deterrent value – nobody had ever tried to break in – but as a high-profile celebrity living in a private home rather than one of the city's numerous high-security condominium developments, it was a necessary evil.

He glanced at the security camera near Vega's front entrance, trained on the four stairs leading to her front door and, after a final look around, moved to the wrought-iron gate of the adjacent townhome's side yard and knelt, invisible in the dark, and picked the lock.

The heavy gate swung open with a soft groan, sounding like a wounded animal's moan on the quiet street. He glanced around as he crept past the threshold, taking care to push the gate closed again so any passing patrols would see nothing amiss.

He knew from his study of the permits online that the property was undergoing renovation, a major job judging by the construction permit value. On his walk he'd seen the windows draped with protection, confirming that the owners weren't in residence while it was being gutted. The small mountain of construction supplies in the walkway and the backyard confirmed his deduction, and he pushed past sawhorses and granite slabs and stacks of imported marble, pausing to grab a fourteen-foot ladder as he made his way to the rear entry. That lock proved harder to open than the gate, but he was shielded from view from the surrounding buildings by a high wall, so he had time.

When the tumblers clicked, he eased the door open, the ladder gripped in his right hand. His eyes rapidly adjusted to the complete darkness as he felt his way down the corridor to the stairs leading to the upper levels. He manhandled the ladder to the third floor and located the attic hatch and in a few minutes was on the roof.

The ladder bridged the ten-foot gap between the buildings with two feet to spare on either side. He'd guessed that the windows on Vega's home would have contact alarms on the second and third floors, the street level protected with bars, but one of the constants of alarm companies was that they overlooked the roofs of anything over two stories out of a combination of laziness and to avoid false alarms from birds or maintenance headaches from the constant battering of the elements.

He looked across the gap and took a deep breath and then carefully inched along the ladder until he was on Vega's roof. The good news was that the ladder was rigid even with his weight. The bad news was that with only two feet of overlap on either side, his margin of safety was slimmer than he'd have liked.

The roof door had no lock, and he swung it open, taking care to ease the hatch onto the concrete so as not to make any noise. The attic below was pitch black, and *El Rey* retrieved a penlight from his pocket and twisted it on. A gossamer haze of cobwebs streamed in all directions, and he picked up a curtain rod by his feet and swept them away. The hatch that led to the third floor was to his right and had a wooden ladder integrated into it that could be lowered like a fire escape for access to the roof.

He leaned over the door and studied the mechanism and then fished out a small can of oil, which he applied liberally to the rollers and hinges. Done, he lowered the hatch and fed out the ladder, which thankfully made little noise due to his precautions.

The master suite was on the second level, the third relegated to guest quarters, and he placed one quiet foot in front of the other as he inched to the stairs. The floors were travertine so he didn't have to contend with wooden planks creaking, for which he was grateful. A quick inspection of the window at the end of the hall confirmed that there was a magnetic sensor on the frame, vindicating his decision to enter from the roof.

He paused at the top of the stairs and listened for any signs of movement below, and when he didn't hear anything, he descended to the second floor. Vega's door was at the end of the hall on his right, her rooms occupying most of the level, along with an en suite office and library. When he cracked it open and stepped through the gap, he found himself in a massive bedroom that even in the dim light from the windows he could see was as sumptuous as any five-star hotel.

Vega was asleep on a pedestal bed, and he froze as she stirred. She rolled over, away from him, her cream-colored satin top shimmering as she moved. He held still as her breathing returned to normal, and then moved toward the bed.

Her eyes bugged out as he clamped one hand over her mouth and pressed on a pressure point on her neck with his other. Her stifled scream was little more than a whimper before she lost consciousness, her brain temporarily starved of oxygen.

El Rey withdrew a syringe and flicked on his penlight. He located a vein in her hand and injected the contents and, after pocketing the syringe, lifted her in a fireman's carry, her body slung over his shoulders. She was surprisingly light, no more than a hundred pounds, he guessed as he crossed the bedroom.

The assassin pulled her bedroom door closed behind him and moved to the stairs, where he paused to confirm the guards were still unaware of the drama playing out on the floor above them. He took the steps two at a time and, when he reached the attic ladder, adjusted his hold, compensating for her weight. Once in the attic, he lowered her to the floor and shut the hatch and then hoisted her again and moved to the iron ladder that led to the roof.

Crossing the gap between the two buildings was the most difficult part of the operation, and his face beaded with sweat in the night air as he shifted his feet rung to rung, a sheer drop to certain death his reward for a misstep.

Once across, he retrieved the ladder, set it out of sight on the roof, and called Cruz.

"I'll be ready for pickup in three minutes," he whispered when Cruz answered.

"I'm two blocks down. See you in three."

El Rey was at the side gate with Vega over his shoulders when the Explorer pulled up, its lights extinguished. He ran to the vehicle, opened the rear door, and placed Vega's inert form on the back seat before climbing in next to her.

"Drive," he hissed, pulling the door closed. Cruz did as instructed and only switched on the headlights once he'd rounded the corner, accelerating as he drove south toward the network of back streets that led to the safe house.

CHAPTER 34

Carla's eyes fluttered open, and her vision blurred in and out, the oscillations of a ceiling fan's blades otherworldly as she attempted to make sense out of what she was seeing. She tried to sit up, but her body wouldn't obey, the muscles in her arms and legs leaden. She wondered absently if this was some sort of a nightmare, a residual effect of one too many glasses of wine with dinner. It didn't feel like a dream, though, because she had a gnawing sense of anxiety in the pit of her stomach, her head was throbbing, and she was desperately thirsty, none of which were in any way dreamlike.

A man's voice reached her as though through a fog.

"She's awake."

She tried to swivel her head, but it refused to accommodate, and the best she could manage was to direct her eyes at the shadowy figure sitting across from her – an older man wearing a baseball hat and sunglasses in spite of the darkness.

"Don't fight it. It can take a good half an hour for the anesthetic to wear off. Just relax," the man said, his voice not unkind. She decided that it might be a dream after all, and closed her eyes, hoping to retreat into the comfortable numbness that seemed just at the edge of her awareness.

What seemed like moments later, the man's voice dragged her back to consciousness.

"Feeling any better?"

This time when she opened her eyes she could focus, and her body told her that she was lying on something soft – cushions, not a bed, judging by the rough texture. If this was a dream, she was imagining a couch – and a not particularly clean-smelling one, she thought as she struggled to sit up. She managed to, but the dreamlike quality, the dissociation, like she was watching herself from outside of her own body, lingered even as she looked at the man, who leaned over and tapped a plastic bottle of water on the coffee table in front of her.

"You're probably thirsty. That's for you."

She tried to reach for the bottle, but her arms had minds of their own, and her hand fell short of the bottle by a half foot.

"Maybe rest and give it another five or ten minutes. From what I remember of coming out of surgery, it can take a while before you're a hundred percent."

Carla cleared her throat, and when she spoke, her voice was a croak. "What is this?"

"I have to apologize for the tactics my associate used to get you here. But there was no other way."

"Kidnapping?" Carla demanded, her mouth having trouble with the syllables.

"Well, yes. For which I'm sorry."

She tried to make sense out of the man's words, but couldn't. Why was a kidnapper apologizing? And how did they get her? Last she remembered she was asleep in bed…

"*Sorry?*" she spat. "You…kidnapped me."

"Yes. But it's not what it seems."

"Not…I…what is this?"

"I'd suggest you take a little more time, and we can discuss things once you're clearer-headed. The water will help. There's no sense in rushing it."

She tried for the bottle again, and this time managed to wrap her fingers around it. Her hands fumbled with the top, and then the cool liquid was coursing down her throat, the feeling more satisfying than she could have believed possible. When she'd drained the water, she tossed the bottle next to her on the sofa, every second returning more of her senses to her.

"Tell me what you want," she said, and her voice sounded more alert than it had moments before.

"I want to ask you some questions."

She stared at him incredulously. "Questions," she repeated.

"Yes. But I want you completely recovered before I do."

"You kidnapped me to ask me questions?"

"That's technically correct, I suppose."

"*Technically?* You took me out of my...out of my bed. What do you mean, technically?" she demanded, her temper flaring as her headache increased.

"*Señorita* Vega, what we did was for your own good. For your safety. I'll explain in time, but for now, I need you to answer my questions honestly."

"What questions? You haven't asked any," she snarled, her strength rushing back into her limbs.

The man glanced off to the left, where for the first time, Carla sensed someone else in the room. She turned her head. A younger man was sitting on a barstool at a kitchen island, also wearing a hat and sunglasses. The younger man indicated that his companion should carry on, and the older man spoke again.

"We're investigating the deaths of several public figures."

Her eyes betrayed her confusion. "Investigating?"

"That's correct."

"You kidnapped me because you're...investigating something?" she said, her tone skeptical. "Who are you?"

Another rapid glance at the younger man by the older one.

"That's not important," the younger man said, speaking for the first time in a quiet voice.

"It is to me," she fired back.

The older man leaned forward. "Miss Vega, I'm an admirer of your work. Tell me truthfully, how are you connected with Admiral Torreon, Archbishop Rene Bolivar, and Robert Perry?"

She processed the names, a range of expressions flitting across her face before her eyes settled back on the older man.

"Connected? You keep using that word. The answer is, not at all. I'm not connected to them in any way."

"You were at the attack on the admiral, and you were at Perry's hotel in Arizona when he died," the younger man said, his tone mild, his demeanor disturbingly pleasant.

"I…I have no idea what you're talking about," she waffled, trying to buy time.

"Miss Vega, I think you do," the younger man said. "I think you're the link between these three men, and you know why they were killed."

The room was quiet except for the soft whirring of the fan. She leaned back and closed her eyes, her head splitting now. "I really don't know what you're getting at," she said, and then her eyes popped open. "What do you mean, why they were *killed*? Torreon died in his sleep. Perry from drugs. The archbishop was accidental. You're not making any sense."

"Answer the question. There's a connection between all three, as well as yourself. And with two others. One of whom was the head of the anti-cartel task force. Captain Romero Cruz," the older man said.

"Cruz? I didn't know the man, I swear. I never met him, and I never met the archbishop, either. I have no idea what you want," she said, her voice cracking at the end. She looked over at the young man. "Can I have some more water?"

He stood, and she noted that he was taller than she'd thought from when he was sitting. He went to the refrigerator, retrieved two water bottles, and walked over to her and placed them on the table.

"There. Now how about you cut the shit? I saw you in Arizona. Stop lying. You were there, and you were at the boat christening."

She reached for a bottle, thinking furiously, and her eyebrows rose in surprise. "Wait – you saw me there? Which means…you were there, too."

The older man stood and motioned to the younger, and they stepped away and had a hushed discussion. When the older man returned, the younger pulled up a wooden chair next to him and sat down.

"Miss Vega, I'm going to tell you a story," the younger man said. "It's the absolute truth, even if it sounds insane. By the end you'll understand why we had to remove you from your house, and why you're in incredible danger. Hopefully you'll be able to help us understand some things that have been eluding us about the connection between you and these others."

"Can we get back to the fact that you kidnapped me?" she snapped.

"Certainly. I'll be happy to explain that. There was no other way to have this discussion with you in a safe place, where you would hear us out."

"You'll go to prison for life."

The younger man smiled, which for some reason alarmed Carla more than if he'd hit her. "Perhaps. But I think first you need to listen to the story and answer our questions. Four men have been killed so far, and you're the only common thread between two of them. And I saw something in your eyes when you first heard the archbishop's name. It meant something to you. I need to know what that is, for your own safety."

"You keep saying that. That I'm safe, that this is for my own safety. But you're kidnappers."

"We're investigating four killings," the older man said. "Four murders."

"Again, those were all accidental or natural causes."

"That's what they were made to look like."

"That's crazy. How do you know? I mean, you claim to know they were killed. How?" she demanded, her investigative instincts kicking in.

The younger man removed his glasses and fixed her with a cold stare, absent any malice, but with a quality like that of a snake eyeing its prey. He was actually quite handsome, she thought, an errant notion that took her unawares, and that she quickly shook off. He leaned forward, resting his elbows on his thighs, and pursed his lips, as though annoyed at the need to explain.

"Because I killed them."

CHAPTER 35

Carla recoiled in shock. She believed him. And the fact that she did scared her more than anything so far.

"You...*you* killed them?"

"*Señorita* Vega, try to resist the temptation to interrupt me with inane repetitions. I'll tell you what I can, and then it will be your turn," the younger man said.

She nodded mutely, not trusting herself to speak.

"I work for a government agency. I'm in the problem-solving business. When this agency has exhausted all other alternatives or has deemed someone dangerous to national security, I get a call. To simplify things, I was instructed to terminate those three men because of their involvement in a drug-smuggling operation. I was given dossiers, information on them you can't imagine, everything I would need about their movements and habits to execute the plan successfully. Which I did."

She was about to speak when the young man held up a hand and shook his head, just once, closing his eyes as though fighting to control his patience. When he opened them, he continued.

"For reasons I found suspicious, they were all to look like accidents or natural causes. Fine. I did my duty. And then I was given another list, with three more names on it. Yours was one of them."

Her eyes widened. "I...I don't understand," she whispered.

"I'm hoping that you do."

"I..."

"The other names were Captain Cruz and a farmer in Sinaloa, whose business is tomatoes and pigs, and who's never harmed anyone in his life, as far as I can tell. His name is Indalecio Arellano."

171

El Rey watched her closely for any giveaways. The name meant nothing to her that he could see.

"What are you saying? That you're going to kill me? Is that what this is about?"

"Are you dead?"

She didn't say anything.

"If I wanted to kill you, you'd have passed on in your sleep at your home. A tragic freak accident of some sort – heart stopped, probably an undiagnosed congenital issue." *El Rey* sighed. "CISEN wants you dead. Not me."

"CISEN? That's insane. They don't go around killing journalists."

Cruz exhaled noisily. "That's correct. Or at least, that was my understanding. But apparently they do. And cops, priests, actors… Now I think it's time you level with us. We need to know what you do if we're going to have any chance of getting to the bottom of this."

"What about me?" she asked.

"If you're honest with us, you can walk away, no harm done," Cruz said.

"Although I have to warn you that they'll just send someone else," *El Rey* said.

"If it's CISEN, I can blow it wide open. If I report what they've done, and that they've targeted me, then they can't do anything. I'd be safe."

The assassin shook his head. "That's not how it works. First, you'll find it never gets aired, for two reasons: no proof – and CISEN has absolute control over the media and can quash a story. And second, you'll be branded a kook. Stories will appear about you drunk, on drugs, having orgies, whatever. And then one day you'll be found overdosed. Or your car will go off a cliff. Or your plane will go down. Or a robbery or carjacking will go wrong, with deadly consequences. I respect your line of thinking, but without proof, you've got nothing, which you should know. Just unsubstantiated allegations."

"You could make a statement. Go public."

"Same problem. I know I killed them, but how do I prove it? Besides which, I have no name. I'm nobody. The invisible man." He sat back. "But we're getting ahead of ourselves. Why were you in Arizona?"

Her eyes narrowed. "Why should I believe any of this? You could be making it all up. Or it could be some kind of trick."

"Trick? To achieve what? We secreted you out of your house to trick you into revealing...what, exactly? Miss Vega, I suggest you think this through. You're on a kill list. As am I. That's why we kidnapped you," Cruz said.

"You?"

Cruz sighed and removed his hat and glasses. "I know we've never met, but you can compare my photos online with me in the flesh. Captain Romero Cruz, head of the anti-cartel task force, at your service."

Her face fell. It was obvious that a part of her had been hoping they'd been spinning her some fanciful tale.

"Do you have ID?"

"Of course." Cruz removed his badge holder from his back pocket and handed it to her.

"But I saw that you died yesterday..." she said, recognition dawning on her.

"Correct. Because if I wasn't dead, they'd still be trying to terminate me." He took his ID back. "Are you starting to understand how serious this is?"

"But if this is true, what can I do? They'll kill me no matter what."

"Maybe not. There's one chance for you," *El Rey* said. "Which is that we figure this out and put an end to it while they believe I'm still trying to get to you."

"I don't understand."

"Tell me what you were doing in Arizona."

Carla inhaled deeply, her breasts swelling against her satin top as she did, and nodded. "I have a source. Inside CISEN. The source indicated that there was something going on with Perry and the admiral. A few days before he died, I also heard that the archbishop was implicated in some way. How, my source didn't know. I went to Arizona to try to get information out of Perry, see what he might be involved in that would connect him to the others. That was the same reason I went to cover the christening. To get to the admiral, whose staff had been stonewalling me." She held Cruz's gaze. "I had no reason to believe any of these deaths weren't what they seemed. I've been such a fool…"

"Then you didn't learn anything new?"

"No, not really. And now that you say Perry was targeted. I mean, he was harmless. A pretty boy. Nothing more."

"Did he have any connection to Mexico or Mexican interests you know of?"

She shook her head. "No. I mean, his father was Mexican, but he seemed ashamed of that and insisted he was Spanish."

"That's it? That's all you got? Some kind of racial guilt?" Cruz asked.

"I only talked to him for a short while. We were supposed to meet for drinks the night he…the night he died. Maybe I would have found out more. Or maybe there was no obvious reason. What I can tell you is that the story about a drug ring makes no sense. Perry was making tens of millions per year. A guy like that isn't in the drug business. No way. He wasn't the type."

"And the admiral and archbishop?"

"Both honorable men, as far as I could tell. And I never found anything in common, although I stopped looking once the archbishop died."

Cruz grunted. "What about this farmer?"

"I have no idea who he is or why he's on the list."

"Who's your source?" Cruz demanded.

She shook her head. "I'll never tell."

"I'm afraid you don't have that luxury."

"It's not a luxury. It's a mandatory condition."

El Rey stood. "This is getting us nowhere."

"You said earlier that I had one chance. What were you thinking?" Carla asked.

"You have to disappear. If you don't, you're dead."

"I can't just disappear. I have a career. Obligations, a home…"

"None of which will do you any good once you're dead."

"Where would I go?"

"That's not the biggest problem. There's a part to this story I haven't told you. It involves an injection," *El Rey* said and gave her an abridged version of his situation with the antidote. When he finished, he frowned. "So you see, you'd have to have a good reason to drop off the radar, to buy me time as an excuse for not terminating you. I can't get you if I can't find you."

"Then I really don't understand what you're proposing," she said.

El Rey laid out his thinking in precise terms. When he was done, the air hung heavy with tension. Carla studied Cruz's face and then the assassin's.

"It could work. Provided I went along with it and didn't alert everyone I could think of the second I was back in my house."

"Which you're free to do. Just prepare a will first, because your life span will be measured in hours at that point. As will mine, and his," *El Rey* said.

Carla sat in silence for a half minute and then leaned forward. "Presuming I disappear, I have one condition. I want an exclusive on this story, whatever it is. I mean, I can help you dig, too. I'm a researcher. It's part of what I do. And with three of us trying to find out what's going on, we might all have a better chance than without me helping."

"Miss Vega, I have a wife I love very much. She thinks I'm dead. Right now her heart's breaking, as is mine. I don't want to have to stay dead, to walk away from the most precious thing in my life. So believe me, if anyone's motivated to dig, it's me," Cruz said quietly.

El Rey looked at Carla. "You can have the exclusive. It doesn't mean that you'll ever get to tell it, though. Our theory that this is a rogue operation within CISEN may be dead wrong, and it may be officially sanctioned at the highest levels, in which case, well…then there's not much you can do but move to Bora Bora and take up bartending."

Carla fixed Cruz with a cool stare. "What do you want me to do first?"

"You're probably not going to like it."

"I think that's safe to say. But do I have a choice?"

"Not a good one."

CHAPTER 36

Carla's neighborhood was deserted at 3:30 a.m., the moon now high in the inky vault of the night sky, and when Cruz dropped *El Rey* and Carla off near her neighbor's townhouse, the street was absolutely still, with only a faint sound of traffic from the nearby Paseo de la Reforma, which was always busy regardless of the hour.

El Rey led her into the building, her feet shielded from the debris by a too-large pair of his running shoes, and guided her up the stairs to the roof. She watched in disbelief as he wedged the ladder in place between the two buildings and gestured for her to approach. She peered down into the void beneath it and shook her head.

"You've got to be kidding."

"It's not that hard. I managed it carrying you."

She closed her eyes. "I'm afraid of heights."

"No time like the present to conquer that fear."

She shook her head again. "I can't do it."

"You want me to try again with you on my back?"

"That would be even worse. Isn't there any other option?"

El Rey considered the question and then nodded and explained the alternative.

She smiled. "I like that one way better."

"You just need to be convincing."

"I'm on TV, remember?"

"All right. Let's do it." He led her back to the ground floor, carrying the ladder, and when they were in the backyard, he leaned it against the ten-foot-high wall separating the properties. "You go first. Sit on the top of the wall while I come up, and then take my hand, and I'll lower you so that it will be a short drop to the ground."

She did as directed, and when both of them were in her yard, he moved to her rear door, his lock picks in hand. Carla watched him massage the deadbolt tumblers until he had it open, and then he stood.

"You know what to do. Give me three minutes to get away. You remember my phone number?"

She repeated it to confirm. "And tomorrow morning...?"

"Just make sure you're on time," he cautioned, and then he was running, a dark streak in the gloom. He seemed to defy gravity as he leapt and pulled himself up and over the wall, all the time as silent as the grave.

Carla counted silently to herself. When three minutes had passed, she twisted the knob and opened the door. Sirens howled a Klaxon wail, and her bodyguards came running, weapons drawn.

Carla waved them off. "Sorry. I forgot about the alarm. I thought I heard something out here."

"*Señorita* Vega, if there's something on the grounds, it would be best if you allowed us to investigate," the shift leader said.

She nodded and ran a listless hand through her hair, having no problem doing a convincing job of being sleepy. "Turn it off, would you? That noise is terrible."

"Of course." He went to the keypad and tapped in a four-digit code. The clamor quieted, and she offered a fatigued smile.

"Sorry, boys. I thought it might have been a cat I've seen back here a few times. I was thinking of adopting it if it's a stray." She covered her mouth and yawned. "Let me know if you see it so I can put out some milk."

She brushed past the men and made for the stairs. They watched her, their faces impassive, and when she was out of sight, the leader rolled his eyes and shook his head.

In her room, Carla opened her floor safe and extracted the money she kept there – twenty thousand U.S. and thirty thousand pesos. She wasn't unusual in keeping cash in her home; the banks in Mexico didn't offer safe deposit boxes, so every house had a good safe. She dropped the banknotes into her purse along with her passport and, after spinning the combination dial, returned to her bed, where she lay sleepless, mind racing, for the rest of the night.

CHAPTER 37

Carla's street looked completely different bathed in cool morning light, Cruz thought as he sat, his expression stony, behind the wheel of a Ford Mustang *El Rey* had stolen several hours earlier. The assassin waited patiently next to him, an old AK-47 in his hands, his attention focused on the front door of Carla's home.

They'd discussed how they would proceed, and Cruz had reluctantly agreed, although he hated the idea of being involved in gunfire in civilian territory. But as much as Cruz disliked it, there was no other way, and it was too late to back out now.

The big V8 engine rumbled quietly as Cruz checked his watch for the fifth time in as many minutes. *El Rey* glanced at him before returning to his vigil.

"Relax. You're making me nervous with the fidgeting."

"Sorry."

"You'd think you'd never operated in the field before."

"It's not that. I'm just not used to being on this side of the law."

"It's no different regardless of which side you're on. Chill out. I need to concentrate."

Cruz took several deep breaths. The assassin was right. He was letting his nerves get the better of him, no doubt due to lack of sleep.

They both saw movement at Carla's front door at the same time, and then the iron gate across her driveway opened, and then a dark gray Chevrolet Tahoe pulled out and stopped at the front curb. Carla had told them that her routine never varied – at 8:30, one of the bodyguards brought the car around and waited as she and the other two men came down the steps for the ride to her office.

"Now," *El Rey* hissed. Cruz slipped the transmission into gear and rolled down the street at a slow pace. Carla stood on her front stoop and programmed the alarm, her two bodyguards looking stiff in their charcoal suits and aviator sunglasses. They seemed to intuit something was wrong as the Mustang slowed just behind the SUV, and both were reaching for their weapons when the shooting started.

El Rey squeezed off a long burst at the house, taking care to avoid hitting Carla or her escorts, spraying the façade next to them instead as well as putting several rounds into the rear door of the Chevrolet for good measure.

"Go," *El Rey* screamed, and Cruz goosed the accelerator as the bodyguards rounded the Tahoe and fired at the car. But hitting a fishtailing vehicle accelerating to high speed with handguns was a doubtful proposition at best, and only a few of their rounds thumped into the trunk as the Mustang carved the corner at the end of the block and disappeared from sight.

"That went well," the assassin shouted, ears ringing from the roar of the weapon. "Two blocks up make a left, and then another three, a right."

"Don't worry. I remember." Cruz gunned the gas and swerved, narrowly missing an Audi sedan backing out of a driveway. "You sure you didn't hit anyone?"

"You do know who you're talking to, right?"

"I'm just asking."

"Every shot went only where I wanted it to go. Although it's dicey with one of these things on full automatic. I mean, they're not the most accurate even on single fire…" *El Rey* turned to look at Cruz's scowling profile. "Don't worry. Everyone's fine."

Two minutes later they coasted to a stop in an alley by a bakery and got out of the car. *El Rey* left the weapon inside and rounded the fender to where Cruz was standing by the driver's door.

"Okay. Just like we discussed. We split up, and I'll meet you back at the house in an hour. Go get something to eat. Buy a good book. The hardest part's over," *El Rey* said, and Cruz nodded. That area didn't have a traffic camera, so they could disappear on foot without leaving a trail. The police would find the car soon enough, leaving them empty-handed.

Cruz walked off in one direction, *El Rey* in the other. At the corner the assassin flagged down a taxi, outwardly calm – a young man on the way to work. Cruz circled the block and at the next boulevard hopped on a bus heading east. He took a seat toward the back and closed his eyes, trying to ignore his stomach growling as the bus bounced toward the far edge of the city, his heart rate only now dropping to a normal level.

The police arrived at Carla's home within six minutes, and in another ten there were five squad cars closing off the street, an officer at each end of the block directing traffic. Carla was inside, on the phone with her publicist, Samantha, her voice tight with an edge of panic.

"That's right. They almost killed me. Thank God nobody was hit. There must have been fifty shots. The house is a disaster," she said.

"Good Lord. Who would do such a thing?"

"I've been working on an investigation into the cartels. I was threatened before, but I didn't take it seriously."

"Threatened! Why didn't you say something?"

"It was just a note. And nothing happened. But I must have struck a nerve."

"My God. What are you going to do?"

"I don't know what I can do. You know the cartels. They're everywhere."

"You have to duck out of sight, Carla. Listen to me. Your safety is more important than your job."

Bingo. Carla knew her friend Samantha well and had hoped she'd arrive at the conclusion she did, making going into hiding her idea, not Carla's.

"I don't know, Samantha. I mean, I can't just drop everything..."

"You listen to me. Get your skinny ass out of Mexico City, now. Take a vacation somewhere the cartels have never heard of. I'll run interference here. In fact, I'll be able to get more mileage out of this than if you were still here."

"Isn't that rather melodramatic?"

"You were shot at and almost killed outside your house. One of Mexico's most beloved television personalities. Are you kidding? This is pure gold. I can keep the headlines going for weeks with speculation about where you're hiding. It's a dream come true." Samantha was reliably consistent and viewed the world in terms of photo ops and sound bites. She was also a gossip, ensuring that long before the evening news the town would be buzzing about the shocking gun battle in its rarefied heart, and the cartel angle would be common knowledge.

"Maybe you're right," Carla said, allowing herself to be talked into it. That it hadn't appeared to have been her idea was even better, because knowing Samantha, she'd take great pains to tell her network of contacts that she'd forced her stubborn client to go underground for her own good.

"Damn right I am. Call me when you're somewhere off the radar. I don't want to know where. You know how I am. Can't keep a secret to save my life."

"That's why I love you, Sam."

"Stay safe. And call."

"Okay. I need to talk to the office and let them know."

"Do it from the road, girl. Get moving. For all you know, they could be watching you right now. God, it's scary. I just frightened myself thinking about it."

"I have to make a statement to the police, and then I'll get going."

"Promise?"

Carla fought the urge to smile. The plan was working perfectly. She'd disappear, her imminent demise a public concern, with proof that the cartels wanted to stop her relentless journalistic probing etched into the mortar of her house façade by every bullet hole. Carla had no doubt that Samantha would be able to get maximum mileage out of the situation, and if anything, when Carla returned to the spotlight, she'd be a bigger name than ever before.

Carla cleared her throat as she caught a glimpse of a detective in a brown overcoat pushing past the uniforms on the front steps, notebook in hand.

"Promise."

CHAPTER 38

Guadalajara, Mexico

The dark-haired man sat on the veranda, staring out at a nearby clearing where a small girl wearing a white sun dress ran with a butterfly net, trying to catch a particularly colorful example as a smiling woman stood watching from the shade of a tree. His head bobbed silently as though he was keeping time to a song only he could hear, and then he held up the morning paper and threw it onto the large outdoor dining table where he was seated across from the fair-haired younger man.

"I don't like it. I smell a rat," the dark-haired man said. The younger man drank his orange juice, displaying no outward emotion, waiting for the older man to finish. "She's been warned, somehow."

"It's possible. Although it's also possible that it's exactly what it seems. Unrelated to our project."

"We can't take the chance. I'm telling you it's gone south on us. Either the assassin spilled the beans, or someone in CISEN did."

"It's going to be virtually impossible knowing which. Assuming you're right. Which, with all due respect, we have no way of verifying."

The dark-haired man's stare hardened as he studied the younger man. "You don't sound convinced."

"What I want to avoid is escalating this any further. As of now, four of the six people we gave to CISEN to handle are dead. The woman's gone into hiding, and the other's disappeared. I'm actually more worried about the farmer than the reporter at this point."

185

"Worry about both of them. We have no idea what the woman knows. She's a potential bomb that could explode in our faces at any time."

"True. But don't forget that the assassin is still hunting her."

"For all we know the botched attack was him trying to snuff her out."

"I highly doubt it. This is a man of skill. He dispatched the others with zero complications. There's no reason he would suddenly go for the obvious, especially since he was specifically instructed to make the deaths look accidental, which he did with all the others. No, it's not him."

"Doubt all you want. I'm saying she found out about it, and this is a ruse."

"You say that because you know we have a contract on her. But absent that piece of information, you'd draw the same conclusion I did, which is that it's a genuine third party who has its own reasons for wanting her silenced. I've already begun investigating, and the preliminary report is that it's one of the cartels. She was working on an exposé of some sort."

The little girl shrieked in delight as she trapped a butterfly in the net, and emitted peals of laughter as she ran toward the woman, who was holding her arms wide. The sound startled two of the horses in the corral near the barn, which snorted and stamped their hooves nervously.

The dark-haired man eyed the paper again, his brow furrowed, and glowered at his companion.

"I appreciate your willingness to disagree with me when you think I'm acting hastily, but I'm making an executive decision here. I can feel something wrong in my bones, and that feeling is rarely wrong. We've been sold out, one way or another. So here's what I want to do: look for a leak in CISEN. Put pressure on your contact there. As far as the assassin goes, assume he's a loose cannon, and that'll have to be dealt with. No arguments. Am I clear?"

"Perfectly. But we have a problem. The assassin isn't an ordinary operative. He's something of a legend. A magician of sorts. I guess what I'm saying is that it's not easy to take out a man like that. I expect he's paranoid, highly skilled, and would see anything coming from a mile away." He paused, allowing his words to sink in.

"That's logistics. I don't particularly care how hard it is to do. I want it done. As to the woman, we'll need to get more people looking for her. We can't assume that the CISEN assassin will deal with her. And with respect to the leak within CISEN, I'd remind you that we have no idea what the reporter actually knows – only that she's nosing around sensitive areas. But we have to assume that someone in the organization tipped her off, or at least pointed her in the right direction. I want that person found."

The younger man shook his head. "Our CISEN contact has no idea of the bigger picture, so it's impossible that anyone inside tipped her to anything, because nobody knows anything to tip. Even if you're correct and there's a leak, what could the informant have told her? Only the names and the phony drug ring story. I'm arguing for caution because each step we take could complicate this matter. That's all."

"Noted. Now do as I've instructed. I'm tired of this debate. I want to go play with my granddaughter, not bicker over how to handle this."

"I'll meet with our man and make your wishes known. It's safe to say it will require more money changing hands."

The dark-haired man gave a small shrug.

"The good news in all this is that there are only two more to go, and if for some reason your intuition is off on this one, it's entirely possible that the assassin will terminate them before we get him. He's been remarkably efficient so far, you have to admit."

"That he has. I hope you're right. But let's plan for the worst. Make arrangements to get someone else on the farmer and the journalist. We need a backup plan, and right now we've got nothing." The dark-haired man stood as the little girl dragged her mother toward the house, the net with her trophy clutched tight in her hand. His face cracked into a reptilian smile and he beamed at the pair, the discussion forgotten as he moved to the steps to greet them.

The younger man slipped into the house, his marching orders issued, already thinking through how to explain to his contact that their assassin would need to be neutralized.

CHAPTER 39

Mexico City, Mexico

Unlike in his nightmares, the morning of Cruz's funeral was picturesque, the air crisp and clear, the sun bright in a robin's egg blue sky devoid of clouds. The memorial ceremony was held in Chapultepec Park only a few blocks from headquarters, the towering glass and steel edifice with the image of a battle-ready federal policeman gripping an assault rifle embossed on one side visible from the grassy field where hundreds of *Federales* were gathered in honor of their captain.

Cruz watched through a pair of binoculars from the parking lot near the Museum of Anthropology, *El Rey* beside him, while the mourners stood in the sunlight as speaker after speaker offered their condolences.

"Quite a eulogy. You must be touched," the assassin said.

Cruz ignored him and kept his eyes on Dinah, who looked pale and drawn, and who spent most of the service leaning on Briones' arm.

"It looks like it'll be over soon," Cruz commented as the blue-uniformed officers broke into groups and stood, clumped, waiting in a rough line to offer the widow their sympathies.

They'd been there for the longest forty-five minutes of Cruz's life, a kind of slow motion torture for him, knowing what his wife must be going through but unable to offer her any reassurance. *El Rey* had turned the radio on low and was humming along with a Mana song, clearly enjoying Cruz's discomfort.

"The coverage on Vega is pretty amazing. Every paper, every news program, it's the top story. Not that your demise wasn't newsworthy," he said.

"I'm sure you shed a tear."

"Are you positive about the bar?"

Cruz had told the assassin that following the ceremony there would probably be a memorial service somewhere else, after which his closest subordinates would likely gather at a bar near headquarters to drink in Cruz's memory. "Yes."

"It would be a lot easier to approach him here than in a crowded room."

"Let's see how it plays. Who was it that was so big on relaxation in the car recently?"

"That was different."

Cruz's eyebrows rose. "If I didn't know better, I'd say that being surrounded by cops makes you a little jumpy."

"Fortunately you know better."

Most of the officers returned to the buses and cruisers that were parked nearby. Cruz wasn't worried about being recognized, not having shaved for three days and wearing sunglasses and a hat. Still, he sank down in his seat, waiting for Briones and his wife to make their way back.

After an unbearable ten minutes, *El Rey* started the engine. "They're over there. Looks like your buddy's driving. So you called that one right."

"No chance of an interception here," Cruz said, his voice glum.

"Nope. Not with Mrs. Cruz in the car. She'd recognize me."

"Fine. Hang back and follow them. Maybe we'll get lucky at whatever hall they're going to."

Briones surprised them both by driving Dinah home. They trailed his unmarked car at a safe distance and pulled into a bus stop when he double-parked in front of the building. Cruz felt a part of his heart tear when Dinah disappeared into the lobby, but shook off the sentimentality. If he ever wanted to be with her again, he needed to concentrate on the matter at hand, not wallow in self-pity. Briones returned a minute later and roared off. *El Rey* cut into traffic to follow him, drawing the ire and a blare of horns from the cars behind him.

"See if you can get next to him. That would be easiest," Cruz said, and *El Rey* nodded.

"He might rear-end the guy in front of him if he sees his dead boss, but you know best."

Briones was driving like a man possessed, and try as they might, they couldn't close the gap in the dense traffic. Eight minutes later, after being cut off by a delivery van, *El Rey* popped the glove compartment, retrieved a new burner cell phone, and handed it to Cruz.

"Do you know his phone number?"

Cruz dialed it, cursing himself for being so preoccupied that he'd missed something so obvious. As he waited for the call to connect, he turned to *El Rey*.

"How do you get all these phones? I thought that with the new laws you couldn't get undocumented cells."

"Laws only affect the law-abiding. Criminals never have a problem getting illegal goods."

Briones answered on the fourth ring. "Hello," he barked.

"Lieutenant? You might want to pull over. I'm having a hell of a time catching up to you."

Silence hung on the line for several pregnant seconds.

"What is this? Some kind of sick joke?"

"Lieutenant, it's no joke. Don't say another word. Pull to the curb at the next light, and I'll be right there."

"I…"

"Not another word. See you in a minute."

Cruz hung up, and they watched Briones' vehicle swerve right and screech to a halt in a loading zone. *El Rey* stopped behind the car, and Cruz jumped out, tossing the phone to him.

"Follow us. We'll find someplace quiet where we can talk."

Cruz trotted to the passenger door of Briones' car and opened it. Briones' face was a study in conflicting emotions: surprise, anger, hurt, relief, confusion.

"Good morning, young man. Can you give me a lift?"

"*Capitan!* I can't believe it. You're alive!"

"Yes, well, it appears the rumors of my demise might have been exaggerated. I'll explain everything, but for now, let's get going."

"Where to?"

"We're not far from Central Park, in the historical section. That should do."

Briones pulled away, obviously shaken by Cruz's reappearance. Cruz buckled in and smiled. "Don't be alarmed if you see we're being followed. That's my guardian angel."

"What's going on, *Capitan?*"

"It's complicated. There's a contract out on me, and the only way to be safe was to fake my death."

"A contract? Half the cartels have a contract on you."

"This is different. Those, I'm used to. This is our own people."

Briones frowned. "I don't understand."

"I'll start at the beginning. It's hard to believe, but we've known each other for a long time, so you have to trust I'm telling the truth." Cruz explained about the killings, CISEN's involvement, his investigation, and finished with the events of the last forty-eight hours. When he was done, Briones was speechless, and they drove in silence the rest of the way. Briones parked in one of the lots north of the park, and they waited as *El Rey* pulled into the slot across from them and got out.

Briones eyed the assassin with his customary distaste, a habit that he hadn't been able to break even after working with him. *El Rey* maintained his usual poker face. They walked slowly down the sidewalk toward the market stalls that were set up all along the periphery of the greenery, and Cruz filled Briones in on how they planned to proceed. When he was done, Briones slowed.

"So you want me to coordinate with you and handle the research from inside. I understand. But I still find it impossible to believe that CISEN would order the execution of innocent people," he said.

"As do I," Cruz agreed. "But there's no arguing the facts. I've read the CISEN dossiers. They're real. And I'm fortunate that our friend here decided to disobey his orders and warn me instead of putting me out of my misery."

"Where do we even start?" Briones asked.

Cruz handed him two sheets of paper. "I've prepared a list. We're looking for anything that ties these people together. And anything you can find on the farmer, who's the only one left alive, other than Vega."

"That's just crazy about her. I saw the news yesterday. The attack."

"That was us."

Briones' eyes widened. "You?"

"We needed to give her an excuse to hide. That was the best we could come up with."

"I'll say. It's all anyone's talking about."

El Rey glanced around and leaned into Briones. "This little reunion's been touching, but the real question is, can you keep your mouth shut? Your captain's life hangs in the balance."

"Sounds like you're driven by self-interest here, too. As usual. Unless I misunderstood, your life's on the line as well," Briones fired back.

"True. But my question stands."

"Of course I can keep this confidential. I'm a professional."

"Right. But you have to play it completely straight. Even a small slip could be disastrous."

Briones glared at him. "Nice to see some things never change. Still arrogant as ever."

"There's a phone number and a blind email address on the list. Use that to contact me," Cruz said, interrupting the exchange. "If you call, do so from a landline, preferably not in your office. I don't think

CISEN would be eavesdropping on you, but at this point, paranoia's in order."

Briones frowned. "I agree."

They ambled along while Briones read the list and then returned to the lot. Cruz shook his hand. "How's Dinah doing?"

"She's in pieces, as you can imagine. I don't get the sense that reality's set in yet."

"Let's hope we can get this licked before it does. If there'd been any way to spare her, I would have. But *El Rey*'s right. She can't know. Not even a hint." Cruz stepped closer. "See to it that the department doesn't demand that she move out of the condo just yet, would you? And if she needs anything, get it for her. Hopefully my credit's good."

"Of course, sir. That goes without saying."

"*Bueno.* I presume you're off to have a drink with the troops?"

"That's right."

"Remember. I'm dead. The world's a poorer place for my passing. Not a word to anyone."

Briones got into his car and started the engine, the door still open. He looked Cruz in the eye and answered without hesitation.

"You can depend on me."

CHAPTER 40

El Rey had arrived two hours early at the rendezvous location where he'd agreed to meet Tovar. He'd watched the pedestrian traffic moving down the sidewalks from his position on the street corner, from where he could see not only the little restaurant but also both sides of the street, including the surrounding buildings. His natural caution had been heightened by the brusque tone the CISEN man had adopted when *El Rey* had demanded a meet.

Tovar's car stopped down the block from the restaurant, and he emerged from the rear, looking annoyed at having to rub shoulders with the great unwashed in the working-class neighborhood. *El Rey* could see his frown of displeasure as he approached the entry and went in. He hadn't spotted *El Rey*, who had donned the clothes of a laborer and darkened his skin, finishing the transformation with a glued-on mustache, sunglasses, and a filthy cap.

The assassin watched the car until it pulled away, and then cut across the street and down the service alley. He stopped at the rear door of the restaurant, which was open for ventilation as the cleaning crew worked. He swung the screen door wide and walked through the kitchen as though he owned the place, and when he emerged into the dining room, he noted the back of Tovar's head at a booth – the only patron.

Tovar started when *El Rey* materialized next to him and almost dropped his cell phone, which he'd been fiddling with. The assassin took a seat across from him and folded his hands on the tabletop. Tovar took in the disguise and pursed his lips.

"Practicing your tradecraft, I see," he said.

"Wouldn't do to get complacent."

"What did you want to meet about?"

"I got Cruz. But I still haven't been able to locate the farmer, and Vega disappeared."

"Yes, I saw that. Bad luck, isn't it?" Tovar said, his tone revealing nothing.

"Your briefing never mentioned I'd be competing with cartel incompetents."

"We were unaware of her involvement with them."

"Well, it's significantly complicated things. A target on alert is much more difficult to reach than an unsuspecting one."

"I understand. But we have confidence in you. Look at what you achieved with the admiral."

"That was different. He was immobilized, and I knew where he was."

Tovar shook his head. "You'll deal with it, I'm sure."

"I need more on the farmer. What you gave me is insufficient to track him down. I've put wheels in motion, and he's not at his farm and hasn't been seen for a week – after a murder there, I might add. So now it's two targets on the run. None of that was in the dossiers."

"It's a fluid situation."

"I need you to run a scan of all the transportation databases. Buses, planes, rental cars. And hotels. He's got to be somewhere. I don't have the resources you do."

"I've already done so. We have a lead in Cancún." Tovar studied the assassin's fake mustache and then slid a sheet of paper across the table. *El Rey* took it and scanned the information, then folded it and put it in his pocket without comment.

Tovar shifted in his seat. "How do you plan to find the woman?"

"That will be harder. But she's an amateur, and she's in a business where she's sure to communicate with someone in her circle. I need you to put a trace on her cell phone. We might get lucky with that."

"Thanks to the internet, even civilians know their phones can be tracked these days. Don't bet on it."

El Rey seemed unperturbed. "I'm not. I just want all bases covered." His eyes narrowed and he paused, eyeing Tovar. "You know, if I didn't know better, I'd think you have another team on these two, and they blew it in both cases."

"You'd be wrong."

"So you say."

Tovar looked at the entrance. "Is there anything else?"

"I'm scheduled for my injection on Friday."

"Then you better get busy."

"With the current circumstances, it's unlikely I'll be able to locate the woman by then, and only fifty-fifty I can set up the farmer in time and be back here. I need time to reconnoiter his situation, presuming your data is correct, and then devise the hit. That doesn't happen in a matter of hours."

"I wouldn't waste any time, then."

"What I'm saying is that I expect my injection on schedule, whether or not I've been able to close out the two contracts."

Tovar sighed. "I anticipated this. Here's what I got authorization for: Get the farmer, you'll get the shot. That's the best I can do."

"That was never our arrangement, and you know it."

"As I said in our last little chat, the arrangement's been changed. We need you to perform. So perform."

El Rey's stare was arctic, and Tovar looked away in spite of himself.

"There will come a time when you'll wish you'd behaved honorably," he said, his voice a whisper.

"Look. I don't make these decisions. So don't blame me or take it personally. I have a job to do and so do you. Let's not make this any harder than it has to be. Go deal with the farmer, get the shot, and then get the woman. Simple for a man of your talents."

El Rey stood. "I'll take it extremely personally if you don't give me my injection on time. Job or no job. I hope I'm completely clear on that. Don't test me."

The assassin returned to the rear of the restaurant and was out of sight by the time Tovar had slid out of the booth and spun around. Tovar's face was white, and he held the edge of the table to steady himself as he considered the assassin's last words. He had no illusion that the threat was an empty one, and he was already dialing a number he had been told to only call in the event of an emergency as he pushed through the entry doors to the street.

CHAPTER 41

Briones' satchel was overflowing with paperwork as he strode across the task force floor to his office. He glanced at his watch, flipped on the coffee maker, and checked his email messages as the device percolated and hissed, and after pouring himself a steaming mug, marched to the conference room, where his kidnapping team waited. The conversation died as he took his seat and tapped the laptop before him. The image of Isabel's face appeared on the wall.

Briones stood and recapped the events of the kidnapping and the subsequent interviews, which had yielded nothing of substance. When he finished, he scanned the faces of the men and women working the case for him as he sat down.

"Isabel was acquainted with the young woman who was the target of the rave kidnapping. It seems obvious that there's a link of some sort between the victims, some thread that will give us a clue as to how the kidnappers knew where their targets were going to be. These were well-planned grabs, which means they had to know ahead of time so they could prepare."

A heavyset man in his thirties with thinning hair and a sheen of sweat on his face closed a file that he'd been studying and looked at Briones. "We interviewed a handful of Isabel's friends, and they weren't particularly helpful," Inspector Guillermo said. "But when I drilled down, they all said that they shared their party information on Facebook."

Briones nodded. "Then that's how they're doing it."

Guillermo shook his head. "That's what we originally thought, but the problem is that they're part of a private group, and you have to be a member to see the information, so it's not visible to the public."

"What about other social media? Twitter? MySpace?"

Guillermo smiled. "Nobody uses MySpace anymore. But to answer your question, a few of them tweet back and forth, but just in general terms. No specifics on locations or times."

Briones turned to a reed-thin man with thick glasses and a buzz cut. "How hard would it be to hack into a private Facebook group, Márquez?" Márquez was their resident tech expert.

Márquez thought about it for several long moments and shrugged. "Depends on the level of sophistication of the person trying. I could probably do it in a few hours. But a layman? It's pretty bulletproof."

"What about a virus or something like that? A key logger? Could they have planted one on one of the group's computers and gotten in that way?" Briones asked.

Márquez shrugged. "Sure. Anything's possible. They could also have hired a hacker. There are hundreds of them out there if you know where to look. Or they might have cracked one of the cell phones. A lot of kids use their phones to access social media these days – if one of them had a phone stolen or lost it, even if they got a new one and canceled that device, the info would still be on it. Or as you posit, they could have somehow gotten one of the kids' IDs and passwords. That's all it would take."

"Let's go down that road, then, because from what I can see we don't have much else. Somehow, the kidnappers have tapped into this group and are using the information they glean to choose not only their victims, but also the venues. That would explain a lot, because they're going from social media photos, which would account for the case of mistaken identity on the rave kidnapping. The victim looked similar to the target, which tells us that the kidnappers didn't know her personally and weren't helped by anyone who knew her at the rave."

Guillermo sat back in his chair. "Makes sense. But how does that help us find Isabel? The clock is ticking on that one, and the senator is extremely concerned about her safety, even if he pays the ransom. He's pleaded for time to get the money – the ransom's three million – and they gave him a few days to round it up, but they won't wait forever."

"How much time did they agree to?"

Guillermo frowned. "Three days. The senator had to liquidate some stocks and arrange for wires. They came to terms the day before yesterday, so the countdown's already started."

Briones turned back to Márquez. "Can we set up some sort of a site that would capture IP addresses of whoever looked at it?"

Márquez nodded. "Sure. Easy to do. What do you have in mind?"

"It this is how they're targeting their victims, even though they have one in play, they'd probably still be thinking about the next one, right? Using that logic, if we set up a site for another big event and have one of the members post it to the Facebook page, then we could log the IP addresses of whoever was looking at the site, correct?"

Márquez smiled. "Ah, I see. Sure. That would work, assuming that they weren't using an IP mask or accessing it from a mobile device."

"If it was from a phone, we couldn't track it?"

Márquez shook his head. "I didn't say that. It's just more heavy lifting."

Briones eyed Guillermo. "How many members does that group have?"

"Couple of hundred. A Who's Who of Mexico City's spoiled and pampered."

"We'll need to cross-reference everyone's IP addresses so we can filter out the members," Márquez said. "It's doable."

They discussed the minutiae of the scheme and, by the end of the hour, had a plan. Márquez would create a site for an event the following weekend, and Guillermo would prevail on one of the members of the group he'd interviewed to allow them to post a link. Then they would sit back and wait, and hopefully the kidnappers would be drawn to the site.

It wasn't foolproof, but they were running short on time. With the senator breathing down the task force's neck, they needed to do something – because if Isabel was returned raped or tortured, heads would roll, Briones had no doubt. And as the acting director, his would be the first on the chopping block.

CHAPTER 42

Cancún, Mexico

A cacophony of music from car stereos and poorly muffled exhausts echoed down Boulevard Kulkulkan, the main artery of Cancún's tourist zone, which was clogged with vehicles crawling to the nighttime entertainment epicenter of the town's party central. The booming bass of a reggaeton beat throbbed from the neon-framed entry of Coco Bongo, where a line of celebrants wearing scandalously little waited to get in. Street performers painted gold and silver stood on milk crates to the delight of the inebriated revelers as midnight rolled around, the party just starting on a strip of the Yucatán that never slept. A throng of drunken American women celebrating a bachelorette outing stood by a massive red statue of a Fender Stratocaster guitar, taking pictures of each other with their phones, *woohoo*ing as they hoisted their beers at passersby, who smiled indulgently at the crazy *gringas*.

Originally a largely uninhabited island that was part of the second largest coral reef in the world, the Hotel Zone had been created by Fonatur, the Mexican government agency chartered with building attractions to lure American money south, and thus a desolate spit of sand and rock had been transformed into the Mexican equivalent of Las Vegas, where nothing was off-limits and anything was available for a price. And lure them it did, millions of tourists each year, making it a perfect place for Indalecio to get lost, just one of many faces in a town that had the memory of a gnat.

Inside one of the discos, the farmer had made a remarkable transformation since hitting town. His bucolic cowboy togs had been exchanged for black dress slacks and a white silk shirt, and he'd quickly gotten into the swing of things, availing himself of the willing young company that catered to lonely gentlemen of secure means. Two young ladies from Veracruz sat on either side of him in one of the VIP booths he'd paid for, a bottle of Johnnie Walker Black Scotch on the table, half-filled glasses before them along with a crystal bucket nestling a bottle of champagne in the ice.

"Oh, Indy, you've got a filthy mind," one of the women giggled as the farmer's hand fondled her ample thigh.

Indalecio grinned sheepishly, his gaze unfocused; hours of drinking had taken their toll on his vitality after multiple nights of exploring the town's many offerings. He'd decided on his first night to try to enjoy himself, and had committed to treating his time in town as a long-overdue vacation. And with pocketfuls of dollars and nothing to do, he'd quickly discovered that the tourist zone came alive after dark, with thousands of locals from the nearby city center making their way across the bridge to celebrate.

"You girls are a lot of fun, you know that?" he slurred, raising his glass in a toast. The second woman winked at him playfully and downed her champagne flute in two gulps before sliding an arm around his neck and massaging his shoulder.

"You have no idea how fun we can be," she assured him with a seductive purr.

"Maybe we find out tonight, eh?" he tried, and was delighted that his companions found the idea appealing, judging by their wiggles.

He was under no illusions that they were anything other than paid company, working girls who'd come south, following the money to the mecca of Mexican sin, but he saw nothing wrong with that. He was willing to part with a few of his hard-earned dollars, and they were more than eager to make his time in town memorable. It was a transaction that was notable for its efficiency and one in which he felt everyone benefited, his stance pragmatic after years of living as a widower. He'd been ecstatic to discover two nights earlier that his appetite hadn't completely disappeared during his sabbatical from romantic pursuits, and he was determined to now make up for lost time.

"Both of you?" he leered. "You are naughty, aren't you?"

"We're as naughty as you can imagine," the first woman assured him, squeezing his thigh again in unmistakable promise.

Indalecio signaled the server and settled the bill, and after leaving a generous tip and taking a last swallow of the expensive scotch, he stood unsteadily, one miniskirted woman on either arm for balance, and made his way to the door, his steps as tentative as a sailor's on the deck of a pitching ship. The doorman and a black-clad bouncer acknowledged him as he brushed by with his entourage, and then they were out on the sidewalk, which was thronged with youngsters hopping from club to club.

"I'm just down here. A block away. I have a beautiful room overlooking the ocean," he said, aware the women didn't require coaxing but enjoying the illusion that they were with him for any but financial reasons.

"Lead the way, *Papacito*," the taller of the pair crooned, and the women giggled good-naturedly, their income for the night guaranteed.

They walked south together, away from the garish lights of the mall and its night spots, the sidewalk uneven as they left the well-lit main tourist area. They passed a darkened stretch near a dumpster filled with construction debris, and a pair of men wearing leather jackets and baseball hats sprang from behind a cluster of plants. The older of the two, a twitchy, emaciated man with sallow skin, wielded a knife, while his accomplice, an equally strung-out youth, waggled a length of rusty pipe.

"Give us your money, pops," the junkie with the knife snarled. The women reared back in fright, leaving Indalecio to face the men down.

"Pops? Screw you, you little prick. Get out of here before I take you apart," he growled, his courage fueled by alcohol as well as fury at being robbed within yards of his hotel.

"You crazy, old man? Give us your cash, or I'll filet you like a fish, *cabrón*."

"Do what he says, *Papi*," the woman on his right said, further infuriating Indalecio.

"The hell I will," Indalecio slurred, and swung a fist at the nearest punk.

When the police arrived five minutes later, alerted by a security guard leaving work for the night, Indalecio was already fading, lying in a black pool of blood, the tapestry of stars overhead a stippling of cosmic light as his troubles receded with his consciousness, his earthly concerns eliminated by the four punctures of a six-inch blade and two punishing blows from an oxidized length of iron.

CHAPTER 43

Mexico City, Mexico

Beatriz left the file she'd been asked to get in the in-box and choked back the fear that blossomed in her stomach. Her thoughts were racing as she checked the time – only an hour to go before she left for the night. She resisted the urge to run from the building, aware that maintaining a cool composure was essential, and made her way back to her station, outwardly calm as she weighed her alternatives.

Carla hadn't picked up the last three times she'd called. Her phone defaulted to an automated message that said she was unavailable. Of course Beatriz had seen the headlines, and she'd never been more worried, but there wasn't much she could do other than commiserate. Nobody at CISEN knew that she and Carla were related, so she couldn't even get emotional support from the few colleagues she was close to at work.

And now a file with every detail of Carla's life had been requested. By the same office that had asked for the files on the other three – all of whom were now dead. Ostensibly from innocent causes, but she had her doubts.

Beatriz sat and focused on her busy work, pushing her speculations from her mind. It was entirely possible that someone had exerted pressure on CISEN to do something to defend Carla against the cartels. She was a national treasure, after all, and it wouldn't do to let criminal elements appear to have control over the country, which was how it looked if even Mexico's most prominent celebrities weren't safe.

Yes, that was probably it, she told herself as she finished up the expense reports, one eye on her computer clock, counting the minutes until she could leave and try Carla again. Beatriz suspected it was hopeless – she was in hiding, so of course she'd have her phone off – but she had to try.

The minutes dragged by, and then it was six o'clock and the rest of her peers were packing their things and donning their jackets. Beatriz joined them and rode the elevator to the ground floor, where she was parked in the employee lot, walled and guarded to keep prying eyes from identifying CISEN employees. Her Chevrolet Chevy started with a grudging cough, and she scolded herself for putting off getting it serviced – she just never found the time, somehow, with life continuing to intrude on her best intentions.

The guard waved to her as she pulled out of the driveway and into the snarl of cars heading home. Mexico City was home to some of the worst traffic in the world, and the commute to her apartment less than five miles away could easily take an hour and a half each way.

She would get home, have a stiff drink, and then go to the nearby internet café and use the pay phone to try Carla. Other than that, she had nothing to go home to, other than a grumpy cat and an empty house since her husband had moved out a year earlier, after deciding that his twenty-something airhead secretary was better company.

Beatriz switched on the radio and listened to the bark of the rapid-fire announcer recounting the day's tragedies and soccer scores, interspersed with overly cheery ads for desserts and hygiene products. Four mutilated bodies had been found in one of the southern *barrios*, victims of an ongoing territorial dispute between drug gangs. The governor of Baja was being investigated for tens of millions gone missing on his watch. The president was explaining why Pemex, the government-controlled petroleum company, had to be bailed out again after losing five billion dollars the last quarter – the only oil company in the world that managed to operate at a huge loss on a consistent basis, well understood by the population to be a massive theft scheme for its management.

Beatriz rolled to a stop at a red light and barely registered the movement near her rear fender before a snarling man with nylons pulled over his head was pointing a revolver at her head and screaming.

"Get out of the car. Now," he yelled. "Do it, or I'll shoot. I swear I will."

Her heart raced as she debated flooring the gas and ramming the car in front of her, pushing her way into the intersection, but she discarded the impulse – her little Chevy would never make it, and it might enrage the carjacker and cause him to shoot her. She held up her hands and tried to speak calmly. "Okay, okay. Take the car. I'm opening the door."

She reached over and unbuckled her seat belt, keenly aware of the can of mace in her purse, but spray versus a handgun at close range was no contest – she'd be dead the instant she went for it. The man was probably a drug addict on his last legs, desperate for a fix, because nobody in their right mind would choose her little crackerbox to steal if they were thinking clearly. Her shaking hand moved to unlock the door, and the gunman fired three times. The window shattered in a shower of safety glass, hollow-tip rounds taking most of the top of her head off at the point-blank range.

He was gone before what was left of Beatriz's face hit the steering wheel, the strident blare of her horn like a death scream as the gunman darted between the cars and down a side street, where he vanished into the bowels of the city, leaving her to be another statistic on the nightly news, missed only by her cat, who would persuade the neighbors into adopting her within a day of missing dinner.

CHAPTER 44

Cancún, Mexico

Heat waves distorted the steaming asphalt as *El Rey* rode in the back of a taxi from the airport. Lush jungle edged the road and the air smelled of ozone and moisture, as clean as Creation Day following a passing tropical cloudburst that had dropped two inches of rain in fifteen minutes. Off to the west, lightning seared the sky with glowing branches through a dark curtain of retreating thunderheads as the storm surrendered the morning to the sun's scorching fury.

After the moderate temperature in Mexico City, the ninety-percent humidity and heat were unbearable, but *El Rey* ignored the discomfort as the sorry car's air-conditioning struggled in vain against the elements, his gaze distant as the landscape rushed by. He was there to kill a man, probably an innocent one. Instead, he hoped to interrogate the farmer and learn what he had in common with the others on the list, and then secret him away after staging another death – probably a boat explosion or a disappearance after swimming out to sea, the undertow having gotten the better of him.

The car rolled over the bridge on the southern end of the island, and the verdant underbrush gave way to miles of gleaming white hotels lining the sea side of the land spit in an endless symbol of man's encroachment. Groups of tourists waited at bus stops along the only road north, pink as freshly boiled shrimp. The driver glanced at the assassin in the rearview mirror and smiled, revealing teeth pocked with decay.

"This your first time here?" he asked.

"No."

The cabby deduced that his fare wasn't in a chatty mood, and instead of regaling him with his customary description of the resort town's delights, concentrated on the road. He pulled onto the sumptuous grounds of a huge hotel, three glass pyramids jutting from its roof – the Melia. A valet came running from beneath the overhang, sweat beading his face, and held the car door as the assassin passed some pesos to the driver and climbed out with the mini-duffle he'd carried on the plane. A bellman swung the hotel entry door wide for him, and he entered the expansive marble lobby, peering up at the inside of the glass pyramid as he approached the reception desk.

His room overlooked the shimmering turquoise of the Caribbean Sea, and after setting his bag on the bed, he opened the sliding glass door and went out on his patio. Six stories below, the surf crashed against the white sand, each swell dissolving with a booming roar before being sucked away from the beach to make room for another – a fitting metaphor for life, he thought, as he watched the infinite procession. Like the waves, humans arrived with sound and fury, mistaking their momentary intensity for substance, only to expire after a brief explosive climax like so many before, replaced by new arrivals equally convinced of their unique importance.

After several minutes of watching the spectacle, he returned to the room, luxuriating in the chill of the air conditioner, and connected his laptop. Once logged onto the network, he went to his email, where there were two messages, one from Carla and one from Cruz. Carla's was from another blind email account, sent that morning at six a.m., and he skimmed it quickly. She'd been researching the names, and had discovered that the farmer was the plaintiff in a lawsuit that had been filed half a decade ago in Baja California Sur, but beyond that and his land ownership, there was nothing more on him in any of the systems she could access. On Perry, she'd learned that his cause célèbre, the turtle charity, was also focused on Baja; but beyond that tentative link, there was nothing else. Neither the admiral nor the archbishop appeared at all concerned about turtles, so other than the four of them having a tenuous connection to Baja, a thousand-mile-long peninsula with a population of millions, there were no other commonalities.

Cruz's message was short: a link to an article in that morning's Cancún newspaper and a curt instruction to read it and call him.

El Rey navigated to the site and absorbed the news and then powered on his burner cell phone, waited for it to connect to the network, and then dialed Cruz's number.

"I gather you saw it," Cruz said by way of greeting.

"Damn. I could have saved myself a lot of flying."

"I hear Cancún's lovely this time of year."

"Like the surface of the sun crossed with a steam bath."

"When are you returning?"

"I'll be on the next flight out. No point lingering here."

"You think it was a competitor that killed him?"

"I'll assume so. Which is alarming, considering that I'm supposed to be the only one with the contract."

"I'll be here whenever you get back. Not like I have a lot of places to go."

"All right."

El Rey hung up and looked at his duffle, still packed. He typed in the address of a travel site and scanned it for flights to Mexico City. The next one was at two p.m., leaving him just enough time for a bite to eat in the hotel restaurant before returning to the airport. His job in Cancún had been done for him, though whether by fate or another contractor, he might never know. The paper had devoted a scant four lines to the farmer's murder, a robbery gone wrong, and contained little detail other than the time and place he was found, and his name.

Hardly anything to show for sixty-four years on the planet. His eyes drifted to the window and the waves outside as he powered his computer down and stowed the laptop back in the bag.

They needed to connect the dots soon, because at the rate things were going, everyone on the list would soon be dead, taking their secrets with them to the grave.

The possibility that he was being played against another party changed his already dim view of CISEN. When he'd agreed to work with them, his conditions had been clear, and this assignment clearly violated the terms he'd laid out. So even the microscopic trust he'd placed in the organization was now gone, and he would have to view them as he viewed all his prior patrons: potentially lethal for no apparent reason.

He'd foolishly thought that having the president's signature on his pardon would ensure that the intelligence agency honored its obligations, but given Tovar's threats, that wasn't a certainty. And now he needed his shot. A bad position to be in, to be sure, but one in which he had no choice.

He shouldered his bag and went to the beach restaurant, where he put his misgivings aside to make room for grouper with a soy-teriyaki glaze, the high point of his day so far. Puffs of cotton-ball clouds drifted lazily offshore as he considered his options, none of which were good, and when he was finished with brunch, his ordinarily placid expression was marred by a frown, which accompanied him to the airport and, later, home to Mexico City and the nest of vipers to whom he'd pledged his life.

CHAPTER 45

Mexico City, Mexico

El Rey approached the downtown metro station cautiously, insulated from any potential foul play by the crowd of people around him on their evening way, either late office workers or early diners. An arid breeze blew from the mountains, concentrating the perennial smog layer that blanketed the city in the western sky, making for a dazzling light show of purple, magenta, and orange as the sun sank behind the craggy peaks.

He'd gotten in touch with Tovar with the news of the farmer's murder and had agreed to a meeting with him in the metro that night. He'd get his vial of antidote, which, as with the last two, he'd take to a lab for testing – a preventative measure to ensure he wasn't injected with poison instead of the correct substance, and that it was the same as his two earlier shots. He'd been warned that it would take three or four injections spaced every six months to clear his system of the neurotoxin that was dormant in his cells, a particularly ugly bit of business CISEN had obtained from the CIA.

His senses were on hypersensitive when he arrived at the station an hour early, after having spent most of the late afternoon familiarizing himself with every inch of the warren of connecting tunnels beneath the streets.

Cruz had offered to accompany him into the metro as backup, but he'd declined. Cruz might have been street savvy for an officer, but there was nobody more adept than *El Rey*, and having the cop around would be more hindrance than help if anything went wrong. He didn't expect it to, but after the events of the last week he had no faith in CISEN's integrity and was taking no chances.

He was on high alert as he descended the steps into the depths of the city, an environment he'd be happy to see the last of after spending hours there. No matter how much money had been spent on modernization, the underground bunker smelled of dank earth and unwashed humanity. Millions passed through it every day, mostly manual laborers who used a bucket and rag for their infrequent concessions to hygiene.

El Rey was dressed as an office worker, wearing a moderately priced sports coat and black dress slacks that effectively hid his SIG Sauer P250 Subcompact semiautomatic 9mm pistol – a small gun with twelve rounds that was devastatingly effective in close quarters yet fit in one of his jacket pockets with only a slight bulge.

He paid his tariff and passed through the turnstile, noting that the pair of transit police that had been stationed near one of the ticket counters had drifted closer to the bottom of the stairs and seemed completely oblivious, their presence more for deterrent value than of any practical use he could see.

As he made his way into the first wide passageway, the tiled tunnel walls shining in the glare of the artificial lights, his eyes roamed over the sea of faces moving toward him – a nightmare from a security standpoint, but equally so from an attacker's. He was unrecognizable with his goatee and modish sideburns, his disguise as a metrosexual hipster complete with a black straw fedora the likes of which were all the rage.

The meeting would take place on the platform beneath an ornate nineteenth-century iron clock at one end of the long span. He repeated his earlier route, his muscles relaxed as he strode purposefully with the rest of the crowd toward the platform. His plan was to take a train north one station, disembark, and then return, so he could study the platform from the opposite side immediately before his meeting, ensuring it was only Tovar as his welcome committee.

He made a left into the middle section of the passageway and slowed with the passengers in front of him, delayed by a homeless man begging from a filthy horse blanket, his castoff clothes covered with grime. *El Rey* eyed him with suitable upwardly mobile distaste, and for an instant their gazes locked before the vagrant looked away.

A flutter of unease rose in the assassin's gut as he continued forward. Something was wrong. The man hadn't been there earlier, which in and of itself didn't mean anything, but it was odd for a beggar to be in the tunnel – the first one he'd seen all day. The hair on the back of his neck prickled as his mind processed the remainder of the thought: the bum would have had to pay to get into that area. Not impossible, because he could have paid at one of the other stations and come that way, but in *El Rey*'s experience, the city's homeless didn't spend their change for metro tickets.

But did it mean something, or was it a harmless anomaly? Perhaps it was worth the few pesos' investment in a ticket for him, the rushing passengers more generous inside than out on the street?

He continued to the platform and waited for a train, eyes roving over the area, watching for anything else that seemed out of place. A group of boisterous teens were talking loudly and listening to music on their phones, annoying bystanders. Nothing alarming there, only irritating. Tired workers leaned against the walls, waiting for the telltale whir from the tunnel, the clatter of steel wheels on rails, the rush of wind that preceded the arrival of a train. An occasional young woman busied herself with her text messaging or web crawling, face downturned, shutting out the world in favor of cyber-connection.

There. Over by the vending machine. A pair of men in windbreakers, talking with each other, but all the while their eyes taking in the arriving travelers in much the same way *El Rey*'s were. He wandered to an old crone he'd seen on his earlier visit, sitting on a wooden crate selling newspapers and gum, and bought a copy of the evening news, perusing its lurid headlines as he glanced at the pair by the machine.

A hum sounded from the tunnel, followed by the clatter of cars rolling down the track, and after a brief honk of an electric horn, the train slowed and stretched along the platform. The doors opened with a hiss, and a trickle of passengers disembarked. *El Rey* moved toward the nearest aperture as he folded his paper. The two men got onto the next car down, and at the last moment, *El Rey* dropped his paper on the ground and darted out of the car to get it, narrowly missing the train as the doors closed and it pulled away. He cursed and glanced at the time, doing an inventory of the platform as he did, looking for anyone else who hadn't boarded – and spotted a hard-looking man with the build of a fireplug thirty yards away.

Possibly someone waiting for his mate or child.

Or not.

He retraced his steps and ducked into the restroom while he waited for another train to come and go. He still had plenty of time to make the loop to the other station and then back, and if he was a few minutes late, Tovar would wait. He nodded to the newspaper vendor as he swept by her and continued to the connecting tunnel, where the crowds were thinning. The hobo was holding his battered tin cup out as *El Rey* moved by him again, and he felt the man's stare linger as he brushed past.

The restroom was clean, with an attendant who washed every surface in exchange for a peso gratuity from patrons. The assassin went into one of the stalls and read the paper, his antennae signaling to him that something was wrong.

He allowed ten minutes to go by and finished up, tipping the attendant as he left. He was walking through the tunnel back to the platform when he realized what was off, recognizing his error too late. He dodged to the left the instant he registered a blur of motion from the vagrant, the incongruity obvious to him even as he cursed silently: the beggar was filthy, but his fingernails weren't. The fingers clutching the cup were clean as a surgeon's – or someone posing as a bum.

A silenced pistol shot barked in the tunnel, and he felt a burn in his upper thigh as he twisted, freeing his gun as a second shot scored a hole through his jacket, missing his kidney by scant inches. A third shot thwacked into his hip as he threw himself to the ground and opened fire at the panhandler, ignoring the screams around him as he emptied the gun. The little SIG Sauer sounded like sticks of dynamite going off in the tunnel, and he was already ejecting the spent magazine and slapping his spare into place as the shooter collapsed in a heap, his pistol clattering onto the concrete beside him.

El Rey didn't wait to see who else was working the surveillance. He forced himself to his feet as screams of terror continued from the remaining travelers in the passageway, most crouched by the ground, all cringing and staring at the assassin as though he was Satan risen from the underworld. He glanced to his left where a short woman was clutching her chest, shot by one of the vagrant's stray rounds. A man was struggling to crawl away, leaving a crimson trail from the wound in his stomach, and *El Rey* pushed past him as he picked up his pace. Blood streamed down his leg from the two wounds, but he'd been shot enough before to know they weren't fatal, assuming he got pressure on them soon enough.

He reached the end of the tunnel and leveled his weapon at an older businessman hugging the wall and clutching his briefcase and overcoat to his chest.

"Your coat. Take it off," he ordered, but the man was immobilized with fear and didn't move. *El Rey* took a step closer and motioned with the pistol. "I said take your coat off. Now."

The man did as instructed, and *El Rey* slid it on. "Thanks," he said and continued around the corner, aware that he was being filmed by the overhead security cameras as he went.

He pulled his burner cell from his breast pocket and called Cruz. When he answered, *El Rey* was typically terse. "Ambush. I've been hit. Meet me where we discussed in five."

He hung up just as the two cops rounded the corner and sped toward him, pushing past the others running from the gun battle. He plunged the gun into the overcoat pocket and pointed with his left hand. "Someone's shooting. There's blood everywhere. Do something, for God's sake. Do something!"

The men looked at him, seeing the blood on his pants, and for a second *El Rey* was afraid he'd have to shoot them. Then they broke into a reluctant trot, service revolvers drawn, the worst day of their three-hundred-dollar-a-month careers in full swing. *El Rey* didn't hesitate or look back. He ran toward the turnstiles with the rest of the panicked throng, using the mayhem he'd helped create to get clear of the station before the police, or the remainder of the hit team, found him.

Each step to the street level was agony, and he felt himself getting light-headed from the blood loss and the pain, but he ignored it and clutched the handrail for support. The rectangle of open air at the top of the stairs looked impossibly far, but he drove himself up, gritting his teeth as he struggled toward it.

Once on the sidewalk he moved more slowly to avoid attracting attention, hoping that the trail of bloody footsteps he was leaving wouldn't be noticed until he was safely gone. He held his hand to the hip wound, and it came away slick with blood. He wiped it on the jacket beneath the long overcoat, which covered him to the knee, and forced himself to keep walking.

Cruz was in the Explorer in front of a McDonald's, double-parked along with a half dozen other scofflaws whose passengers were inside buying dinner. *El Rey* pulled himself into the back seat and closed the door behind him and then lay flat as Cruz pulled away.

"How bad is it?"

"Lot of blood. One in the leg, which went through, the other in the hip. That one's still in there. You'll need to dig it out and stitch me up. Hope you don't faint easily."

"Can you make it till we're back at the house? It'll be at least fifteen minutes."

"Give me your belt. I can slow the bleeding from the thigh. Can't do much for the hip other than ball up my jacket and keep pressure on it."

Cruz did as asked as he pulled around the corner. The assassin improvised a tourniquet and lay back for a moment, drained, then struggled out of the overcoat and jacket. Cruz hit a rough patch of pavement, a particularly ugly series of the city's infamous potholes, and *El Rey* flinched and drew in a ragged intake of breath.

"Try to avoid the worst of it, would you?" he said.

"Will do. Just hang on. I presume you have a field kit at the house?"

"What's the saying? Don't leave home without one…"

Cruz grinned humorlessly and eyed the assassin in the mirror, taking in his ghost-white face and eyes squeezed shut against pain Cruz knew too well from his prior brushes with death. *El Rey* was as tough as they came, so if anyone could make it even shot to pieces, he could; but judging by the amount of blood pooling on the Explorer floor, it would be close. He increased his speed and returned his attention to the road, anxious to get the cutting over with before he lost the patient for good.

CHAPTER 46

The following day, Cruz went to meet Carla at an out-of-the-way hotel they'd agreed to use as a rendezvous. Cruz checked in, paying cash, and once in the room called her and told her the room number. She arrived fifteen minutes later, and he was taken aback when he opened the door. She looked little like she had at their last meeting — more like a student now, in sweats, her hair dyed almost black, and the disguise completed with sunglasses that covered most of her upper face, and a cap. She smiled as she entered and glanced at the bed, and then she removed the glasses and sat at the small two-seater square wooden table by the window. Cruz joined her and, after offering her water, sat back as she described her research progress.

"I looked harder at Perry's charity, since that's the only real solid connection with anything Mexican. I ran a background on his father, but it's unremarkable, and frankly, there's not a lot there. Got a green card in the eighties. Worked as a manager at a custom metal fabrication shop. Died six years ago of lung cancer at the age of sixty-one."

"And the mother?"

"American Latina, from Los Angeles, born and bred there. She was twelve years younger than dad. Worked in an office, now retired and living off her son's largesse."

"Remind me I need a son who'll support me when I'm in the autumn of my years."

She eyed him over the top of the phone she was reading from and smiled, and for an instant he saw the international superstar again.

"That leaves us with the charity. It's kind of like Greenpeace, fighting to preserve whole stretches of Mexican coastline for sea turtles."

"Anything shady about it? Or any connection between the charity and any of the names on the list?"

She shook her head. "Unfortunately, not that I can find."

"What about its other supporters? Any links there?"

"Not really. Just a hodgepodge of the usual celebrity friends. Perry was the largest contributor."

"Then how does it help us?"

"It doesn't. But it's something we can scratch off the list."

Cruz groaned inwardly. Carla was doing her best, but it didn't appear it was going to be a big help.

"Good. What else have you come up with?" he asked.

"The archbishop also did a lot of charity work. His cause was the rights of the indigenous people or, more broadly, of the little guy."

"But no turtles."

"Not even little ones, no. His replacement appears to have done a 180 in terms of policy, though. His new proposals aren't at all supportive of the young archbishop's work, which isn't that strange, but is a little sad. The young archbishop was a progressive. This one appears to be a step backward."

"Who is he?"

"Franco Arriola. Fifty-seven. A hardline conservative, according to his reputation." She held up her phone so Cruz could see an image. He drummed his fingers against his leg absently as he stared at it.

"He looks familiar."

"He's one of the more influential members of the Church in Mexico City. A political mover and shaker, too. Kind of has to be to get his own diocese, given his conservative stance. That's sort of out of favor these days as the Church tries to remake itself for a modern Mexico."

"Interesting. Anything tying him to the others?"

"No."

"What about the admiral or the farmer?"

"I've spent the most time on the admiral since he was the one that was attacked. I figured there had to be something in his closet, some rivalry or indiscretion, but there's nothing beyond a career of exemplary service and a loving wife. Three kids, all girls. No scandals, all married."

"Maybe blackmail was a motive, and when he wouldn't buckle, they took him out?" Cruz said, thinking out loud.

"If so, it's a secret that's so well-hidden I haven't gotten a whiff of it. I mean, the man was a model officer, his men loved him, and he was incorruptible. And he came from family money, so there was no shortage of cash. My guess is you couldn't buy him."

"Maybe that was the problem?"

"Anything's possible."

"He was in charge of the Pacific fleet, correct?"

"Yes. For the last eight years."

"Including the ports?"

"Of course."

"A lot of drugs move through those ports," Cruz observed.

"I'm sure they do. But I'm not seeing the link between him and the others."

"No interaction with the archbishop of any sort? A common cause? Social circle? Maybe through the wife or one of the kids?"

"Nothing."

Cruz sighed. "And the farmer?"

"There's literally nothing remarkable about him. Even his land isn't particularly attractive. I was thinking it might have something to do with the cartel wanting his land, or a cartel link between the four of them…"

"Actually, the six of them. You and I are on the list too, remember?"

"Right. But we have zero in common, much less a connection to the others. No, I'm afraid if there's anything linking us, I still haven't found it."

They discussed the results of Cruz and *El Rey*'s research, such as it was, which had also yielded nothing of note, and before long it became obvious that they had little to discuss.

"Where are you staying?" Cruz asked.

222

"At a shithole hotel that doesn't ask questions over on the other side of town. But I need to move again. I don't feel comfortable staying in one place for any length of time. How about you?"

"We have a safe house. So far so good."

"Do you have room for one slightly unemployed journalist? I'm worried about being recognized. This all falls apart at that point, and if you're correct, I'm dead."

"I...I'd have to check with my associate."

She smiled. "Great. Let's do it together."

Cruz stiffened. "I'm not sure that's such a great idea."

"Why not? It's the place you brought me when you kidnapped me, right? It's not like I haven't already been there. I sort of remember where it is." She mentioned the neighborhood.

"It's not a good time."

"Right. And for me, having to run for my life and drop everything, it is. Look. I don't want to stay in the hotel any longer, I have no place else to go where I feel safe, and we're all in this together, right? So what am I missing? I can sleep on the couch if you don't have any room. But right now I'm going stir-crazy, staring at the hotel walls by myself. Give me a break, will you?"

Cruz looked away. "My associate was wounded. He's recovering."

"Wounded! How?"

Cruz gave her the short version.

She stared at him openmouthed and then slapped the tabletop with her open hand. "That settles it. We absolutely need to stick together. *Capitan* Cruz, I'm not taking no for an answer on this."

"I'll need to check," Cruz waffled.

"Make the call."

Twenty minutes later they were on their way to the house, *El Rey* uncharacteristically amenable to another roommate. As he drove, Cruz thought about their lack of progress and the implications for any of them living out the week. His glum mood deepened with each block. And there was still something about the new archbishop that was like a pebble in his shoe, something he was missing, a thought that danced just out of the periphery of his awareness, that when he tried to focus on it, flitted away.

Probably sleep deprivation, he thought. He'd been up for hours with the assassin, stitching him up and doing a crude field operation on the hip wound, ultimately digging out the slug with a pair of bloody forceps as *El Rey* bit down on a rolled-up washcloth. Lacking plasma, Cruz had brought him liter after liter of water and fruit juice so his body could rebuild the resources it had lost, and for a while it had been touch and go. But this morning he'd looked better, his color returning as he dozed, so he would make it. He was young, and Cruz's bet was that he'd be back in action in a day or two, perhaps not a hundred percent, but sufficiently healed to do whatever he needed to deal with CISEN.

He hoped so. Because as of now, they were no closer to piecing together the reasoning behind the agency ordering the executions than when they'd started, and unless they had a breakthrough, it was only a matter of time until their survival became known to their adversaries, and then there was no place in Mexico they could hide.

CHAPTER 47

Briones looked up from his paperwork as Márquez knocked on his open door, using the tentative courtesy rap his subordinates had taken to using since he'd been put in charge of the task force pending an official consideration of a new commander. Briones set his pen down and leaned back in his chair, rolling his head to ease the stiffness in his neck that was one of the rewards of working at a desk all day.

"Come in. What have you got?"

"Good news, I think. I filtered out all the IP addresses that belong to the group's members, and there are two that we can't place."

Briones perked up. "Really? And where have you traced them to?"

"One is an internet café near the city center, so that's a dead end. But the other is a warehouse out in Naucalpan," Márquez said, referring to a district in the western reaches of the city.

"A warehouse? I presume you've run the ownership info?"

Márquez nodded. "I have. It's a corporation out of Monterey."

"Are there any red flags when you pull up their shareholders?"

"Corporate shareholders, all offshore."

Briones offered a satisfied smile. "Typical cartel setup, eh?"

"There aren't a lot of legit businesses that feel the need to create layers of shareholders in foreign jurisdictions that keep their ownership secret."

"How many times have they hit the site?"

"Three so far. The first was last night, late. Then two this morning."

"Like someone in charge might be taking a harder look at it."

"That was my thinking."

"Good work, Márquez. Call a meeting for the group, and then we'll brief them and get surveillance in place. I want any cell calls originating from that building, directional mics, round-the-clock surveillance, the whole nine yards."

"I anticipated your request. The meeting will convene in" – Márquez looked at his watch – "seven minutes."

"I'll see you in the conference room."

Márquez turned and walked out of the office with a smug expression. Briones let him have his moment of triumph – if the warehouse really was the kidnappers' headquarters, he more than deserved it. The senator was planning to hand over the ransom the following day at noon, and had been exerting every bit of his considerable muscle to ensure that the *Federales* were treating the kidnapping as their top priority. He'd made it clear that if a single hair on his baby daughter's head were harmed, he'd hold the department responsible, and he had the clout to make that a meaningful threat.

There weren't a lot of reasons Briones could think of for an unknown party to be accessing a URL known only to a closed group of Facebook friends, and for the first time his hopes rose that they could put an end to this gang's reign of terror, preferably in time to rescue Isabel. The delicate part would be alerting the senator that they planned to take the warehouse in an armed assault. Briones knew how power and politics worked, and in the end the senator would decide whether they would get the green light on going in.

But for now they needed to understand what they were up against, and that would mean setting up a listening post, mobilizing technicians, coordinating with the phone company, getting blueprints for the building and any surrounding structures, and ultimately developing a strategy for taking the kidnappers without risking Isabel's life – no mean trick in a hostage situation.

For the hundredth time, as he pushed back from his desk, he wished Cruz were there to help with the planning and to make the hard decisions he was so good at. But he wasn't, and this one had landed squarely in Briones' lap – for better or worse, the kind of high-visibility case that made or broke careers. He got his fourth cup of coffee of the morning and marched across the task force floor to the conference room, his shoulders square, no trace of the crisis of confidence he was feeling in his brisk, assured stride.

~ ~ ~

Assistant Director Rodriguez carried his tea into the ground-floor office of his Mexico City home. A victim of the flu that was going around, he'd been on sick leave for the last three days. His whole body felt like he'd been beaten with a board, and his head throbbed despite the drugs he was taking, which seemed to serve no purpose but to mask the worst of the symptoms.

A rustle sounded from near the floor-to-ceiling curtains, and he glanced at the window and shook his head – the damned wooden frames swelled when it rained and contracted when it was hot, making for a leaky and drafty time when the wind was up. He sat behind his desk and froze when a soft voice greeted him.

"They say that illness is a function of a poor constitution," *El Rey* said as he stepped from behind the curtains, SIG Sauer trained on the senior CISEN official's head.

Rodriguez shook his head sadly. "I see the reports are true."

El Rey took a seat across from him, weapon steady in his hand. "I'll play along. What reports?"

"That you've gone rogue and are working for the cartels again."

"Nice try. I went to get my antidote day before yesterday, and it turned into a shoot-out in the metro. A wet team was waiting to ambush me. So your pathetic pretense that you've behaved honorably and that I'm the problem doesn't wash."

A look of genuine surprise flashed across Rodriguez's face. "What are you talking about?"

"As if you didn't know. I was supposed to meet Tovar. Instead, I got shot. Twice, actually. But like so many of your operatives, the shooters weren't up to the job, and I left most of the gunman's brains on the subway wall."

"I...I read about that. That was you?"

El Rey let out a hiss of breath. "I'm tiring of this game, Rodriguez. Give me one reason I shouldn't shoot you right now."

"I have a report here on my desk that details your role in the assassination of five different people, among them Captain Cruz. You're going to try to deny that's your handiwork?"

El Rey's eyes narrowed almost imperceptibly. "Of course it's my handiwork. You ordered me to do it."

"*I* ordered you?" Rodriguez blurted.

"CISEN. Tovar. I was given CISEN dossiers and a story about how they were involved in a meth ring. I was told to terminate them, making the deaths look like accidents or natural causes, or I wouldn't get my antidote."

Rodriguez's expression hardened. "I don't believe you. What proof do you have of this?"

"You? *You* don't believe *me*? Did you miss where you tried to have me murdered in the subway? I'd say you aren't in any position to judge me."

"So you say."

"I've got the bullet wounds to prove it."

Rodriguez picked up a file and tossed it to *El Rey*. "I presume you haven't lost your ability to read."

"What's the point?"

"Humor me. You're the man with the gun."

El Rey eyed Rodriguez warily and then flipped the file open. "Keep your hands on the table where I can see them."

Three minutes later he closed the folder.

Rodriguez sneezed and glared at the assassin. "We know all about your side jobs."

"You have a problem, Rodriguez. Listen very carefully, because you don't seem to be good with comprehension right now. CISEN sanctioned those hits, as well as one on Carla Vega. If the order really didn't come from you, then you have a rogue in your organization. If I had to bet, it's Tovar. The sanctions came from him. And he set up the meet for the antidote, which was an ambush."

"Carla Vega? The journalist?"

"At least you got that part."

"That was a bungled cartel hit…"

"Sure there was. That was me. I smelled a rat when I got the second list of names and hers was on it."

They sat staring at each other, and Rodriguez broke the uncomfortable silence. "I don't believe you. I think you invented your story to throw suspicion off yourself. It's essentially non-disprovable."

"Why would I do that if I was doing cartel hits?"

"Because you screwed up in your little scheme and forgot about the antidote, or you didn't think we'd get wise to the fact it was you doing the executions. So now you want your injection, but you know you won't get it since you violated the terms of our agreement."

"I violated them? Your men tried to gun me down in the metro. Was that in our agreement? Tovar refused to give me the antidote until I'd executed everyone on the lists. Was that in our agreement?"

"That's your story." Rodriguez reached for a box of tissue, eyes still on the assassin. "But let's assume you're telling the truth, which I don't for a moment believe, but can't entirely discount. Bring me proof, and I'll get you your antidote. That's the only deal you're going to get. Shoot me and you get nothing, and you'll die in horrible agony within, what, a week or two?" Rodriguez scowled at him. "Ball's in your court."

"How? How am I supposed to get you proof?"

"You can start by explaining why anyone would want those six people killed."

"I don't know that. It's what stopped me from proceeding. I didn't buy your official explanation," *El Rey* said.

"Right. So you don't know why Tovar or whoever wants them killed, and you can't prove that he told you to kill them. Did I leave anything out?"

El Rey nodded. "Because of course, if it wasn't you, and it was Tovar, he'd deny everything when questioned, which would leave me looking like a liar."

"It wasn't me. But your problem is that I don't believe you."

"And I don't believe *you*. Although I'm starting to. Maybe you didn't know anything about this. You're not a good enough poker player to pull that off. Which means you've been duped and one or more of your subordinates is running an off-the-books operation without your knowledge." He paused. "I have the CISEN dossiers on the targets."

"That proves nothing. You could have figured out how to hack into our records section. I've read your background, remember? Or you could have bribed someone. In fact, one of our administrative people was killed recently in a carjacking. How convenient, no? If you paid her off, there was only one way to end the trail. Seems like vintage *El Rey* to me."

"Now I'm killing your staff?"

Rodriguez eyed him without blinking. "She's dead. If the shoe fits."

"Let's say I play nice. What would it take to prove what I'm saying is true?"

"A confession would be nice. But barring that, a reason why Tovar, or his superior, or anyone, would want to run an op to execute an admiral, a media star, our top cop, a religious dignitary…and an actor. A celebrity foreign national, I might add."

"You forgot the pig farmer."

Rodriguez threw a black glare at him.

El Rey stood. "I'm feeling generous, so I'll let you live. Here's what I'd suggest you do. Tap Tovar's phone and his boss's phone, and go through their bank records for any large deposits. You may not believe it, but you've got a serious problem. In the meantime, I'll see what I can do about getting proof. But you have the capacity to do a lot of the heavy lifting yourself, and despite your doubts about my veracity, you'd be well advised to do so."

Rodriguez considered for a moment. "I suppose there's no harm in that."

"I'll contact you when I have the proof," *El Rey* said, moving to the window.

"Knock next time. Try the front door."

El Rey stopped by the window. "If I find out you lied to me, you'll never hear me next time."

CHAPTER 48

Carla clomped down the stairs in her sweats and hiking boots and sat at the dining room table, where *El Rey* was working on his computer. She gave him a warm smile, and he stopped what he was doing, distracted by the beauty sitting across from him. He reached out, grabbed his water glass and took a long drink, and then raised one eyebrow in silent inquiry.

"I've got more on the farmer," she said, sounding pleased.

"Really. Such as?"

"I tracked down where the lawsuit he was involved in was filed, but it's in La Paz," she said.

"In Baja."

"Correct. And of course, everything's hard copy. Nothing's in the computer. I don't think they've even heard of computers there."

Cruz looked up from his position on the couch. "It's an antiquated system. We have to struggle with it all the time when we try to get any info out of them. Like pulling teeth."

El Rey nodded. "Nobody's in a hurry in Baja. I spent enough time there to know the drill."

"Right. Well, anyway, if I want to know what the suit is about, I have to get on a plane, go to the courthouse, and get a paper copy myself."

"You really think it's worth it?" Cruz asked.

"Do we have anything else to go on?" Carla fired back.

El Rey smiled. "She has a point. The farmer's a complete mystery, and the only thing he's ever been involved in of any note is this suit. Other than that, he's a zero."

Carla glanced at him briefly, acknowledging his support, and continued. "Look, we can safely assume that they want to get rid of me because I was poking around Perry and the admiral. When you told me about the administrative assistant that had been shot during a carjacking, it all fell into place. That was my cousin. She was the one passing me the leads. She obviously didn't know what she'd gotten me into, or she would have never done it. As it was, it backfired and cost her her life."

"I'm sorry, Carla," *El Rey* said, and Cruz thought he sounded like he meant it.

"Thank you. Anyway, that's the link between CISEN, me, and the men on the list. They put two and two together and figured out that I must have been getting tips from inside the agency. Which explains my presence on the list."

"But there's still no explanation for me," Cruz observed.

"Or the farmer," she said. "But we have the chance to discover what the suit was about, and that might point us in the right direction." She looked at *El Rey*. "How long does it take to fly to La Paz?"

"Couple of hours."

"When's the next flight?"

El Rey tapped the computer's keys, stared at the screen, and looked at his watch. "There's one at four."

"Which would put me there at…six. Too late to make it to the courthouse."

"Seven," *El Rey* corrected. "They're in a different time zone."

"What about first thing tomorrow morning?"

"There are no first-thing flights. La Paz isn't a big destination, so it looks like there's the afternoon flight and a late morning one, but that would put us in too late, too. So we'd be better off spending the night and hitting it first thing in the morning."

Carla eyed the assassin. "We?"

"Not to alarm you, but your name's on that list, and given what we know, I think we can safely assume that CISEN has someone else working it. So anywhere you go outside of this house puts you at risk. Which means I need to go with you as backup, because if anything goes wrong and you're recognized, you're dead."

She looked at Cruz, who held up his hand. "Don't ask me. I hate flying."

El Rey leaned forward. "This isn't a negotiation. I agree it's worth a trip. For both of us."

"Okay," she said slowly.

The matter decided, the assassin sat back. "You need ID to get on the plane. Do you have any that doesn't say Carla Vega?"

She brightened. "I actually do. A fake driver's license I had made for one of my investigations. I needed to be undercover."

"Let me see it."

She ran up the stairs and returned shortly with the license in hand. *El Rey* looked over both sides of it and tossed it to Cruz, who examined it more carefully and then nodded. "Not bad," he said. "That should work. *Señorita*...Constance Leon."

"Has a ring to it, doesn't it?" she said.

"Then it's decided. We'll fly out this afternoon and be at the courthouse when it opens," *El Rey* said.

"How are your wounds?" Carla asked.

El Rey shrugged. "I heal fast."

"Still. Shot twice..."

"I'll book the tickets. You good for a ride to the airport?" the assassin asked Cruz, brushing off Carla's sympathy.

"Wouldn't miss it for the world."

Carla returned to her room to pack while *El Rey* made the reservations and searched for accommodations near the courthouse. He booked a decent-looking hotel and switched the computer off, stood stiffly, and joined Carla upstairs to pack his overnight bag.

Cruz was tired when he returned to the house after dropping the pair at the airport. He'd slept uneasily, his dreams troubled by visions of his wife being thrown out of the condo by his enemies on the force. When he stepped across the threshold, he decided to take a nap – a time-honored tradition on his day off. And it certainly didn't get much more off than hiding out in a slum with nothing to do.

He opened a Modelo beer and drained it in four swallows, belched loudly, and shuffled to the sofa. Within minutes he was snoring loudly, his mouth open, one arm folded across his chest, the other dangling off the edge of the sofa, the overhead fan orbiting with a dull whir.

He almost fell off the couch when he sat up abruptly forty-five minutes later, his eyes wide, his heart palpitating.

"Damn. The archbishop. I knew I'd seen him somewhere," he murmured. He forced himself up, swung his legs off the sofa, and went in search of his phone. When he found it, he called Briones.

"Briones."

"Lieutenant, call me back at the number I gave you." Cruz hung up. Five minutes later, the little cell buzzed like an angry wasp.

Cruz didn't waste time with preamble. "Briones, I need you to get a sketch artist as soon as possible."

"A sketch artist? Why?"

"I interrupted a carjacking a few weeks ago. I didn't think a lot of it until just now. But I think I know why I'm on the list."

"I'm not following you."

"There were two people in the car. One of them is the new archbishop of Tijuana."

"Who was the other person?" Briones asked, his voice quiet.

"I don't know. But what do you want to bet that meeting somehow jeopardized something – that nobody was supposed to see them together? It's the only thing that makes sense. I have exactly no connection with anyone otherwise. That's the only intersection with one of the victims."

"I'll see how quickly I can get someone. Where do you want to do this?"

"Has to be someplace quiet, where we won't be disturbed. Hotel?"

"Fine." Briones mentioned a place near headquarters. "I'll get a room."

"Great. Call when you know a time. Think you can come up with a mask for me to wear? We probably don't want anyone from the department seeing my face."

"I'll bring one of the assault team balaclavas."

"Leave it at the front desk in the name of *Señor* Terranova. I'll pick it up."

"Perfect. Let me get working on this. It's been hectic here. We've located the kidnappers, and we're preparing to take them down."

"Congratulations! When?"

"I'm waiting for the go-ahead from the brass, but if we get the okay, probably early in the morning."

"All right, then. I won't keep you. Just let me know when to show up."

CHAPTER 49

The hotel Briones had selected had a faux mission-style motif, walls sponge-painted bright oranges and yellows with wagon wheels and cow skulls adorning the walls. Cruz parked a block away and threaded his way through the rush-hour pedestrian traffic, the stream of humanity dense and determined to get home.

A courteous young woman with her hair in a bun greeted him at the front desk and, after checking for a package, returned with a padded envelope. He thanked her and took the stairs to the second level as he opened the parcel and removed a black balaclava. He discarded the envelope in a trash bin at the end of the corridor and rolled the knit mask onto his head, wearing it like a sailor's cap so as not to alarm any guests as he made his way to Briones' room.

Cruz neared the door and, after glancing in both directions, knocked and rolled the mask down over his face. Briones swung the door open moments later and gestured for him to enter. A heavy woman in her thirties wearing a mannish blue suit sat at a circular table at the far end of the suite, and Briones led Cruz to her and indicated a seat.

Briones cleared his throat. "Thank you for coming, *Señor* X. This is Lorena, our top sketch artist. She'll try to get the drawing as close as possible for us. Right, Lorena?"

Lorena, who looked as though there were any of a thousand places she'd rather be at dinnertime than sitting in a hotel room with a masked mystery man, nodded demurely and flipped the cover page over, revealing a fresh sheet of paper.

"Okay, *Señor*...X. Let's start with the facial shape, shall we? Many find it's easier to envision the face and give a good description if they close their eyes and imagine looking at the person like they're watching a movie they paused. Just pick a time when you had a good look at him, pause it, and let's begin."

Cruz nodded as Briones moved to the chair near the door and sat down, thumbing through emails on his phone as preparations for the warehouse assault escalated, and Cruz began the lengthy process of describing a man he'd seen for maybe thirty seconds several weeks earlier, under highly charged circumstances.

An hour and a half later Lorena sat back, looking drained. "Is there anything that doesn't seem right?"

Cruz studied the finished drawing for several long beats. "No, that's him. You got it perfectly. Even the eyebrows." One of the man's distinguishing features, besides his obviously dyed dark hair, were his eyebrows, also dyed, but bushy. Cruz eyed the portrait – this was a man whose power and arrogance showed through any civilized veneer he constructed. A man who would kill without hesitation or, rather, have his underlings do his dirty work while he sipped a martini.

Briones thanked Lorena, who placed the drawing on the table, collected her purse and tablet and, after nodding to *Señor* X, hurried from the room. When the door had closed behind her, Cruz removed the balaclava and handed it to Briones and then rubbed a tired hand over his face. Briones pocketed the mask and examined the portrait.

"I'll take this and run it through that new software that the Americans sent us. It's supposed to be good at getting closest matches to Identi-Kit drawings. No guarantees, but it's a place to start. It's a fairly unusual face, so hopefully that will narrow it down."

"We're looking for someone with a lot of clout. Money or power, or both. You can discard any card sharks or burglars that come up."

"I'll bear that in mind. Now, if you'll excuse me, I have to get the assault team on deck and go over the plan. I got the go-ahead while you were giving her the description. We're going in at five a.m."

"That's great. I'm sorry to pull you away for this, but it's obviously time sensitive."

"I understand. No problem at all. I'll call you as soon as I have something."

"How long will it take?" Cruz asked.

"No way of knowing, but I'd expect something by tomorrow. It has to be cropped and then scanned and then input correctly, and the person who knows how to do that well won't be in until nine." Briones paused. "My hunch is tomorrow afternoon if we're lucky."

"So far that hasn't been the case."

"Always a first time," Briones said.

Cruz stopped at a corner stand three blocks from the house to get asada tacos to go. He ate a lonely dinner of chewy beef at the dining room table, reading the newspaper as he washed his meal down with two beers, and then packed himself upstairs to sleep, tired from the alcohol and full stomach. He stood at the window, looking out at the harvest moon, and after a long pause lay on the bed and closed his eyes, for the first time in days satisfied that he'd done everything he could to return to the arms of the one he loved.

CHAPTER 50

La Paz, Baja California Sur, Mexico

Carla met *El Rey* outside the hotel restaurant, where they had a quick breakfast before driving to the courthouse in their rental car. He'd disappeared the previous night for two hours, and when they'd met for seafood dinner across the street from the beach, he was armed – there was an infamous source for illegal goods in La Paz, an old man who could get any request filled in minutes, and he'd prevailed upon the arms dealer to sell him a Glock 9mm with two spare clips for only double the going rate in Mexico City.

"That's highway robbery," the assassin had complained, inspecting the heavily used piece.

"It's inflation. Everything goes up each year."

"It looks like it went through the revolution."

The old man had shrugged pragmatically. "No extra charge for the historical value. You want it or not?"

"You drive a hard bargain."

"It's a dangerous world. A smart man is a prepared one."

The courthouse was a mile and a half from the bay. The heat and humidity were cloying as they walked from the parking lot to the main records building next to the courthouse. They pushed through the double doors and followed the signage to the main reference desk, where several bored clerks were attending to a large waiting room filled with attorneys and plaintiffs, all trying to get updates or documentation for their cases. Carla took a number, and they waited half an hour, and when it was called, a short man with salt-and-pepper hair and steel-rimmed spectacles greeted them with bored resignation.

240

"We need to see the records for case A9-4721-2009, please," *El Rey* said. "Arellano vs. Juvenetud."

The man scribbled the number on a scrap of paper and disappeared without a word, and they returned to their seats. Twenty minutes later, he reappeared and signaled to *El Rey*, who approached the desk while Carla remained seated.

"We're looking for the file. It wasn't where it was supposed to be," the clerk explained. "Are you sure that's the right case number?"

El Rey repeated the number, and the clerk returned to the vaults. Almost an hour went by before they saw him again. When he emerged from the back, the assassin strode to the counter, where the man waited, ill at ease.

"I've looked at all the places it might have been misfiled, but it's not there. I'll keep looking, but it's going to take longer than usual. Perhaps you'd like to come back after lunch?"

El Rey checked the time. "We really need the file. We'll wait here. Are you sure you wrote the number down correctly?"

The clerk held up the paper scrap nervously. "That's it, isn't it?"

"Yes."

"Like I said, it isn't there."

"Is that common? For an active court case to go missing?"

"With a manual system, it's not as uncommon as you'd think. All I can do is keep looking."

A tall man with a goatee neared, carrying an armload of folders. "Is there a problem, Ernesto?" he asked with a supervisorial air.

"Misfile."

"What's the case number?"

El Rey repeated it, maintaining an even tone even as his annoyance with the incompetence and sloth of public sector employees grew. Their only job was to file and safeguard court documentation and retrieve it when asked. How hard could it honestly be?

The goateed man glanced to the side. "Ah, yes. I remember that one. Title dispute, I think. Rather a thick one, which is why it impressed me."

"Title dispute?"

241

"Yes. A large tract of land near Magdalena Bay. Someone from mainland claiming it didn't really belong to the *ejido* – you know, the agricultural collective – due to a preexisting title grant from the Spanish governor. We don't see many of those. Usually it's a more recent title issue contesting the legitimacy of the transfer. This one caused a local stir, as I recall."

"A stir?"

"I don't remember all the details. Sorry. But let's see if we can find the file, shall we?"

El Rey returned to his seat and told Carla what the supervisor had said. Another hour dragged by before both clerks returned, the goateed one looking befuddled.

"I have to apologize. According to the sign-in ledger, the last time the file was viewed was two weeks ago. It's definitely been misplaced. We'll find it eventually, but it could take some time," the supervisor said.

"How much time?"

Ernesto shook his head. "I have no way of knowing." He turned to the assassin. "Again, I'm sorry for any inconvenience. If you'd like to give me a phone number, I'd be happy to call you when it's located."

El Rey eyed the supervisor. "You mentioned that the case caused some controversy?"

"That's right. I remembered a little more. It claimed that a significant chunk of beachfront land wasn't the property of the *ejido*, and that a land grant from the 1700s preceded the allocation of the land to the *ejido* after the revolution. One of the local papers covered it. The same thing happened in Cabo – a family claimed that the entire Cabo and San José del Cabo tract had been deeded hundreds of years ago, which obviously jeopardized many billions of dollars of properties."

"How did that turn out?"

"Some sort of a settlement, I believe. It just sort of dropped off the radar after the governor left office. Rumor was he was financially supporting the family for a slice of the proceeds, but who knows?"

A question occurred to *El Rey*. "What happens if the person bringing the suit dies before it's adjudicated?"

"Well, I'd expect that the next of kin or the estate would take the position as plaintiff."

"What if there was no successor? If the plaintiff had no descendants or family?"

The supervisor thought about it. "I'm not an attorney."

"Of course. I was just curious. I wouldn't hold you to anything."

Ernesto wiped a trickle of sweat from the side of his face as his supervisor and he exchanged a glance. The supervisor leaned closer. "I'd guess in that case, it would expire. If there's no harmed party, under Mexican law, there's no case. It's possible that the attorney could figure out a way to pursue it, but I'd think it would be almost impossible."

El Rey's expression didn't change. "Interesting."

Ernesto tried again. "Sir, can you leave me some contact information so I can get in touch when we find the file?"

The assassin considered the request as if for the first time. "What? Oh, no need. I'll be back tomorrow. Let's hope for better luck then."

"It would be no trouble."

"Don't worry about it. Just keep looking for it. You open at nine?"

"Every business day," the supervisor confirmed. "Sorry we couldn't accommodate you today, but we'll keep searching. It's got to be around here somewhere. I don't see it signed out by the judge, but I'll check that next. Sometimes one of their clerks pulls a file and forgets to follow procedure, in which case it's sitting on a desk somewhere."

Carla rose as *El Rey* returned to her and explained the situation as they made for the exit. "A title dispute near Magdalena Bay, huh? When we're online, I'll do some more looking at what specific area Perry's charity is concerned with. If it's anywhere around that tract of land…"

"Then this is all about property."

"Which is really about money."

They reached the car, and *El Rey* hesitated as Carla climbed into the passenger seat. "If the case expires, according to the clerk, nothing would happen and it would remain the *ejido*'s land," he said.

"And *ejidos* don't kill people. So there's got to be something else going on." Carla buckled in as *El Rey* started the engine, and directed the air vents at her face, a gesture against the oppressive heat. "You know, I'm familiar with Magdalena Bay from when I was a child. There's nothing there. I mean, seriously, nothing but a few fishing shacks, a sliver of a town, an airstrip, and a gas station. I can't imagine anything there would be worth more than a pack of gum. It's not exactly Rio."

El Rey pulled out of the lot and accelerated along the dusty road. "Curiouser and curiouser, as the saying goes. But that's got to be the key. Now we just need to figure out why anyone cares about a plot of land in the middle of nowhere, and how the archbishop, Cruz, and the admiral fit in." He glanced at the rearview mirror and sped up and then cut hard right down a smaller street leading into a barrio.

"Easy there," Carla said, her voice playful.

"Don't look back, but I think we might've picked up a tail."

"A tail?"

He looked in his side mirror. "Yes. A pickup truck. And it just made that same turn, so it's not a *might* anymore." *El Rey* floored the accelerator, and the economy car's motor strained as the speedometer wound past 100 kph. "Hang on," he warned and then twisted the steering wheel left, nearly putting the car on two wheels as he took another corner at reckless speed.

The big pickup's V8 more than compensated for its lack of agility, and as the assassin executed another turn, he could see that it was gaining on them. The rows of small cinderblock homes with black plastic cisterns on their roofs receded in the mirror as the neighborhood changed into industrial, and he dared a look at Carla, who was clutching the dashboard with a death grip.

A sedan swung out of a street ahead and stopped in the middle of the road, blocking most of the dusty asphalt strip. Two men got out.

El Rey saw the pistols before Carla did, and whipped his from his jacket as he yelled to Carla, "Get your head down."

She ducked below the dash level as *El Rey* floored the accelerator. The men began firing as he roared toward them, and *El Rey* simultaneously slammed on the brakes and twisted the wheel hard right as he neared them, sending the rental car into a controlled sideways skid as it slowed thirty yards from the shooters. The vehicle hadn't come to a halt yet when *El Rey* squeezed off a dozen shots, only stopping when the slide locked in the empty position. Both men went down, one of them pitching backward, arms akimbo, the other slumping to the ground as though suddenly tired, his weapon dropping from his hand as he pawed at the three ruby blossoms that had appeared on his bright yellow polo shirt.

El Rey gunned the engine, pointed the wheel at the car blocking their way, and then rammed its rear end, shifting it enough to scrape by. The boom of a shotgun roared from behind them, and the rear window shattered as he stomped on the gas, losing control on the loose dirt that blanketed the road before the tires gripped and the car straightened out.

Carla's voice sounded panicked. "Oh my God—"

"Stay down. It isn't over yet," he warned, jerking the wheel left and then right, presenting an erratic target. Behind them the truck barreled past the sedan, smashing into its rear quarter panel in a shower of sparks, and then accelerated after them. A glance at the mirror told *El Rey* everything he needed to know – there were three men in the cab, with one leaning out the passenger window with a shotgun. His gaze returned to the street, and he spotted a dirt road leading across the empty scrub ahead on his left. He ejected the pistol's spent magazine one-handed and held the wheel steady while he rummaged in his pocket for the spare.

"What are we going to do?" Carla cried, cringing as the dull roar of another shotgun blast reached them through the rear window.

He slammed the magazine home.

"Hang on. It's going to get a little rough."

"Going to?" she said through gritted teeth, and then they were flying down the washboard dirt road, a haze of reddish dust fogging the track behind them as he opened the throttle. The little car bucked like a bronco as it crashed and bounced over the track, the tires skidding on the dirt like they were on black ice. He eyed the mirror, and all he saw was an opaque beige wall.

"Keep down. If I get hit, crawl behind the wheel and floor it the hell out of here."

"How will I know you're hit?"

"I'll stop shooting." He glanced at her. "Brace yourself.

"What are you—"

El Rey yanked the emergency brake and turned the wheel, locking up the rear tires as the car drifted to a stop at the side of the dirt road. He was out of the vehicle and moving around the front fender as the truck bore down on them, and when it blew through the dust, he waited as the driver stood on the brakes and tried to stop, momentum carrying it forward without slowing. He fired three times at the left front tire and was rewarded by the sight of the rubber shredding to pieces as the truck pitched forward onto the rim, completely out of control. The wheel plowed into the rise that framed the dirt road. The truck flipped end over end in a gravity-defying somersault and then slid for another twenty yards on its crushed roof.

El Rey held the Glock in a two-handed grip as he walked toward the mangled wreckage, the cab half staved in. He saw movement inside the cab – the driver was trying to get his seat belt unbuckled, hanging upside down, blood streaming down his face, the deflated airbags sagging from the dash.

A lump of blue streaked with bright crimson lay nearby – a passenger, who'd been thrown from the vehicle as it flipped, now an impossibly twisted parody of the human form. *El Rey* continued to the truck and watched as the driver continued his fruitless efforts, apparently not realizing that both of his arms were broken, his hands useless to free him.

The third passenger's body was crumpled in the cab, head twisted at an unnatural angle. *El Rey* sniffed the air before kneeling by the driver and pocketing the Glock.

"Smell that? Gas. I hear burning alive's about the worst way to go," he said softly.

The driver's blurry gaze moved to the assassin's face, which was as untroubled as an altar boy's. The man tried to speak, but all that he managed was a wet cough that drenched his upside down features with blood before he shuddered and fell still, sightless eyes frozen open.

Carla was still tucked behind the dash when he returned and slid behind the wheel. "Looks like I should have taken the rental agent up on the additional insurance," he said and put the transmission into gear.

"What happened? Are they…are they dead?"

He nodded as they bumped their way back down the road, the shocks protesting every rut. "That's a safe bet."

"Oh, God."

"It gets worse. They were cops."

"What?"

"Police. At least those three were. But that's not an official vehicle, so they were probably off duty or ducked out to take us on. No doubt they were dirty. The question is, who's paying them?"

"You killed cops?"

"I killed three men who were trying their damnedest to kill us. They happened to be wearing uniforms." He snorted, impatient with himself. "I should have known there was something off about that clerk. He was skittish. My bad."

"What do we do now? Go back and question him?"

"That's not how this works. No, what we do is steal a car, drive south to San José del Cabo, where there are plenty of flights, and take the first one anywhere in Mexico. Because they're going to have roadblocks and a manhunt going for the cop killers in no time, so we're racing the clock. The only break is that I didn't see any surveillance cameras in the records building. So it'll be a verbal description of a man with a goatee and sideburns, and a woman with sunglasses and a baseball cap. An attractive one, but still, difficult to describe accurately." He felt at the edge of his goatee and winced as he ripped it free of the contact cement that held it on, and then repeated the act with his sideburns.

She eyed him with a combination of fear and awe. "You're so…calm. How can you be so calm after that?"

He shrugged. "You can panic for both of us." He slowed as they reached the pavement and turned on the first street. "I'll drop you off somewhere so you can take a bus north to Loreto. If there's an APB, they'll be looking for a couple. So we split up. We'll rendezvous in Mexico City tomorrow."

"Really? I can't come with you?"

The trace of a smile tugged at the corner of his mouth. "I'd have thought you had enough excitement for one day. No, we split up, you'll be in Loreto by late afternoon, and if anyone stops you, which they probably won't, you show them your ID and tell them a sob story about a sick friend or a boyfriend who did you wrong. Whatever you want." He glanced at her. "Don't worry. You'll be fine. You're a natural. Just lose the hat. Buy a new one at the station and some different shades." He slowed more when he spotted an eighties-era Plymouth coupe. "That should do. Follow me once I've got it started, and we'll ditch the rental a few streets away. No point making it easy." He glanced at his bag in the rear seat. "Get one of my shirts out and wipe down every surface you touched. Dash, door, seat, windows, whatever. I'll finish it when we ditch it."

She stared at him like he'd asked her to eat a fistful of live tarantulas, and then twisted to get his duffle.

CHAPTER 51

Mexico City, Mexico

Briones watched the ghostly outline of the warehouse on the monitor in the back of the surveillance van parked two blocks from the target. He'd been in position for three hours, and the incursion team was primed and ready to move on the building. Three SUVs and a van were parked haphazardly in the walled complex's lot, and there had been no sign of movement or life since the last appearance by one of the building's occupants four and a half hours ago at the back door, where he'd smoked a cigarette while drinking a liter bottle of Pacifico beer, commonly referred to as a *ballena* – a whale.

Briones leaned over to the sergeant who would lead the assault team.

"All right. The mics aren't picking up any movement inside, so they're asleep. It looks like there are motion detectors there and there," Briones said, pointing to two areas circled in red on a color printout of an aerial view of the building. "You'll want to cut the power once the men are in position and go in through both entrances. Use explosive charges to get them open if they're locked and you can't pick them quickly. Chances are we'll only have a minute or two from the time the power goes out until they're awake and checking why the AC went off, so we want to use those seconds wisely."

They'd agreed that cutting the power was a necessary evil, but given the area's penchant for outages, the hope was it wouldn't cause instant alarm. Their layout expert had looked over the visible structures and assured them that there was no backup generator in evidence, so the plan was to black out the building, get in, and engage the kidnappers using flash bangs wherever possible – nonlethal stun grenades that would be devastating indoors.

The squad was equipped with night vision goggles, offering the men a significant advantage over anyone inside the darkened building. The forty highly seasoned men that were waiting nearby were veterans of countless similar assaults and could be counted on not to make mistakes.

Still, there was always a chance that they'd overlooked something. That was the constant worry when determining the approach and the tactics to use. They'd counted seven men inside after round-the-clock surveillance, and it was obvious the gang was using the building as living quarters as well as their headquarters. No employees arrived during the day, no deliveries or shipments came or went, so the warehouse was either empty or out of use for commercial purposes – which made sense if it was the staging area for multimillion-dollar kidnappings, which paid the rent better than bags of fertilizer or wholesale gardening supplies, the business registered at that address.

"Yes, sir," the sergeant said and, after checking his earbud, shouldered his way out of the van, night vision goggles in place.

Briones watched the jiggling greenish image being sent from the sergeant's helmet camera on a split-screen monitor as he approached his men, who were all similarly equipped: bulletproof vests, NV gear, stun grenades, and standard-issue Beretta 9mm pistols and M4 assault rifles. Four of the men were demolitions certified and would be tackling the doors.

He glanced at the digital readout of the clock next to the console and leaned back, turning to one of the technicians next to him. "Ready to cut the lights?"

"Yes, sir. On your order."

Briones tapped the comm line live. "Sergeant, get moving. I'll give the signal on the power when you're inside."

The helmet image swept the compound front gate, framed on either side by a high concrete wall and held in place by a length of chain with a padlock, and then an officer carrying bolt cutters knelt by the lock and snipped it off. He stood and pulled the barrier partially open, and the officers darted through, now using hand signals to communicate. Two halogen lights brightened the parking lot from atop a tall metal pole, and the sergeant paused just inside the gate, waiting for them to go out.

Briones turned to the technician again. "Cut it."

The technician murmured into his headset, and two seconds later the parking lot lights went dark.

The helmet image brightened as the sergeant and his men sprinted to the rear door, another team moving to the front. It was immediately evident both were locked, and after watching the specialists trying to get them open for a half minute of the clock's relentless countdown, Briones gave a whispered order.

"Blow them."

Fifteen seconds later the charges were in place, the sergeant communicating with his counterpart at the front door via the comm line, and Briones watched as a blinding flash lit the screens and the doors blew inward, the hinges and locks vaporizing from the blasts.

The sergeant's camera followed a half-dozen men into the smoking gap, and then they were in a large warehouse, mostly empty except for a few pallets loaded with bags of soil. The men ran to the office structure at the far end of the space as the front door team burst through, and then muzzle flashes lit the pitch black from the office doorway.

Two flash bangs detonated near the door, and twenty *Federales* pressed their temporary advantage, moving in running crouches, nobody firing, their discipline serving them well as they approached. The lead officer tossed another flash bang through the doorway and waited as it exploded, and then the squad was through, dozens of men pouring into the offices.

Several gunshots sounded from within, another two grenades detonated, and then nothing for half a minute. When the sergeant's voice came over the speakers, it sounded tight but calm.

"The area is secured. Repeat. The area is secured."

Briones thumbed the microphone to life. "What about the girl?"

Everyone in the van could hear the sergeant's breathing. "In a back room. Unharmed from our end. Three hostiles are dead, one wounded, the other three in custody. Go ahead and turn the lights on."

Briones exhaled a long sigh of relief and waved to the tech, who gave the order with a smile of satisfaction on his tired face. Briones stood and pulled his jacket on, emblazoned with *Federales* across the back, and barked instructions to the others. "Get the ambulances in and secure the perimeter. I don't want anyone getting within a quarter mile of that place until I give the okay. And if I hear a hint of a leak, as in media crews showing up, I'll personally fire everyone in this room, am I clear?"

He didn't wait for an answer, knowing that it would be just a matter of time before the buzzards arrived to get their footage for the morning news, but it was an obligatory warning and might make them think twice before placing a cell call. He strode from the van toward the warehouse gate, and two officers joined him. The operation had been a decisive success, ensuring that they'd all have jobs tomorrow, as well as the senator's appreciation. A line of vehicles raced toward them, emergency lights flashing, bringing the coroner's staff and medical technicians and forensic crews, as well as the van that would take Isabel to headquarters for a statement and a reunion with her father, who would be the first phone call Briones made once he'd verified with his own eyes that she was alive and well.

CHAPTER 52

Jorge Tovar finished his breakfast of toast and black coffee and placed the dishes in the sink, where his housekeeper would attend to them on her alternating day's stint at his house. He looked outside, checking the weather again, as if he distrusted what his eyes had taken in from his earlier peek at the sky, and then moved to the hallway, where his briefcase rested by the front door.

The house was neat, a three-bedroom dwelling in a good section of town, inherited from his parents, who had been successful business people. Tovar had never had any desire to follow in their footsteps, though, and had sold the company when they'd died in a bus accident while touring Guatemala, preferring a career that had called to him ever since he'd been a young boy, up late under the covers every night reading the translation of the latest le Carré or Ludlum novel.

A spy was what he'd sworn to be, and he'd jumped at the chance to work in CISEN when he'd been tentatively recruited while in university, after having made it clear to anyone who would listen that he wanted the lifestyle of a Bond, James Bond, with all the shaken-not-stirred cachet it held.

Reality had been disappointing, but still eventful enough to keep him engaged, and he'd never regretted his decision, even though the last six years had been spent piloting a desk, with rare exceptions – like his running the assassin, which had turned into a disaster in the last few days.

He groaned as he bent to retrieve his case, and scooped his keys out of a ceramic bowl. He'd have to do something about *El Rey*, but he didn't want to take any further steps until he had a consensus determination from the intelligence committee that oversaw the man's case. His superior, Bernardo, had agreed to convene a meeting within the next forty-eight hours. The only holdup now was getting Rodriguez to it, his schedule packed since returning from sick leave.

Tovar locked his front door and made his way down the quiet sidewalk to the lot where he kept his car. The streets in his area were clogged with automobiles, making parking impossible in front of his house. The air felt sticky and thick, and his skin seemed to be coated with a fine dusting of grime by the time he made it to his vehicle – one of his few luxuries, an Audi A7 sedan that would do zero to a hundred kilometers in just over five seconds.

He waved to the attendant and continued into the depths of the three-level garage as he checked his email on his phone. Sensitive communications were routed to his work computer, but still, he routinely had to field twenty or more queries every morning before hitting the office.

The car chirped at him as he neared. He tossed his briefcase on the passenger seat before sliding behind the wheel, and paused to check his shave again in the rearview mirror – a neurotic habit like many others that had grown on him over time, like moss on a mature tree.

The Audi exploded in a blast of orange flame, lifting all four wheels off the ground in a shower of fire and shattered glass, and the chassis distended like a pregnant Dachshund as the surrounding vehicles' alarms sounded.

By the time the fire trucks had stifled the blaze, there was little left but the smoldering frame. A later examination would locate enough of Tovar's dental plate lodged in the blackened dashboard to make a positive ID. His passing warranted two inches in Mexico City's second largest paper, which described him as a career bureaucrat with the Ministry of the Interior, and it would be a week before the forensics report came back and confirmed trace elements of C-4 plastic explosive in the twisted wreckage. None of which made it to the media, which had already moved on to other news.

~ ~ ~

El Rey sat in the living room with his computer on his lap, speakers on, munching on a corn tortilla. Classical music filled the room as he tapped in a query. Carla came down the stairs and eyed him before moving into the kitchen to get coffee. When she'd filled her cup, she sat at the dining table, staring at him.

"What is that you're listening to?" she asked.

"Bach. Cello Suite in D Minor."

"It's depressing. Like a requiem."

"I like it," he said and returned his focus to the screen.

She'd caught a prop plane out of Ciudad Constitución that had taken her as far as Culiacán, and then an evening flight to Mexico City. They'd both managed to evade any roadblocks, and he'd theorized that the local police had been caught flat-footed – La Paz didn't see the violence that mainland Mexico did, so when something big hit, reaction times were glacial as lazy and apathetic cops scrambled to remember what real police behaved like.

Cruz appeared in the stairwell and sniffed the air. "Smells promising. Coffee and...?"

"So far just coffee," Carla said.

"There are tortillas on the counter," *El Rey* said.

Carla glanced at Cruz. "Come on. I'll make some eggs and fix a proper breakfast. You can't live on tortillas alone. At least I can't."

El Rey shut off his computer and went upstairs while Carla worked in the kitchen. He turned on the cell phone he used to communicate with CISEN, and dialed Rodriguez's number via Skype so the phone's location couldn't be traced. When Rodriguez answered, he still sounded congested, but alert.

"*Bueno.*"

"Rodriguez. I think I've figured out some of what this train wreck is all about, but it's not ironclad proof yet." The assassin paused. "In the meantime, if you're telling the truth about CISEN having no part in this, that only leaves whoever is in the chain of command beneath you as possible culprits. I'd start with Tovar. He doesn't strike me as particularly stern stuff."

"Yes, well, it'll be hard to do that. His car blew up this morning, with him in it."

El Rey digested the news. "Who else is in the command chain?"

"Bernardo."

"Only Bernardo? Nobody else?"

"Are you hard of hearing today?"

"Then he's your man. I'd do round-the-clock surveillance and scrutinize every record you can find. Especially bank records. Unless you want me to use my powers of persuasion to interrogate him."

Rodriguez's tone was flat. "Thanks for the tips on fieldcraft. And no, that won't be necessary. I'm not going to okay you doing anything to my staff."

"Very noble, but he's the only one left, which means he's orchestrated the deaths of at least eight people, counting myself. If you're not going to put the screws to him, it's my ass on the line, so I will."

Rodriguez let out an exasperated sigh. "We're not stupid, you know. I've had them both under surveillance since our discussion."

"And?"

"And so far, nothing." Rodriguez paused. "It occurs to me that if you wanted to eliminate your handlers so you could point to them as the culprits, something like a car bomb would be the way to go."

"You can't think I had anything to do with Tovar."

"I don't know what to think. But I do know that you haven't proved anything, and now one of the possibly guilty players is a smudge. Convenient for you, isn't it?"

"Convenient in the sense that I don't get my antidote because you're blackmailing me? Or convenient in some other way that escapes me?"

"You mentioned learning the motivation for the killings?"

"That's right. It involves a lawsuit." *El Rey* told him about the farmer's case. "As to Vega, she's targeted because she's nosy and was digging into the admiral and Perry. Cruz is a little more complicated, but I think he witnessed a meeting he wasn't supposed to."

"Wait — so you're saying that whoever is doing this not only has co-opted CISEN senior staff but is ordering hits because someone might have seen something?"

El Rey described the carjacking with the archbishop. Rodriguez said nothing and then cleared his throat.

"When did you discover this?"

"It's not important. What's important is that I did."

When *El Rey* hung up, Rodriguez didn't sound swayed, but it was obvious that his mental gears were meshing. Only not enough to authorize the injection. That would require something more than supposition and theory, which Rodriguez had more than made clear.

El Rey returned to the ground floor just as Cruz was hanging up his burner cell phone. He glanced up at the stairs, an excited look on his hangdog face.

"Lieutenant Briones got a match on the sketch. It's a real estate developer named Jacinto Ynez. Out of Guadalajara. There were eight other possibles, but nobody else that fit the profile."

"How is he involved? Any idea?" *El Rey* asked.

Carla moved to the stairs. "I'll be right back. I want to get my computer. Two screens are better than one."

El Rey approached his laptop and powered it back to life. "We'll see what Carla can come up with. Meanwhile, I have my own resources."

Carla returned a minute later and sat near the assassin. The two of them were silent as they scoured the internet for information on the developer, and at the end of an hour Carla stood and stretched. "I need to make some calls."

Cruz glanced at her. "About?"

"I want to check a theory of mine. To do that, I need to talk to a friend of my father."

"Care to share?"

She smiled. "He's a career naval officer. Not a huge fan of our admiral, but it's a big navy. He's stationed in Veracruz, but he might be able to verify what I think might be going on."

El Rey eyed her. "Which is?"

"I don't want to distract you. Continue doing whatever you're doing, and I'll be back in a jiffy."

Both men watched her move to the stairs and take them two at a time. Cruz exchanged a glance with the assassin. "Quite a woman, isn't she?"

El Rey returned to the screen. "I hadn't noticed."

CHAPTER 53

Dinner that evening was a celebratory affair. The identification of Ynez had boosted everyone's sense of purpose. Cruz had gone to a nearby *taqueria* and bought a kilo of barbequed steak accompanied by grilled onions and charro beans, and after changing his dressings, *El Rey* joined Carla and Cruz at the table.

"How's the healing going?" Carla asked as she nibbled on an onion.

"I've been through worse."

"Any sign of infection?" Cruz asked.

"No. I'll live," *El Rey* said.

Carla's phone rang, and she leapt to get it. She had a hushed discussion in the kitchen and frowned when she hung up.

"What?" Cruz asked.

She sauntered back to the table and sat down slowly, her brow furrowed. She gazed at the food absently and flipped her computer open, lost in her inner world. Cruz glanced at *El Rey*. The assassin shrugged and kept eating. Carla would tell them when she was ready. Fifteen minutes later the spell broke, and she was all smiles again. *El Rey* looked at her with a quizzical expression.

"Well?"

"That was my friend from the navy. A big project was recently approved to put a naval base on the Pacific coast of Baja, in between Magdalena Bay and Cabo San Lucas, at a place called Punta Conejo. It'll transform the area – they're going to create a harbor, bring in power and water, paved roads, infrastructure... And get this. Admiral Torreon was absolutely against the project. In fact, he was the main opponent, and since it's on the Pacific coast, it needed his blessing, which he continually refused to give because he didn't agree that there would be any benefit to Mexico. The base would really be a concession to the United States, to help with their war on drugs – to allow Mexican naval ships and helicopters to work the shipping lanes up the coast."

"Why would he be against that?"

"He didn't see why Mexico should have to spend billions to fight the U.S.'s battles. His view was nationalistic – that if the Americans can't keep their population from being the largest consumers of drugs in the world, they can foot the bill to try to stop them, not us." She paused. "He viewed it as a demand issue, not a supply issue."

El Rey nodded. "And now that he's out of the way…"

"Exactly. It's been fast-tracked."

"That will completely change the value of the surrounding land, I'd imagine," *El Rey* said. "The difference between arid land without power or water and a new harbor with all the amenities is incalculable."

Cruz frowned. "Sounds like Ynez got a heads-up."

"It happens." She gave the assassin a sidelong glance. "Why do you look so pleased with yourself?"

El Rey eyed her. "Is it that obvious? I went into the government's central database and researched the parcel that the *ejido* owns to see if there was anything that might shed more light on the farmer's lawsuit. Turns out it's in escrow." He waited a beat for the information to sink in. "To a company that's a subsidiary of Ynez's development corporation."

Carla's eyes widened. "If there's a dispute over the title, it could jeopardize his entire project, especially if the claim was legitimate. Banks don't like to fund things that could turn out to be vapor. But with the farmer dead, that problem goes away…"

Cruz began pacing, a habit that was by now familiar to them all. "And the actor's charity?"

"What do you want to bet that the stretch of shoreline the parcel fronts onto is one of the beaches the charity committed to protecting? I'll go look up the details, but I remember it was concerned about the Pacific coast." Carla smiled at Cruz. "Did you know that a sea turtle will return to the beach where it was born, thousands of miles, no matter where in the ocean it is, when it's time to lay eggs? Alaska, Hawaii, Japan, doesn't matter. The turtle will find its way back, every time, to within yards of where it hatched. If it's a hatchery, development of that beach with hotels and condos and timeshares would destroy the habitat. Perry, for all his faults, was committed to lobbying to make it off-limits to ever develop in those areas."

El Rey turned to Carla, a contemplative expression in his eyes. "It would make sense – that's why he had to go. With nobody really high profile and passionate about the issue, it dies with him."

They fell silent, the food largely forgotten. Cruz shook his head. "I still don't understand the archbishop. That makes no sense."

El Rey motioned at his computer with his water bottle. "Of course it does. He was big on ensuring that developers didn't take advantage of the little guy. What do you think his reaction would have been to the *ejido* selling its land at giveaway prices to a developer who then saw a windfall because he had access to inside information? The archbishop was popular and influential enough to create real problems."

"He sure was," Carla agreed. "And you'll note that his replacement shares exactly none of those ideals. He couldn't dismantle his predecessor's work fast enough and pimp his own pet causes. Want to bet there's a bonus in it for him somewhere down the road from Ynez?"

"The naval base brings it all into focus," Cruz said in a low tone and then his demeanor brightened. "Carla, you're a genius. Without that piece, it might have taken us months to put this together on our own. Months we don't have. We'd have had to wait until the base became public knowledge to make the connection." He looked away. "Assuming we were still alive."

El Rey took a swig from his water bottle. "Slim chance of that without my injection," he said.

"Which you'll get now, won't you?" Carla asked.

The assassin shook his head. "This isn't proof. It's all circumstantial. Compelling, sure. But it's not evidence. If I'm going to get CISEN to honor its commitment, I need more. I know Rodriguez. He'll stall to buy himself time to check everything, and each day I go without my shot I lose the ground I gained over the last two injections."

"But he can't deny you with all this…" Carla protested.

"Sure he can. He thinks I may have killed one of his men. I read the report he's working from – it looked pretty ugly. I can understand his thinking. He doesn't know what to believe, and he's a company man, so he'll waffle. Which is dangerous for me. But he's got me over a barrel. What choice do I have but to wait?"

"I can break the story," Carla said.

"That CISEN mistakenly killed a bunch of prominent people? 'Oops, don't mind us, our bad?' I told you – it'll never make it on the air," *El Rey* said.

"I can break the part about the developer."

Cruz grunted. "Getting a great deal on a land parcel? Is that really news?" Cruz asked in a bitter tone. "Without the killings, it's not really much of a story. Okay, maybe something stinks about how he found out about the base, but that's typical politics, and nobody's going to lift a finger to stop it. If you can't talk about the executions, you've got nothing. And your editor will tell you as much. Meanwhile, you'll never be safe, because a guy who's willing to kill this many people isn't going to hesitate to have you taken out. Maybe not tomorrow. But it'll happen."

El Rey stood. "Unless."

"Unless what?" Carla asked.

"What are you going to do?" Cruz asked, knowing the assassin well enough by now.

El Rey hesitated, and when he spoke, they had to strain to hear his words. "Where did you say he's from? Guadalajara? It's been forever since I was there. Beautiful town."

CHAPTER 54

Guadalajara, Mexico

The horses neighed and stamped their hooves in the stable, waking Jacinto Ynez, who spent his nights at his estate with his windows open and the ceiling fan spinning. He looked over at his wife, who was snoring, and exhaled heavily before sliding his legs over the side of the four-poster bed and slipping on the worn huarache sandals he used for slippers.

Outside, a moderate breeze rustled the trees. The moon streaming through their branches cast a ghostly luminescence over the compound. He moved to the window and squinted in the dark, seeing nothing suspicious. In the distance by the corner of the stable, he saw one of his security men leaning against the wall, smoking a hand-rolled cigarette, his pump shotgun beside him.

Ynez licked his lips and shuffled to the bathroom. Now that his plans were coming to fruition he'd only managed a few hours of rest each night, too much adrenaline in his veins from the rollercoaster of emotions for sustained slumber. Ynez was a wealthy man, but the downturn in the U.S. coupled with a tightening of his credit lines had driven him into uncomfortable circumstances, where he was overleveraged on his other projects, and he'd been forced to turn to less savory sources of funding to buy the *ejido* parcel. As he knew all too well, when you slept with dogs, you woke up with fleas, and the cartel that was his lender of last resort was now in bed with him on the project, like it or not. Twenty-five million of its money was laundered in his deal, but with a pressure to perform like none he'd ever experienced, the clock ticking on the interest he'd agreed to pay even as the project stalled because of the damned admiral.

He eased the heavy cedar bedroom door open and padded to the kitchen, where a pitcher of jamaica awaited his nocturnal thirst. He'd just finished pouring a glass to the brim when he heard a scrape from his office – an area that was off-limits to everyone but his inner circle. Ynez cocked his head and listened, and heard it again. Unmistakable, coming from the hall that led to his study.

Taking care to be quiet, Ynez returned to the bedroom and retrieved a .357 magnum revolver from his nightstand drawer. He eased back through the door and down the hall, his drink forgotten, and cocked the hammer on the loaded gun as he neared his office.

His hand settled on the antique lever, and he drew a long breath, the pistol clutched with whitened fingers. He twisted the lever and threw the door wide, sweeping the inky room with the gun as he entered, searching for a target. The scrape sounded from the far side of the room again, and he lowered the weapon and flipped on the light switch. It was only the window, blown open by the wind. He must have forgotten to close it.

Ynez walked over, pushed the two hinged panels shut, and latched them in the middle. The antique bronze mechanism was dull from the years and loose in the slot. No wonder it hadn't closed properly before. His eye caught a glint from the miniature model of the three towers of the Punta Conejo project on a table set up to showcase it – hundreds of rooms in each phase to be sold as timeshares.

The economics were staggering – for sixty million of earnest money and using reinvested profits to build each phase, he'd see over a billion, assuming he got the construction loans at a reasonable rate. With the current environment that was a given, because once the base was announced and the four-lane road was started, it was only a matter of time until a real airport went in and land values went through the roof.

His gaze drifted to his desk, where the files on Tovar and Bernardo lay, the latter chronicling the payments he'd made to the CISEN official as well as the blackmail material. That was strange. He could have sworn he'd filed them. Then again, he was of an age when the mind softened and memory wasn't what it had once been.

Perhaps he'd referenced them and forgotten. He glanced at the row of bottles of tequila on his bar, where he routinely had several nightcaps after dinner – maybe it was best to cut back to only two or three.

Ynez turned and moved back to the door and shut off the light, feeling sheepish with the heavy gun in his hand. He'd be glad when the escrow was closed and he could break ground on the project. His nerves were shot from the stress of making it all come together, more so on this deal than any he'd cobbled together.

But he'd done it. The rest was inevitable.

He smiled in the dark. He'd be hailed as a genius, as he had been in his heyday, when Baja was booming and Cabo had swelled from a tiny fishing hamlet into an international resort destination. With the navy harbor would come a private marina – he'd already made deals with those responsible for planning. The taxpayer would shell out to dredge twice as large an area as was needed for the base, build a longer breakwater, provide all the necessary services, and a few officers would be able to buy second homes in the hills. It was the way things had been done since he'd arrived on the planet. He chuckled to himself as he returned down the hall at the thought of his competitors' expressions when the news of his coup broke. That alone was worth the risks he'd taken and the toll paid.

Because in this world, you were either hunter or prey.

And Ynez was too seasoned and too savvy to be prey. Not so his adversaries, who would be forced to watch as he built yet another fortune while they stood by, powerless to stop him.

If life got any better than that, he didn't know how.

~ ~ ~

Mexico City, Mexico

At CISEN headquarters, Rodriguez eyed the monitor displaying *El Rey's* video footage from Jacinto Ynez's office a final time before turning the playback off. The assassin sat across from him, his countenance placid, seemingly unconcerned by the struggle visible on the older man's face. Rodriguez stood and moved to the window – double-paned, bulletproof glass – and looked out at the city as the assassin waited patiently for a response.

Eventually Rodriguez turned to him. "Seems I owe you an apology."

"Then you agree this is sufficient proof for me to get the antidote with no further delay?"

"Yes. Of course."

"Because I'd happily go back to his house and skin him alive and capture the proceedings for you as he confesses. Just say the word."

"That won't be necessary. I think the files paint a clear enough picture."

"You're sure?"

"Quite."

"What about Bernardo?"

Rodriguez's jaw muscle clenched, and his eyes narrowed. "I'll take care of it internally."

"A lot of people are dead because of him."

"I'm more than aware of that. I said I'd take care of it," Rodriguez repeated, steel in his voice.

"Fine. When do I get my vial?"

"I'll have someone search Tovar's office. There's no reason to suspect him any longer, given the contents of the dossiers. They obviously decided to execute him to end the trail to Bernardo – it would seem natural that you killed him, and then we'd be after you. Everyone neutralized, end of problem."

"Then you don't have it?"

"I know it was delivered. But where he put it after the subway shoot-out is unknown." Rodriguez sat back down and leveled a frank gaze at him. "Don't worry. You'll get your antidote. If I have to, I'll have the Americans send more."

"If you don't mind, I'll wait here for your people to conduct the search. I'd really prefer having it in my hand when I leave today."

Rodriguez inclined his head. "Fair enough."

Half an hour later, nothing had been found. Rodriguez seemed uncomfortable having the country's most lethal assassin's eyes boring holes through him as he waited. When it became obvious that there was no antidote, Rodriguez made good on his promise and called his counterpart in the CIA. After twenty minutes of delays, he got the okay and hung up.

"There. I have to complete some paperwork, but it will arrive first thing tomorrow morning. I'll have one of my people pick it up at the airport, and we'll call you. If you like, we can drop it off at the lab of your choosing."

"I'll come by for it," *El Rey* said, his tone skeptical.

"Suit yourself." Rodriguez hesitated, and his tone grew formal. "On behalf of CISEN, I apologize for all this. I obviously had no way of knowing. In the future, I'll be your contact. Nobody else."

"I think after this, I've discharged my obligation. I more than kept my side of any bargain."

Rodriguez looked off at a kit of pigeons flapping into the sky outside the window, and followed their flight as they veered south toward the cathedral. He seemed, for a split second, lost in his big office, and then he returned to the moment and turned to the assassin.

"We'll take it day by day."

CHAPTER 55

Guadalajara, Mexico

A jet streaked a white horsetail across the cobalt sky as the ranch hands finished their coffee in preparation for starting their morning. There was no shortage of work to be done on the grounds, and the men were used to beginning early and continuing until dark, as their ancestors had done for hundreds of years. Today would be fence mending on the eastern perimeter, replacing the degraded wood used for posts.

The foreman moved to the old Dodge pickup parked adjacent to the stand-alone four-car garage, and when he reached the vehicle, he paused, listening. His men straggled behind, but when they reached the truck, they could see the concerned expression on his face.

"What is it?" Tobias, his cousin, asked.

"Do you hear that?"

"What?"

"An engine. In the garage." The foreman moved to the entry door and tried it. Locked. He fished in his pocket and extracted a fistful of keys on a worn ring and, after finding the one he wanted, inserted it in the lock and twisted.

The door swung outward, and a pall of exhaust fumes belched from inside. He leaned to the side, took a deep gulp of fresh air, and entered the building. The Land Rover was idling, its engine thrumming steadily, the Mercedes and Escalade silent next to it. He took a few tentative steps toward the SUV, his eyes burning from the fumes.

The Land Rover door was locked. The foreman moved to the toolbox in the corner and removed a hammer and, after a glance at the entry, ran back to the vehicle. The glass shattered on the first blow, and he jerked the door open.

The foreman and his cousin dragged Ynez onto the ground outside the garage, the developer's gray face slack in the warm sun as they coughed, eyes watering. Ynez was cold to the touch, and after a few minutes of halfhearted CPR, the foreman looked up at the men and shook his head.

He stood and dusted off his pants, the sour expression in his eyes matching the scowl on his face.

"I'll go tell the *señora*," he said quietly and left the men standing in a circle around their longtime employer's lifeless body, hats clutched in their hands, heads bowed.

~ ~ ~

Mexico City, Mexico

Cruz stood outside of headquarters, staring up at the image of the officer in assault garb that stretched to the roof far above, and smiled. It was good to be back in the land of the living, even if that meant a return to twelve-hour workdays. He'd had a conference call with the brass the evening before and explained his subterfuge in faking his death – he and Briones had invented a plausible scenario where it had been necessary as part of an undercover sting operation against the Los Zetas cartel, which required everyone believe Cruz was dead.

His superiors had been both relieved that he was alive and furious that they'd been duped. Cruz had offered his resignation, effective immediately, which had been summarily rejected. After some discussion, everyone agreed that Cruz was to be commended for his unorthodox approach and that he was to be reinstated with back pay, signaling the end to the matter. Mainly, he knew, because nobody else would be willing to take over the task force, risking his life on a daily basis, living on the run.

Cruz walked through the entryway, his uniform crisp, head held high, and paused to shake hands with the duty officers. When he emerged from the elevator at the task force level, he was greeted with a standing ovation from his staff and, after a few impromptu words, marched to his corner office, stopping every ten feet to shake hands and accept congratulations.

Briones was waiting nearby, and after Cruz's receptionist released him from a teary embrace, he waved the younger man in.

"Good morning, Lieutenant."

"Good morning to you as well, sir. Nice to have you back."

"It's nice to be back. I think," Cruz said, taking in the overflowing stacks of paperwork on his desk and the conference table. "Bring me up to speed. What's been going on during my little sabbatical?"

Briones took his customary seat. Cruz shifted two piles of documents from the tabletop to his desk and pulled up a chair opposite him. "The kidnapping ring was responsible for at least a dozen high-profile abductions, as part of Los Zetas' expansion into that. We got a confession from one of the survivors, so there's no doubt. Whether this will mark an end to the cartel's efforts or not remains to be seen, but I wouldn't bet on it."

Cruz nodded. "Too much easy money to be made."

"Exactly. And as they get squeezed on the drug trade, they'll be more aggressive in their other endeavors. No, we haven't seen the last of this, although the violence and abuse appears to have been the work of the cell leader, not a systemic tactic."

"Isabel wasn't...harmed?"

"No, thank God. And we have a very grateful senator in our debt. We saved him millions and got his daughter back – it doesn't get much better than that."

Briones updated him on the remainder of the open cases and then raised the topic he'd obviously been waiting to breach. "Did you see that the developer committed suicide?"

"Yes. It was on the news this morning. Sad, isn't it?" Cruz said, his expression unreadable.

"You don't think *El*...our friend had a hand in it, do you?"

"No way of knowing. But I can't say as I'm heartbroken about his demise." Cruz straightened his collar. "And it does save CISEN from considerable embarrassment. There's no way he could have been prosecuted."

"So really, just karma."

"I suppose one could view it that way. Perhaps his guilty conscience got the better of him. I hear that can happen."

Briones fell silent for a moment. "I saw that his chief financial officer broke his neck, too. Fell down a flight of stairs."

"Yes, well, it's a reminder to us all to watch our step."

"Indeed."

"What will happen with the *ejido* land? And the base?"

Cruz shrugged. "Beats me. But I was thinking that a senator with the right connections might be able to call into question the wisdom of spending a fortune on a base that Mexico really doesn't need."

"It would be his patriotic duty, I'd say."

Cruz allowed himself a small smile. "We can only hope."

That night, Dinah snuggled with Cruz on the sofa as Carla finished her special TV report about the new Tijuana archbishop, and Cruz smiled the same smile. He'd told Dinah most of the story, but left out living in the same house as Carla for the better part of a week. Dinah's anger at his faking his death had gradually faded, and as she'd thawed, she'd seen the logic in keeping her in the dark.

"I couldn't risk it," he'd explained. "I couldn't risk you."

"You put me through hell."

"I know. And I've never been sorrier about anything in my life. But it was to protect us both." Cruz punched at the remote, muted the sound, and turned his face to hers. "How does an early bedtime sound to you?" he asked.

"Good." She kissed him, and then her eyes drifted back to the program. "Did you follow that whole thing with Vega while you were dead, about the cartels being after her?"

"How could I miss it? It's all that was on the tube."

"She's brave to have decided to go back to work in spite of the threat. Reminds me of how we've been living. Sword of Damocles hanging over our heads every day."

"That's not the kind of thing to be taken lightly," Cruz agreed.

"I thought it was interesting, didn't you? Her exposé on the archbishop? How do men like that get positions of power in the Church? Are they all pedophiles?" Carla had broken a story about the new archbishop's child pornography collection, discovered by the police after an anonymous tip had alerted them to its presence on his computer.

Of course the man had denied everything, but he had no explanation for the hundreds of images found, and as the Tijuana police chief had said on camera, it was unlikely that the devil's minions had come during the night and placed them on his hard disk.

Cruz bit his tongue, sensing *El Rey*'s hand in the matter, and kissed Dinah again, this time with more heat.

"The world can be an ugly place. All we can do is try to be happy, and leave it a little better every day that when we awoke."

She pressed against him. "Time to leave me a little better."

He switched off the TV.

"I'll do my best."

CHAPTER 56

The tall young woman working the front counter at the lab looked up at *El Rey* as her associate emerged from the back, where the lab equipment and spectrum analyzer were kept. The associate did a last check of the readout in her hand and, after making a clicking sound with her teeth, nodded at the seated assassin.

"Mr. Barossa?"

"Yes," *El Rey* said.

"We have the results of the analysis. They match the report from last time," the associate said. *El Rey* studied her striking bottle-green eyes and smiled with genuine relief.

"Oh, good. Nothing new, then?"

"No." She held up the remainder of the vial, which was still more than he needed for his booster, replaced it in the small polystyrene container, and slid it across the counter to him. "Will there be anything else?"

"Just the bill."

He pocketed the antidote and paid and then was out on the street, eyes moving constantly behind his sunglasses. He'd do the injection himself – had already gone to the pharmacy and bought a syringe – and would endure alone the hours of weakness and nausea he typically experienced after the injection, as was his preference.

Rodriguez had come through for him, and their ongoing cautious truce was tentatively reestablished, although their level of mutual trust was slightly below zero. Still, one kept one's friends close and one's enemies closer, so he would still pretend to be CISEN's creature as long as he needed – which, he hoped, would be no more than another six months, when a blood test would conclusively show that his system was clean. If not, another final shot would be

273

necessary, after which he would be a free man, discharged from his involuntary cooperation with the agency.

He picked up his pace as he weaved through the mass of lunchtime pedestrians, thick as ants, focused on their own petty dramas and aspirations, the assassin just another in an anonymous swarm, unremarkable except for a certain confidence to his bearing and a glacial calm in his dark eyes. At the corner he seemed to hesitate as he glanced in both directions and then bolted across the street as the light turned yellow, making it impossible for anyone to follow him without giving himself away.

On the far side of the boulevard he stopped and looked back, the sun warm on his face as he eyed the waiting throng and, after confirming that nobody had crossed the street after him, turned and disappeared into the crowd.

About the Author

A *Wall Street Journal* and *The Times* featured author, Russell Blake lives full time on the Pacific coast of Mexico. He is the acclaimed author of many thrillers, including the Assassin series, the JET series, and the BLACK series. He has also co-authored *The Eye of Heaven* with Clive Cussler for Penguin Books.

"Capt." Russell enjoys writing, fishing, playing with his dogs, collecting and sampling tequila, and waging an ongoing battle against world domination by clowns.

Visit RussellBlake.com for updates
or subscribe to: RussellBlake.com/contact/mailing-list

Co-authored with Clive Cussler
THE EYE OF HEAVEN

Thrillers by Russell Blake
FATAL EXCHANGE

THE GERONIMO BREACH

ZERO SUM

THE DELPHI CHRONICLE TRILOGY

THE VOYNICH CYPHER

SILVER JUSTICE

UPON A PALE HORSE

The Assassin Series by Russell Blake
KING OF SWORDS

NIGHT OF THE ASSASSIN

RETURN OF THE ASSASSIN

REVENGE OF THE ASSASSIN

BLOOD OF THE ASSASSIN

REQUIEM FOR THE ASSASSIN

The JET Series by Russell Blake

JET

JET II – BETRAYAL

JET III – VENGEANCE

JET IV – RECKONING

JET V – LEGACY

JET VI – JUSTICE

JET VII – SANCTUARY

JET – OPS FILES (prequel)

The BLACK Series by Russell Blake

BLACK

BLACK IS BACK

BLACK IS THE NEW BLACK

BLACK TO REALITY

Non Fiction by Russell Blake

AN ANGEL WITH FUR

HOW TO SELL A GAZILLION EBOOKS

(while drunk, high or incarcerated)

CPSIA information can be obtained at www.ICGtesting.com
Printed in the USA
LVOW11s2311240316

480609LV00001BA/260/P